Bright Lights
of
Summer

By
Lynn Ames

BRIGHT LIGHTS OF SUMMER
© 2014 BY LYNN AMES

ISBN: 978-1-936429-10-3

OTHER AVAILABLE FORMATS

eBOOK EDITION
ISBN: 978-1-936429-11-0

PUBLISHED BY
PHOENIX RISING PRESS
PHOENIX, ARIZONA
www.phoenixrisingpress.com

CREDITS
EXECUTIVE EDITOR: LINDA LORENZO
AUTHOR PHOTO: JUDY FRANCESCONI
COVER DESIGN: TREEHOUSE STUDIO

Dedication

To my dear friend, Dot Wilkinson, National Softball Hall of Famer, 19-time All-American, 3-time World Champion. You have the biggest heart of anyone I know. I love you. You will always be family to me.

To Estelle "Ricki" Caito, National Softball Hall of Famer, 3-time All-American, 3-time World Champion, and Dot's partner of 48 years. Thank you for gracing the cover of this book. As Dot often tells me, that's what a real softball player should look like.

Acknowledgments

A work of historical fiction such as *Bright Lights of Summer* requires copious amounts of research. I was most fortunate to have access to numerous original source materials—newspaper clippings, photographs, game programs, and first-hand accounts. The single book I used for background information was the excellently researched and written, *The Path to the Gold*, by Mary L. Littlewood.

I have no words to explain what Dot Wilkinson means to me. Quite simply, Dot is family. Her remarkable memory, incredible collection of historical artifacts, and her willingness to make all of it available to me made the richness of this account possible.

As is true with all of my books, I owe a debt of gratitude to my beta reading team. I am so blessed to have folks who read along with me, critique the story, give me detailed feedback, and make my work so much better.

Then there's my extraordinary editor, Linda Lorenzo. We've been working together for the last half-dozen of my titles. With every book, I learn more as a result of Linda's skill and ability to explain the whys and wherefores of every change/correction. Her steady guidance and sharp eye give me absolute confidence in the finished product—this book you're holding in your hands right now.

To Ann McMan, the genius behind TreeHouse Studio, who created the beautiful cover and all supporting materials for *Bright Lights of Summer*, I am so blessed to have you and your lovely wife, Salem, in my life. Working with you is a dream. Thank you for making everything I do look like a million bucks. I love my North Carolina family.

Finally, to you, the readers, I extend my deepest gratitude. You are so generous and kind. Thank you for reading, thank you for recommending my books to others, thank you for sending me feedback and posting reviews of my work, and thank you for joining me on this journey.

Enjoy *Bright Lights of Summer*.

Author's Note

It is my distinct honor to call National Softball Hall of Famer Dot Wilkinson "family." Our love, respect, and deep affection for one another transcends generations, geography, and all other differences.

Considered by many to be the best female catcher in the history of softball, Dot generously and graciously spent countless hours and days with me discussing her life during the heyday of the game. She provided me with copious amounts of research material, introduced me to her ball-playing friends, and gave me permission to add fictitious players to the roster of her team, the vaunted, 3-time World Champion P.B.S.W. Ramblers.

That brings me to this very important point. This is a work of fiction. Diz and Frannie are fictional characters and wholly my creation. Any interaction between them and the real individuals within the story is fictitious.

While Dot magnanimously allowed me to add fictitious players to the Ramblers, I am by no means implying that Diz and Frannie's experiences were the experiences of anyone, living or deceased, connected to the Ramblers or any other softball organization at the time.

Much of the framework of this book is historically accurate and factually authentic—the teams, many of the games played, the trips taken, the locales, etc. Ford Hoffman managed the Ramblers from the team's inception in 1933 until into the mid-1950s. The team's roster in the 1940s included Amelina "Amy" Peralta, Marjorie Law, Louise Curtis, Virginia "Dobbie" Dobson, Jean Hutsell, Jessie Glasscock, Kathleen "Peanuts" Eldridge, Zada Boles, Mickey Sullivan, Mildred Dixon, Delores Low, Shirley Wade, and, of course, Dot Wilkinson. Every game I describe is factually correct in terms of the score, the opposing pitcher, and opposing players. In many instances and wherever I could find supporting research, I recreate the exact manner in which games were won or lost. The locations of games and the mode of transportation used on road trips also are accurate.

And yet, as the disclaimer on the copyright page of the book reads: This is a work of fiction. Names, characters, places, and incidents are the product of the author's imagination or are used fictitiously, and any resemblance to actual persons, living or dead, businesses, companies, events, or locales is entirely coincidental.

I do hope you enjoy *Bright Lights of Summer*, my extended love letter to Dot and to all of her teammates and contemporaries who gave so much to the game.

~ Lynn Ames

Foreword

By Dot Wilkinson
3-time softball world champion, 19-time All-American,
member of the National Softball Hall of Fame

About the Game

Softball means everything to me.

My parents gave me the genes and my coach and mentor Ford Hoffman taught me to be a good athlete and a successful businesswoman. Softball gave me many, many special friends and a great partner for forty-eight years, Ricki Caito.

I love the game and hope I have given back as much as I received in pleasure and friends. I wish I could do it all over again.

It's not about winning, it's who you meet and keep along the way.

About My Friendship with Lynn Ames

My relationship with Lynn Ames began several years ago when she picked up me and fellow Hall-of-Famer Billie Harris to do an interview on women in sports for her television show.

Later, Lynn gave me one of her books to read. I really enjoyed that and have read all of her books since, many times over.

We go out to lunch once a week and spend some special times together, like Thanksgiving and Christmas. Lynn and I talk about many things. We are family.

I know this book is going to be special for me, as it will be for many other women who have played softball and other sports.

Thanks, Lynn.

Love you,

Dot

CHAPTER ONE

Phoenix, 2014

Thank you for agreeing to see me, Ms. Hosler. I can't tell you what it means to me to be able to talk to a Hall of Famer like you."

"Oh, please. Call me Diz, dear. Mrs. Hosler was my mother." Diz smiled, and the blue of her eyes stood out in sharp relief against the wrinkles in her face. Her gnarled fingers curled around a cup of steaming coffee. She leaned in and blew on the liquid. When she looked back up, her eyes were clear, her vision focused on the woman sitting across from her. "I don't get much chance to talk about the old days anymore. Almost all of my friends are gone and most of those that are left aren't doing that well in the memory department." She tapped the side of her head to emphasize the point.

The interviewer leaned forward in the booth. She reached out and laid a hand on Diz's arm. "That's exactly why I want to do this. I want people to know what the heyday of women's softball was really like, not the made-for-the-movies version."

Diz laughed, the sound soft and low.

"Did I say something funny?"

"I can't remember the last time I met someone your age who was so passionate about the history of the game."

"Well, I—"

"I like your earnestness and the fact that you recognize that the darned movie only covered the smallest fraction of what was going on at the time. It's all anyone seems to know about women's softball from the 1940s. Aggravating." Diz harrumphed.

"I imagine it is. So let's set the record straight."

Diz narrowed her eyes and cocked her head to the side, studying the other woman. "You've got spunk. Good. We're going to get along just fine."

A blush crept up the side of the interviewer's neck and she removed her hand from Diz's arm. She fumbled in the bag at her feet, pulled out a tape recorder, and set it on the table. Eventually, when the red faded to pink, she lifted her head to meet Diz's amused gaze. "Is it okay if I record this?"

"Of course, dear." Diz smiled kindly. "I'm sorry if I frazzled you."

"No. No, not at all." The interviewer busied herself with the controls on the recorder. "Testing. Testing, one, two. This is Julie Newsome. Today is Monday, February 17, 2014, and this is session number one with Theodora 'Dizzy' Hosler."

"My. That all sounds so formal." Diz winked.

"I assure you, that's by far the most 'official' part of our program." Julie returned the wink and held the recorder to her ear to block out the ambient noise as she played back the test to ensure that the recorder was working properly. Apparently satisfied, she replaced the recorder on the table and set it to record. Then she flipped through the pages of a dog-eared notebook. Every page was filled with scrawled handwriting. She tapped her finger on a date outlined in red and surrounded with a black rectangle. "How about if we start at the beginning with a question that's been nagging at me?"

"Sounds like a good place to begin."

"I know Dot Wilkinson was a big influence on your career. My notes say you've known each other for seventy-six years."

Diz nodded, then bent toward the microphone. When she spoke, her voice was several decibels louder than it had been before. "I met Dottie in 1938, although I was aware of her before that. Everyone knew who Dottie Wilkinson was. She was the best catcher in the game." Diz sat back.

"I could be wrong, but it was 1941 when you joined the Ramblers, correct?"

"That's right."

Julie's brow furrowed. "But you met Dot three years earlier."

"I did."

"So…"

"Ah." Diz raised an eyebrow. "It's a math problem. You don't see how it adds up."

"Well, yeah." Julie pulled an iPad from her bag. As she did so, she said, "By the way, you can just sit back. The microphone will pick up your voice. There's no need to make yourself uncomfortable by hunching over the tape recorder. I'm only using that as a backup in case I miss anything while I'm taking notes. I just want you to relax, and we'll have an easy conversation. Okay?"

"Works for me." Diz's fingers trembled as she grasped her mug. She used her other hand for support and lifted the cup to her lips, blowing once more to cool the coffee before taking a sip. "Now, where were we?"

"You were about to solve a math problem for me."

"Ah, yes. Indeed." Diz slurped another mouthful of coffee. "My older sister, Elsie, and I played ball in the field near our house every morning before school. In 1938, Elsie tried out for the Ramblers and made it. That's when I met Dot. After school, I would run as fast as I could to the field to watch the girls practice. I went to every home game with our folks. I just wanted to be around softball."

Julie nodded as she tapped on the keypad.

"Then, right before we left for the national championships in Chicago, we got the news that the team was going to New York City to play in Madison Square Garden. I begged my mother to let me go along."

"Wait!" Julie held up a hand. "The Ramblers played in Madison Square Garden? In 1938?"

"Yes. It was the largest crowd ever to watch an indoor softball game." Diz sighed and put down the cup. "I remember that trip like it was yesterday."

13

Chicago, 1938

"Please, Mother. Please let me go with Elsie. It's New York City! I might never get to see it if I don't go now." Diz pressed her hands together in front of her face in a prayerful pose. "You said yourself that she needs a chaperone."

"Don't be so dramatic, young lady. You may think you're all grown up, but let's not forget that you're thirteen years old. You've already missed the first week of school by coming here to Chicago for the national championships. You'd be missing another entire week if we let you go on to New York."

Diz opened her mouth to respond, but her mother shushed her. Diz frowned. Desperate times called for desperate measures. She bit her lip. If she said it and it didn't come true, she'd be in big trouble. *In for a penny, in for a pound.*

"Mr. Hoffman said I could help with the equipment if you give me permission to go. I'd be working, Mother. It would be good experience for me. You're the one always wanting me to be more responsible. Please?" She drew out the word and gave what she hoped was her most angelic expression.

"He did, did he?"

"Yeah." Diz's voice squeaked a little, and she hoped that her mother hadn't heard it. It was a white lie, really. Diz *was* planning to ask the coach if she could carry the bats and balls for the team.

She tried not to squirm under her mother's piercing stare.

"That's 'yes,' young lady. Proper grammar counts."

"Yes, Mother."

In the ensuing silence, Diz calculated how fast she could run over to the field where the championship game was being played. Although the Ramblers already had been eliminated, she knew that Mr. Hoffman was in the stands, watching the game. If she could just get to him in time, she could talk him into taking her along, and then what she'd told her mother would be the truth.

"You know I'll be checking with Mr. Hoffman myself?"

"I know, Mother."

"And if you're not telling the truth…"

"I'm telling the truth." Diz crossed her fingers behind her back.

"We'll see about that," her mother muttered.

14

"Can I go watch some of the game?"

"If you promise to go right over to the field and come right back here as soon as the game ends."

"I promise," Diz said. She dashed out of the motel room, opening the door just wide enough to clear the threshold. Her feet barely touched the ground as her legs ate up the distance to the field.

"Mr. Hoffman. Mr. Hoffman." Diz bent over and put her hands on her knees, trying to catch her breath.

"Slow down, Theodora."

Diz winced at the use of her given name. "Can…can I ask you something?"

"Sit down." The coach patted the seat next to him. "And slow down."

Diz took a deep breath. On the field, Alameda was at bat. "My mother says that I can come with you to New York, if it's okay with you." Diz stared at the tops of her sneakers. When she didn't hear anything, she dared a peek at Mr. Hoffman's face. He was scrutinizing her. She tried her best not to look as desperate as she felt.

"Are you telling the truth, young lady?"

"Why wouldn't I be telling the truth?" Diz swallowed hard.

"An excellent question."

The coach continued to stare at her, and Diz's shoulders slumped. If he said no…

"What would you do on the trip, exactly?"

Diz straightened up again. "Anything. I'd do anything." Her slim body vibrated in the seat. "I could carry the equipment for you. I'd iron the uniforms. I could keep score. I could—"

"Stop." Mr. Hoffman put his hand on Diz's arm. "Stop."

"But—"

He patted her arm. "I'll talk to your mother about it. If…"

Diz jumped up and stopped just short of throwing her arms around the coach. "Thank you! Thank you. You won't be sorry."

"Wait a minute," Mr. Hoffman said. "Let me finish." He put a little pressure on her arm, signaling her to sit back down.

For the first time, Diz looked around and realized that she was blocking the view of the game for the people behind her. "Sorry," she said, and slumped back into the seat.

"I'll talk to your mother. If, and that's a big if, she says it's okay, then you can come along and carry the equipment."

"Thank you! Thank you! I promise I'll do a great job."

"You know the equipment is pretty heavy, don't you?"

Diz flexed a bicep. "I'm stronger than I look." Why did everyone think she was a weakling? It was true that she was several inches shorter than Elsie, but she was still growing, wasn't she?

"I'm sure you are." He turned his attention back to the game. "I'll talk to your mother after the game and then we'll see about New York."

"Yes, sir." Diz heaved a big sigh of relief. She had told her mother the truth, after all.

⊰⊱

New York City, 1938

Diz rolled over and put the pillow over her head. The sun was streaming in through the hotel-room window and the rollaway bed on which she was lying was lumpy. She rubbed the sore spot on her side where a protruding spring had left a bruise.

"Hey, sleepyhead."

Diz swatted at the annoying fly...

"Theodora Hosler, if you do not get your lazy bottom out of that bed right this second..."

Diz's eyes popped open as she registered Elsie's presence and the hand that was shaking her shoulder. She bolted straight up. "Am I late?"

"You will be if you don't get up right now. Go brush your teeth and get yourself clean. We have a big day today."

"Oh, gosh, yes." Diz swung her legs around and stuffed her feet into the slippers she'd left next to the bed. She grabbed a towel, a comb, and her toiletry bag and hustled down the hall to the bathroom. Today was going to be the best day ever, starting with a trip to Mayor Fiorello LaGuardia's office and then a tour of the grounds for the upcoming World's Fair.

Diz let the buzz of conversation wash over her. The girls were oohing and aahing over the buildings on the grounds of the World's Fair, but Diz was busy replaying the game the Ramblers won the night before over the New York Roverettes. She'd never seen anything like it. More than 12,500 fans. She overheard someone say it was the largest crowd ever to see an indoor softball game. It sure had looked and sounded like it. The cheers had reverberated off the terrazzo floor and echoed in her ears when the Rambler players stripped off their cowgirl outfits after warm-ups to reveal their regular short-short satin uniforms underneath.

"Oh, my goodness!" Diz winced as Elsie squeezed her arm too hard. "Look at that! Have you ever seen anything like it?" Elsie pointed at a spherical object juxtaposed against a gargantuan pointy structure. The entire thing was surrounded with scaffolding.

The perky guide smiled indulgently at Elsie. "That," she said, "is the Trylon and Perisphere. It will house Democracity, a utopian city of the future. It's going to be the lynchpin of the Fair."

"I'll bet."

"Who's ready for lunch?" Mr. Hoffman asked.

As if on cue, Diz's stomach growled. "Me," she said and patted her stomach for good measure.

"Good, because we've got something really special planned."

The "something special" was a real-life giant of the sporting world—Heavyweight Champion of the World Jack Dempsey. His restaurant was directly across the street from Madison Square Garden.

Diz bit into her burger and moaned with pleasure. It was rare and juicy, just the way she liked it.

"Hiya, pal. Whaddaya think? Pretty good, huh?"

The burger slipped out of Diz's suddenly boneless fingers as she looked up into the rugged face of Jack Dempsey himself.

"It's…" Diz finished chewing the bite she had in her mouth and tried to find her voice. "It's really good, Mr. Dempsey."

"Call me Jack." He clapped Diz on the back. "I'm glad you like it." He held out a glossy, eight-by-ten inch, black-and-white photograph. His eyes twinkled as he gazed down at her. "This is for you."

"It is?" Diz looked at the photograph. It was Dempsey, throwing the punch that won him the title from the reigning champ, Jess Willard, on July 4, 1919. Her eyes widened.

"Yep, it is." Dempsey whipped out a pen. "What's your name?"

"Theo— Um, Dizzy, sir."

Dempsey threw back his head and laughed. "Dizzy, huh?"

Diz squirmed in her seat as heads turned in their direction from nearby tables.

"Why do they call you Dizzy? Do you have trouble standing up?"

Diz's face grew hot and her ears reddened. "No, sir," Diz mumbled. "It's on account of Dizzy Dean is my favorite baseball player."

"He is, is he?"

"Yes, sir."

Dempsey tilted his head, sizing her up. "Are you a pitcher?"

"No, sir. I'm an outfielder."

The boxer crossed his arms in front of him as he continued to size her up. "Are you even old enough to play?"

Diz felt, rather than saw, the eyes of several of the nearby Ramblers watching the interchange. She straightened up in her seat and lifted her chin. "I'm not playing with these girls yet, sir. But I will be soon."

Elsie, who was sitting next to her sister, guffawed, and Diz glared at her.

"Yes, she will be, Mr. Dempsey."

Diz turned her head just in time to see Dot Wilkinson's wink. Her heart thumped hard in her chest as gratitude flooded through her.

"And you are?" Dempsey asked.

"That's Dot Wilkinson. She's the best catcher in the game. Nobody messes with Dot," Diz gushed.

"Is that so?" Dempsey asked. "She must be pretty tough."

"She is," Diz agreed.

"So, Dizzy-who-is-soon-to-be-a-player, do you want me to autograph this picture for you?"

"You bet, Mr.—er, Jack."

Dempsey signed the photo with a flourish. "To Dizzy, Keep punching. Jack Dempsey."

"Thank you, Jack."

"Now, how about a picture with me?"

"For real?" Diz jumped up out of her seat.

"Absolutely." Dempsey motioned to a photographer who was standing by. The boxer put his arm around Diz and the flashbulb went off, temporarily blinding her.

As they left the restaurant a short time later, Diz hustled to catch up to Dot. "Hi."

"Hi, yourself."

"I just wanted to say thank you for sticking up for me in there with Mr. Dempsey and not letting me look like some loser little kid."

Dot reached over and patted Diz on the back. "You're welcome. Besides, what I said was the truth. I've seen you throw the ball. You've got a good arm. Keep practicing and learn how to hit that drop ball, and I'm sure we'll find a place for you in the lineup."

"You really think so?"

"Yep. I really do."

For the rest of the day, all Diz could think about was the conversation with Dot. Even when they met the famed Radio City Rockettes and took pictures with them on the roof of Radio City Music Hall, Diz's imagination was busy conjuring visions of her hitting homeruns off the drop ball and rounding the bases to the cheers of the crowd.

The next night, when the Ramblers wrapped up the two-game set by beating the Roverettes again, this time in a raucous, 2-0, 18-inning affair, Diz paid even closer attention than normal to everything Dot Wilkinson did.

When Dot got the game-winning RBI on a walk in the top of the 18th inning, Diz cheered louder than anyone else in the record-breaking crowd of 13,500. She stood at the end of the line of Ramblers waiting to congratulate Dot after the game. "That was terrific, Dot. Did you see the way the crowd reacted to you? I swear, half of them wanted to kill you and half of them wanted to hug you."

"I didn't notice."

Undeterred by Dot's lack of enthusiasm, Diz prattled on. "What a neat trip this has been, huh?" She skipped alongside as Dot strode purposefully toward the Ramblers' cars. They were parked outside waiting for the team to make the long drive home to Phoenix. "Jack Dempsey, the World's Fairgrounds, the Rockettes, the Pittsburgh Pirates-Giants game. This has been so much fun."

Dot stopped short and rounded on Diz, her blue eyes piercing and serious. "If you want to make this team and be a Rambler, you need to remember something, kid."

Diz instinctively backed up a step. She hadn't been overstating Dot's ability to intimidate. "O-okay."

"The game is the only thing that matters. All of this fancy stuff is fine, but when it comes right down to it, softball is the only thing I care about. That's true for every player on this team, including your sister. So, if you want to be one of us, the game better be your number one priority. If it isn't, you can forget playing and go find something else to do with your time."

Diz simply nodded. *Softball first, last, and always. Got it.*

Phoenix, 2014

"That sounds pretty harsh," Julie said, as Diz pushed aside her now-empty coffee cup.

Diz waved a hand dismissively. "Not at all. It was the single most important thing Dottie ever said to me. I still thank her for it whenever I see her. Those were words to live by, you see." Diz's hand fluttered to her throat. "I'm sorry, dear. I'm not used to talking so much." She cleared her throat.

"After New York, I wanted to make the team even more than before. It became sort of an obsession with me. I began to practice harder. I learned to hit a drop ball." She shook her head. "I hated that damned drop ball. But I'd be dipped if I was going to let it keep me from making the team."

Diz coughed again, and Julie handed her a glass of water. She checked her watch as Diz sipped.

"It's no wonder your voice is worn out. We've been talking for two hours."

"Oh dear. We have?"

"We have. I shouldn't have kept you so long." Julie frowned, flipped closed the cover of the iPad, and shut off the tape recorder.

"Don't worry about it. I'm not as fragile as I look."

Julie chuckled. "Diz, there are many things I might say about you, but that you were fragile? That's not anywhere on the list."

"Good." Diz sat back and took her measure of the woman across the table. "I like you. I like you a lot. You're a good person, and that goes a long way with me. Especially when you're a real fan of the game."

"I'm glad. And again, I want you to know how much it means to me that you're willing to talk to me."

"It's my pleasure. Like I said, I don't often get to talk about the old days." Diz cocked her head to the side. "Remind me how you know Dot?"

"She knew my mother."

"Was your mother a player?"

Julie nodded. "When my mother died a few months ago, I was going through her things and I found a picture of her in a softball uniform. Apparently, she played for the Queens. In the picture, she was sliding into home and Dot was applying the tag."

"No kidding!" Diz exclaimed.

"No kidding."

"Well, I'll be darned."

"The handwriting on the back of the photo indicated that the play occurred during the 1940 regional softball championships. I was stunned. Although my mother was the one who taught me

21

how to play, she never, ever mentioned that she played at such a high level."

"I wonder why she didn't tell you?" Diz asked.

"Me too. Why would she hide that part of her life from me? I felt cheated, somehow, that there was this whole side of my mom that I knew nothing about. So I decided to get to the bottom of it. I tried to find anyone left who played for that Queens team in 1940, but they're all gone."

"Mm. Like I said earlier, there aren't many of us ball players left from that time," Diz said.

"I know, and because of that, I thought I might never figure it out. Then I looked at the picture again and decided to see if I could find the other woman in the photo."

"Dot," Diz said.

"Right. So I looked Dot up and showed her the picture. She remembered playing against my mother, but she didn't know anything about her, really."

"I'm sorry she couldn't help you." Diz patted Julie's hand.

"Thank you. That's so sweet." Julie smiled. "Anyway, as Dot and I started talking in general about what it was like to play back then, I got completely caught up in that world. The stories were fascinating."

"It was a different time, that's for sure."

"It wasn't just different. You gals were amazing!"

"It goes back to what Dot said to me all those years ago. The game was everything. That kind of commitment and passion doesn't seem to exist in today's players."

"I think you're right. So I really wanted to explore that and write about it. But I also began to wonder about something else." Julie wiped the condensation off her glass and took a sip of water as if gathering herself.

"What's that?" Diz asked. "And why, all of a sudden, do you seem uncomfortable?"

"Well, it's just…" Julie bit her lip. Instead of looking at Diz, she stared at the table. "This is a little bit awkward and I'm not sure what you'll think about it."

"Try me. Whatever it is, I'm sure it's nothing I haven't heard before."

"It's softball. And where there's softball, at least nowadays, there are lesbians." Julie met Diz's eyes. "I couldn't believe that there wouldn't have been any players back then that were gay. So I started researching."

"I'm sure you didn't find any mentions of that in old newspaper articles or write-ups." Diz's eyes twinkled.

"No, I sure didn't. But I did find a couple of interesting present-day items that told me I was on the right track."

"Such as?"

"Obituaries," Julie said. She reached into her bag, grabbed a folder, and pulled out a photocopied newspaper clipping. "First, I found an obit for Ricki Caito. That one listed Dot as her longtime companion." Julie slid the document across the table for Diz to see.

"You're a smart girl, I'll give you that."

"Thanks." Julie took the document back. She fingered a second piece of paper, started to take it out of the folder, hesitated, shoved it back inside, and returned the folder to the bag.

When she glanced back up from what she was doing, Diz was watching her knowingly.

"What is it you want from me?"

"While I started out just wanting to know about my mother and her time playing softball, I can see now that there's a more interesting story that needs to be told, one that's so obviously different than the perception created by the movie. That's why Dot pointed me in your direction."

"I see. So, have I been wasting your time for the past two hours, not giving you what you need?"

"Are you kidding me?" Julie gently squeezed Diz's hand. "You gave me exactly what I was looking for. That was an incredible memory."

"But what you really want to talk about is what it was like to be gay back then. You want to talk about me and Frannie."

Julie leaned forward, obviously warming to the subject. "I want to hear about all of it—the game, the times, being gay back then, your relationship. I'm guessing all of those things are intertwined for you. Are they?"

"They are."

"Are you going to be okay talking about it with me?" Julie asked.

"I guess that depends on what kinds of questions you have."

"I don't want to ask you anything you don't want to answer."
Diz pursed her lips in thought. "Well, Hell's bells. I'm eighty-nine years old. What do I care what people think anymore? Truthfully, it will be a relief to talk about it."

Julie sat back, pulled out her iPhone and opened the calendar app. "So, can we talk again soon?"

"Sure."

"Next week?"

"You bet." Diz peeked at Julie's notepad. "What's the next question on your list? I might need to prepare." Diz winked.

"As if." Julie scanned the page. "I want to talk about how you got your start playing for the Ramblers."

"That's easy."

"And, if you're comfortable about it, I want to talk about how you met Frannie."

Diz's hand hesitated as she reached for the water glass. "Oh. Going to get right to it, are we?"

"Is that okay? I really think that it's an integral part of the story."

Diz's eyes misted over and Julie put a hand over hers. "I'm sorry. I shouldn't have—"

"No, no. It's fine. Really." Diz smiled kindly. "But if we're going to talk about that, I think we'll need to take a field trip." Her eyes met and held Julie's gaze. "Are you up for that?"

CHAPTER TWO

Phoenix, 2014

The morning sun glinted off the bleacher seats at University Stadium and Julie slid her shades into place to block out the glare.

Slowly, deliberately, she pushed Diz's wheelchair forward. The wheels crunched on the gravel, the sound echoing loudly in the emptiness of this graveyard of champions. When they arrived at home plate, Diz reached back and tapped Julie's hand.

"Stop here."

The chair straddled the plate, offering a view of the entire diamond. For long moments, the only sound was the plaintive call of a red-tailed hawk as it circled overhead.

Julie stepped around the chair. Her eyes widened at the sight of tears streaming down Diz's face. She crouched down in front of Diz, a hand on each of the older woman's knees.

"What's the matter?"

Diz didn't answer. Her eyes tracked around the stadium, stopping and lingering briefly at various spots.

"Diz?"

"Hmm?"

"If this is too hard..."

Diz wrapped her fingers around Julie's hand. "No. I want to tell you. And I needed to see this place one last time." Diz took a deep, wheezing breath. "This is where it all started. It was the first place I saw her. She was so damned cocky. So sure."

"Who...Frannie?"

"Hmm?" Diz, who had been staring in the direction of left field, focused on Julie as if just realizing that she was there.

"You were saying something about this being the first place you saw somebody. Do you mean Frannie?"

"Why, yes. Of course. Who else would I be talking about?"

◈◈

Phoenix, 1941

Diz dug her cleats into the dirt and tried to get herself comfortable in the batter's box. She used her sleeve to wipe her forehead where beads of sweat formed and threatened to drip into her eyes.

Amelina "Amy" Peralta, who had helped pitch the Ramblers to the national championship several months ago, was on the mound. Dot Wilkinson was behind the plate. Mr. Hoffman stood off to the side, his arms crossed. Elsie was in right field, a sprinkling of other regulars were in their positions around the diamond, and the other three girls who were vying for a spot on the roster rounded out the field.

"Okay, kid. Let's see what you've got," Dot said, as she squatted down and patted her glove.

Diz squinted into the afternoon sun as it hung low and large over the pitcher's right shoulder. When Amy reached the top of her motion, the ball disappeared completely.

By the time Diz spotted it again, it was hitting Dot's glove with a pop. Diz's bat never moved.

"What was wrong with that one?" Dot asked, tossing the ball back to Amy. "You waiting for an engraved invitation to swing? Get the bat off your shoulder."

Diz swallowed hard and stepped out of the batter's box. She sucked in some air, took a practice swing, and settled herself in the box again. "Blasted sun's in my eyes."

"Better get used to it," Dot said. "It'd be the same in a game."

"Would not," Diz mumbled. "You guys play all your games here at night." She adjusted her hands on the bat and focused. This time, she swung at the spot where she thought the ball should've been. Her heart sank at the sound of the ball hitting the catcher's glove again.

She slumped her shoulders. At this rate, she'd never make the team.

"Listen, kid. Normally, I'd tell you to watch Amy's arm the whole way. But, with the sun where it is, try this—don't watch Amy's motion. If you do, you're just going to be guessing every time. You'll never hit the ball that way."

Although Diz kept her eyes forward, all of her attention was on what Dot was saying.

"Pick a spot, the place where you think Amy's going to release the ball, and focus only on that. Watch her hip. You'll be able to pick the ball up there. That's the release point. That's all you need to worry about."

"Okay," Diz said. "Thanks." She screwed her metal spikes deeper into the dirt and gravel and locked her eyes on the pitcher's right hip.

This time, when the pitch came, Diz saw it plain as day. She swung easily and grinned at the unmistakable and satisfying crack of the wooden bat connecting with the ball.

Her smile faded as the center fielder raced back, turned, and made a spectacular, diving catch. All eyes turned to the outfield and several players whistled and clapped.

"Nice grab, center!"

"Center," Mr. Hoffman yelled, "you're up."

"Great," Diz said. She walked back to the dugout, disgustedly threw the bat onto her bag, and picked up her glove. The Ramblers only had one opening in the outfield. If this girl could hit, whoever she was, chances were the coach would pick her.

Diz climbed the dugout steps, her head down, her hopes fading, and slammed directly into the center fielder. Instinctively, Diz reached out and grabbed the girl to keep her from falling. "Sorry," she muttered.

"That's okay. Don't worry about it."

Finally, Diz looked up. She blinked. The girl's hair was a lovely shade of red. Her eyes were a vivid shade of green. Her face was dusted with freckles and her smile…

"Miss Hosler! Center field. Sometime today, please."

Diz blinked, realizing that she hadn't relinquished her hold. "Um." She let go of the girl and shuffled to her left so that she had a clear path to the field.

"I'm Frannie," the girl called out.

"Dizzy," Diz answered. *Frannie.* Even her name was pretty.

With her first swing, Frannie lofted one deep to left. Although it was caught, the show of power was unmistakable.

Diz fussed with the strings on her glove and toed the grass as Mr. Hoffman walked out to the mound and said something to the pitcher.

"Hey," Elsie elbowed Diz.

"What?" Diz didn't bother looking at her sister.

"Snap out of it, that's what. You're standing around looking like you lost your dog."

"Have you seen what that girl can do?"

"I'm here, aren't I?"

"Then why are we having this discussion?"

"Because you're acting like a spoiled child instead of someone who wants to be a Phoenix Rambler."

"What do you want me to do?"

"I want you to play like you play with me every morning. Put some pep in your step and find your confidence. You can do this, Sis. But you have to believe it."

Diz straightened up. Elsie was right. She could do everything Frannie could do, just as well or better. Diz pounded her fist into her glove and peered in as Amy launched the next pitch. It was a rise ball, and Frannie timed it perfectly, connecting with the meat of the bat and sending it deep to center.

Diz turned and ran, glancing over her shoulder to spot the ball. It was several feet to her left, her backhand side. Realizing that it was too far for her to run, she launched into the air, laid herself out, and prayed. She hit the ground hard, her teeth clamping together from the impact, her belly skidding along the dry grass, her left palm scraping the bare patches where the cover had worn thin.

When she came to a stop, she rested her cheek on the ground and smiled. The ball was snuggled firmly in the pocket of her glove. Diz pushed herself back up, dusted herself off, and tossed the ball to the shortstop, who had come out to take the relay throw.

"That's what I'm talking about!" Elsie said, clapping Diz on the back.

Diz grinned. Elsie wasn't one to heap praise, so Diz figured the catch must've looked really impressive.

When Mr. Hoffman called the four prospects back in after each of them had seen three pitches, Frannie jogged up alongside Diz.

"Nice grab out there."

"Yeah? Well, yours was better."

"Nu-uh. Yours was backhanded."

"If you girls are done admiring each other's prowess in the outfield, I'd like to see what you can do at other positions. Francine, take third."

Frannie trotted out to third base.

"Miss Hosler, grab short."

The coach sent the other two girls to first and second base.

"Dot? Put them through the drills."

Dot picked up a bat and a bucket of balls and began to swat balls at every infielder in turn.

"Turn two," Mr. Hoffman yelled out, as a ball careened to Diz's right.

She fielded the hit cleanly, pivoted, and fired a throw to second base.

So it went for the better part of half an hour. Sweat dripped from Diz's face, down her neck and into her shirt and bra. She couldn't remember ever being this happy.

"Okay," the coach yelled. "That's enough for now. Bring it in."

All four prospects trotted over to where Mr. Hoffman and Dot Wilkinson stood chatting quietly.

Diz imagined they were sharing notes as the coach tried to decide which of the girls would make the team. Her stomach roiled. She'd acquitted herself well in the field, but Frannie was stronger at the plate and had that spectacular catch.

"Nice job, everybody. You haven't made my job easy here." Mr. Hoffman looked at each girl in turn. "First and second, thank you for coming. You're free to leave."

Diz worried at one of the rawhide knots holding her glove together. She was afraid to breathe, afraid to hear the coach's next words.

"Francine and Theodora, we have an exhibition game here tomorrow. I'd like you both to come so that I can get a look at you in a game situation."

≼ؘ؞ٙ

"Theodora? You've barely touched your dinner. What's the matter? Are you feeling alright?"

"Yes, Mother." Diz speared a green bean and shoved it in her mouth.

"Chew with your mouth closed, young lady."

"Yes, Mother."

"And don't talk with your mouth full."

"Yes, Mother."

Diz finished chewing. "May I please be excused?" Her knee bounced up and down under the table. It was almost dark. If she hurried, she could fit in another hour of practice before the ball would be too hard to see. She looked at her mother's intransigent face and her heart sank. She turned to her father, sitting at the head of the table. "Daddy?" Diz pleaded. "Please? You know how important tomorrow is to me. I need to go practice."

"Sure. But be back here before full dark."

"Ted! She hasn't even finished her meal."

"Relax, Beverly. There's no harm in it. Elsie and I are going up in the Valiant after dinner, anyway."

"Thanks, Daddy." Diz jumped up, nearly toppling the chair.

"Theodora!"

"Sorry, Mother," Diz called as she grabbed her glove from the table in the vestibule and yanked open the screen door. She winced as the door clattered shut behind her. She could imagine what her mother said about that. Fortunately, she was too far away to hear.

An hour later, Diz was sweaty and tired. She'd fielded imaginary ground balls and turned imaginary double plays. She'd chased down imaginary balls in the outfield and threw the ball home, no doubt getting the runner out. When she had trouble finding the last ball she'd thrown because it was getting too dark to see, she headed back to the house.

She ran into Elsie, who was just closing the door to the barn where their father stored their 1932 Chevy. "How was your flying lesson?"

"The best." Elsie swung her leather flying cap and goggles as they walked.

"Where is Daddy?"

"Already inside. He's flying the San Francisco route again tomorrow, and he needs to get a good night's sleep."

"What's so fun about it?"

"Flying?"

Diz nodded. Although her father had been a pilot for Transcontinental and Western Airlines for five years and kept his own Piper Cub Trainer on the side in which he gave flying lessons, she'd never flown with him. She was afraid of heights.

"Oh, Diz. It's the *most* up there. It's so freeing. The ground falls away and there's nothing but the wind, the sky, and the clouds above. And Daddy is such a patient teacher. You really should try it."

"No thanks. I'll keep my feet on the ground where it's nice and safe."

"Scaredy-cat. Other than playing softball, there's no place I'd rather be than in the cockpit."

"Lucky for you, Daddy treats us like the sons he doesn't have."

"Lucky for both of us. Can you imagine being stuck inside learning how to sew and bake?"

"Eww." Diz shuddered. She threw open the screen door and preceded Elsie inside.

"Theodora? Is that you?"

"Yes, Mother," Diz called, in the direction of the living room, where she knew her mother was listening to the radio.

"Did you see Elsie out there?"

"I'm here, Mother."

"Good. Go get cleaned up. It'll be full dark in a few minutes. I need you girls to bring the wash in off the line and fold it, please."

Diz groaned and rolled her eyes.

"Yes, Mother," Elsie answered.

"About tomorrow," Elsie said a few minutes later as they finished folding a linen tablecloth, "try not to be too nervous. Just play your best. Don't show off."

"I know," Diz said, putting the tablecloth in a nearby basket. "I'm not a kid anymore."

"Yes, you are." Elsie poked Diz in the side.

"Hey, cut it out!"

Elsie danced away, just out of Diz's reach. "No matter what, you're always going to be my little sister."

Diz couldn't argue with the truth of that, so instead she stuck out her tongue.

Elsie laughed and they finished folding the laundry in companionable silence.

Diz stepped to the plate for the first time against the Southern Arizona Champion Tucson Jewels. Despite her outward bravado, her palms were slick with nervous sweat, making the bat hard to grip. She asked the umpire for time, stepped out of the batter's box, wiped her hands on her shorts, and took a deep breath.

Somewhere in the background, she could hear her teammates cheering for her from the dugout. While the support should have made her feel more comfortable, in this case, it only made Diz more jittery.

"Watch out for the curve," Diz heard Dot yell.

"Keep your eye on the ball," Elsie chimed in.

"Right," Diz said, more to herself than anyone else. She stepped back into the batter's box and dug her cleats into the dirt.

The first pitch, a rise ball, sailed by her before she could even lift the bat off her shoulder. "Curve ball my eye," Diz mumbled.

"Steee-rike one!" the umpire yelled.

Diz took a practice swing and focused once again on the Tucson pitcher. The next delivery was headed directly down the center. Diz cocked the bat, strode into the ball, and connected with air. The ball curved at the last possible moment, putting it just out of reach.

"It's okay, kid. You'll get this one," a fan called from behind home plate.

"She's rattled," Diz heard someone else yell, no doubt from the Tucson dugout.

"Easy out. Strike her out, Wimpy!"

That last comment made Diz's ears turn red. She squinted at Wimpy Lansaw, the Tucson pitcher, standing supremely confident on the mound, and something shifted inside. Nervousness morphed into steely determination. And when the third pitch in the at-bat winged its way over the inside of the plate, Diz swung for all she was worth.

She felt the solid thwack of the ball meeting wood, heard the shouts of the crowd, and glanced out of the corner of her eye as the right fielder dove for, and missed, the catch. Diz ran as fast as her legs would carry her, rounding first as the first base coach waved her on to second. She spied the third base coach signaling her to slide and she launched herself, feet first, at the outside corner of the bag.

Diz looked up through the cloud of dust to see the umpire's signal.

"Safe!"

He granted her time as she popped up and shook the dirt out of her shorts. When she peeked into the dugout, she saw every single player, including Frannie, standing at the edge of the dugout, clapping and cheering.

Two batters later, Frannie slapped a single through the left side of the infield. Diz, moving with the hit-and-run on, scored on an errant throw from the left fielder.

In the end, Diz's run on Frannie's hit turned out to be the winning margin. When Ramblers' pitcher Amelina Peralta recorded the last out of the game with a strikeout, Mr. Hoffman called the team together.

"Good job, everyone. I saw a lot of things to be proud of tonight. I'd like to see our bats a little more lively, so we'll be taking a lot of batting practice in the next week or two before the regular season starts. Still, overall I thought we acquitted ourselves well for this early in the spring.

33

"Which brings me to a happy dilemma. Theodora, here, provided a key hit, showed excellent speed on the bases, and scored the winning run." Mr. Hoffman put a beefy hand on Diz's shoulder and Diz tried not to squirm at the attention as all eyes turned to her.

"Francine," the coach pointed at Frannie across the way, "supplied the game-winning hit.

"Both girls played errorless ball in the outfield, hit all the cutoffs, and generally fielded their positions well." The coach looked first at Frannie, and then back at Diz. "You two are making this decision hard for me."

Diz swallowed the lump in her throat. What if he chose Frannie? How would she ever show her face around the Ramblers again? And what if he didn't choose Frannie and Diz never got to see that brilliant smile again?

"So here's what I'm going to do," Mr. Hoffman said. "I'm going to keep both of you for now. You two will rotate playing time until one of you shows a clear advantage over the other."

Diz's legs buckled. She'd done it; she'd made the squad. She was a member of the vaunted P.B.S.W. Ramblers, the defending world champions. She blinked back tears as they welled in her eyes.

All of the girls moved in to surround Diz and Frannie to congratulate them.

"I'm not done yet," Mr. Hoffman said, and all of the players froze in place.

Diz wrestled her emotions under control.

"If one of you performs so spectacularly that there's no longer a question which of you is the better player, the other one of you will be dismissed. Conversely, if one of you clearly fails to live up to what you've shown thus far, you'll be let go without preamble. Do I make myself clear?"

"Yes, sir," Diz and Frannie said in unison.

"Okay. Now you may celebrate." He squeezed Diz's shoulder and backed away.

Diz was inundated by well-wishers. Every player patted her on the back, slapped her on the butt, or mussed her hair. In the midst of all the chaos, she fought to catch a glimpse of Frannie, who was similarly besieged.

Eventually, when the fuss died down, Diz spotted her. She wove her way over until they were standing face to face. Once there, Diz was completely tongue-tied. So she held out her hand for Frannie to shake.

Frannie ignored the proffered hand and threw herself into Diz's arms, wrapped herself around Diz, and squeezed hard. "Congratulations," Frannie breathed in her ear.

Diz's head swam. She registered that Frannie's hair smelled like lilacs in bloom and that her body was firm and warm.

"Aren't you going to say something?" Frannie asked. "We made it. We both made it."

Diz leaned back as far as she could so that she could have some space. If she thought that was going to help, it did not. Instead, she found herself gazing into Frannie's mesmerizing eyes. She was completely flummoxed. "I… Um… That's great. It's just great."

"Well, I think it is," Frannie said, frowning. She released Diz, pivoted, and walked away.

Diz blinked. What had she said wrong? Whatever it was, surely she could undo it. She took two steps toward Frannie's retreating form when she ran headlong into Elsie.

"I'm proud of you, Sis. You did great."

"Thanks," Diz said, tilting her head to look past Elsie toward where she had last seen Frannie.

"Wait until Daddy gets home tomorrow and hears. He's going to be thrilled."

"Yeah," Diz said. "Listen, I'll be back in a minute, okay?"

"Where are you going? Mother will be waiting up for us. We have to get home."

"I know. I'll only be a second," Diz said, and took off running in the direction Frannie had gone.

She caught up to her just as Frannie was about to get in a car with some girls Diz had seen in the stands behind the dugout during the game.

"Wait!" She skidded to a stop in front of Frannie. "I…" Now that she was here, Diz had no idea what it was she wanted to say. So she blurted out, "I hope I didn't offend you back there. I really

35

am happy we both made the team. I hope you didn't think otherwise." Her face turned beet red.

"I don't quite know what to think about you, honestly. But I suppose I'll give you the benefit of the doubt and just assume you're shy."

"Come on, Frannie. We're going to be late," one of the girls called from inside the car.

"Look, I've got to go."

"Oh. Okay. Um... Well... I guess I'll see you at practice tomorrow."

"You bet!" Frannie winked.

Diz stood by as Frannie climbed into the car and watched as it pulled away, leaving behind a haze of dust. She wasn't sure why it was so important what Frannie thought of her. She just knew that it was.

CHAPTER THREE

Phoenix, 2014

D iz's hands shook as she tried to twist the cap off a
bottle of water.

"I'll get that," Julie said. She liberated the plastic
bottle from Diz's grasp and removed the cap.

"Thank you." Diz accepted the bottle and drank greedily. "It's
going to be another scorcher today."

"I'm afraid you're right about that." Julie looked up, surprised
to see that the sun had traveled so high and so far across the sky
from the time they had arrived at the stadium. During the time Diz
had been talking, Julie had relocated them twice in order to find
shade. Now, it was just before noon, and the only shade to be
found was in the non-handicapped-accessible dugouts.

"I'd best be getting you back," Julie said. She undid the brakes
on Diz's wheelchair and rolled her in the direction of the exit.

"Wait," Diz said. She put a foot out as if to halt the chair's
progress.

"Whoa!" Julie came to an abrupt stop. "Careful, Diz. I don't
want you to hurt yourself."

"I thought we had this discussion? I'm not a delicate flower,
you know, just because I'm old."

"I'm sorry. That was a reflex. I'll try not to make that mistake
again."

"And I'm sorry I snapped at you. I hate being in this damned
chair."

"I can imagine."

"But I like being out with you. It's not that I don't like going places with my aide, but she hovers. I don't need someone who hovers."

"Noted," Julie said. "So, why are we stopping?"

"Take me over there." Diz pointed to the third base dugout.

"To the dugout?"

"Yeah." She lifted her leg with both hands and repositioned her foot on the foot-rest. "All moving parts are now in the vehicle, if you're worried about that. We can go now."

Julie laughed. "Aye, aye, captain." She pushed Diz toward the dugout until they were right in front of the steps that led to the benches, then stopped.

Diz wrapped her fingers around the arms of the wheelchair and began to push herself up. "Better hold onto this thing and keep her steady."

"What are you doing?"

"Checking on something in the dugout."

"You're going to walk?"

"I can, you know. For short distances, anyway."

"Diz, those are steps."

"Very observant."

"You're planning to walk down the steps?"

"Do you have a better idea? Surely you don't think you can carry me? And, unless this chair has wings, it's not getting down there."

"Are you allowed to do that?" Julie set the brakes and hustled in front of the chair to stand in front of Diz and support her.

"Are you planning to try and stop me?" Diz's arms shook with the effort of raising her body to a standing position.

Julie hesitated. What if she wasn't strong enough to support Diz's weight? What if Diz fell?

"Are you just going to stand there like a deer in the headlights? Or are you going to help me?" Diz was halfway out of the chair.

"Do I have a choice?" Julie stepped forward, wrapped her arms around Diz under the armpits, and lifted until Diz was standing upright.

"You can let go now. The getting up is the hardest part."

Julie continued to hold on as Diz swayed unsteadily. "Nothing doing. Not until I'm sure you're not going to fall."

Diz sighed. "You're as stubborn as I am."

"Probably."

"All right then, take my arm and support me that way. We'll do this together."

Julie shifted so that they were side-by-side and threaded her arm through Diz's. Together, slowly, painstakingly, they made their way down the three steps and into the dugout.

Diz ran the fingers of her free hand along the back wall. The forest green paint was peeling in places and fissures in the brick spoke to the age of the structure and the years of neglect.

When they arrived at the far end of the wooden bench, Diz stopped, extricated herself from Julie's grip, and bent over. "Mmph."

"What are you trying to do?" Julie asked.

"I need to see the underside of this bench."

"You—"

Before Julie could get the words out, Diz leveraged herself by placing a hand on the bench and dropped to her knees. She craned her neck and peered up.

"Diz!"

"It should be right..." Diz squinted. "There! There it is. Oh, Frannie, it's still here." Her trembling fingers caressed the wood.

Julie knelt down to catch a glimpse of what it was Diz saw. She read, "8/24/41." She glanced at Diz. Silent tears slid down the elderly woman's cheeks, tracing a path through the furrows and lines and dropping onto her blouse.

Without a word, Julie locked her arms underneath Diz's armpits and helped her up and into a sitting position on the bench. She sat down next to Diz and hugged her. They stayed like that for a long time, Julie rubbing Diz's back as her body shook with emotion. Finally, when Diz pulled away and wiped her eyes with a proffered tissue, Julie asked, "Is that a date, Diz? What does it mean?"

"Everything, dear girl. That date meant everything."

⧸❦⧹

Phoenix, August 24, 1941

Mr. Hoffman held the bat against his shoulder and a ball in the other hand. All of the Ramblers were gathered around him in a circle. "Okay. Look lively, ladies. When we leave for Detroit tomorrow, I want you all to forget that we're the defending world champions. In fact, I want you to forget everything except for how to hustle, how to make plays, and how to smack this little round thing where the other team isn't."

"Hey!" Diz winced as Elsie elbowed her in the ribcage. "What was that for?"

"Are you paying attention?"

"Of course—"

"Shush!" Jessie Glasscock, the shortstop, glared at the sisters.

Diz lowered her voice. "Of course I'm paying attention."

"You are not," Elsie whispered harshly. "Your mind is a million miles away."

"Is not. It's just that…we both know I probably won't even be going with you guys."

"You don't know that. Mr. Hoffman hasn't made up his mind yet whether he's taking you or Frannie on the trip."

"Frannie's been hitting the cover off the ball. And she hasn't had an error since July."

"Shush!" Jessie said again.

"Neither have you, Sis." Elsie lowered her voice further. "When are you going to get it through your fool head that you are every bit as good as Frannie?"

Diz rolled her eyes.

"You are. And Mr. Hoffman knows that. Now, if only you had Frannie's confidence, you'd be fine."

"Right." Diz frowned. Although the coach had been good for his word, splitting starts equally between them in center field, Frannie's batting average was a few points higher than Diz's, and she had a half dozen fewer strikeouts. The only thing Diz had working in her favor was her speed. She was far and away the faster base runner. As a result, she was better at stealing, better at successfully staying out of double plays, and had scored more runs.

"Okay, then. Everybody take your positions. We're going to run some game situations. Theodora," Mr. Hoffman pointed at Diz, "center field. Francine? Take left."

Diz's eyes widened in surprise. Both of them? In the outfield at the same time? And Frannie in left field? Usually, they took turns playing center.

"Sometime today, ladies."

Diz turned and trotted toward the outfield. Frannie came up alongside.

"What do you suppose this is about?" Frannie asked.

"I don't know." Diz took note of the other girls around them. "But I don't see Jean anywhere." Jean Klont, who for years had been the Ramblers' shortstop, of late had been moved to the outfield to make room for Jessie.

When they reached the outfield grass, Diz headed for center field.

"All right." Mr. Hoffman stood at home plate. "Runners on first and second, one out. Hit the cut-off." He hit the ball, and Diz ranged back and to her right.

"I've got it. I've got it!" She glanced quickly to check her proximity to the wall and to Frannie, who was running toward the ball from her position in left. Diz hauled the ball in just in front of the fence, got set, planted her right foot, and let the ball fly.

The throw was directly at the shortstop's head and in line with third base.

"Good job, center!" Coach Hoffman launched another long fly ball, this time to left, and then one to right. "Okay. Runner on third, one out. Runner is tagging…"

When they'd run through five more scenarios, the coach called the girls back in. "Outfielders, get running. Infielders, with me."

Diz groaned. Like all of the girls, she detested running laps around the field. The only thing that made it bearable was Frannie, who would run with her.

"Well, this is something, huh?"

"You mean us both practicing with the starters at the same time?" Diz slowed her pace slightly to allow Frannie to keep up.

"What else would I be talking about, silly?"

"Um…" Diz blushed and Frannie shoved her playfully, almost unbalancing her.

Frannie laughed. It was that deep, rich "I love life" laugh that made Diz's heart beat just a little faster.

"You have to be the shyest girl I've ever met."

The comment only made Diz redden more. She sped up.

"You can't outrun that cute blush, you know. And I'm making it my business to keep up with you."

They ran a few paces in silence.

"So, the way I see it, you can either keep trying to kill us both, or you can slow down a little so I can talk without huffing and puffing." Frannie wrapped her fingers around Diz's arm. "Come on, I'm dying here."

Diz relented and slowed her pace.

"There. That's much better. Now, where were we?"

"We were talking about us both being in the starting outfield at the same time."

"Right. So, what do you make of it?"

"I'm not sure."

"Ugh." Frannie shook her fists. "You are maddening, you know that?"

"Why would you say that?"

"Maybe it's because we've been playing on the same team for almost an entire season and I still can't figure you out. Sometimes I think we're going to be great friends. And then other days, like today, it's like you don't say more than two words to me." Frannie stopped running and, winded, bent over and put her hands on her knees.

Diz hesitated, thought about staying with Frannie, but decided to finish the two remaining laps by herself. "What am I supposed to do? How am I supposed to act?" she asked when she was out of earshot. Being around Frannie was…well, Diz wasn't sure what it was, but it was sure confusing. She felt like such an awkward oaf. Besides, she and Frannie were competitors. Yes, they were teammates, but, in the end, they were fighting for the same spot on the roster. Surely Frannie didn't expect Diz to be her best pal.

Diz sighed. If she was honest with herself, that was exactly what she wanted. "Out of the question," Diz said to herself. "She's what's standing between you and a starting position in the outfield."

Still, every time she was around Frannie, she felt alive and happy. When she wasn't with Frannie, she was thinking about the next time she would see her.

Diz finished the last lap and the coach motioned her to join the rest of the team on the bleachers.

"Okay. Listen up. This was a productive practice today and good preparation for what we're going to face in Detroit." Mr. Hoffman made eye contact with each player in turn. "Most of you have been in the big tournament before. A couple of you have not." He locked eyes first with Frannie, and then with Diz.

"Which brings me to this announcement."

Diz closed her eyes and prayed. *Please, God. Please let me be the one going to Detroit. I want to play in the national championship.*

"Some of you may have noticed that Jean isn't with us today. Unfortunately, she has some family matters to attend to."

A few of the girls murmured to each other. Diz blinked, wondering if she'd heard correctly.

"That means we'll be taking both Francine and young Theodora with us to the championships."

Diz gasped. From somewhere nearby, she heard Frannie give a little whoop. They were both going to Detroit? It was too good to be true.

"I expect those of you who have been down this road to help these two girls along. They've been real assets to us all season. I know that will continue. I'm counting on all of you," Mr. Hoffman looked pointedly at Dot Wilkinson and Marjorie Wood, "to take them under your wings and show them what it means to be a Rambler on the big stage."

"Yes, sir," Marjorie said.

"We will," Dot chimed in.

"Okay. That's it then. You all have a list of what to pack. We'll meet here in the morning and be on our way."

The girls all started to head toward the parking lot. Elsie wrapped an arm around Diz's shoulder.

"See? What did I tell you? You're coming with us. I knew it."

"Well, that makes one of us. I can't believe it."

"Hey, Diz." Frannie trotted up from behind. "A couple of my friends and I are going to go celebrate with a burger. Want to come?"

"Me?"

"You know anyone else named Diz?"

Diz looked to Elsie. "Can I? Do you think Mother would mind?"

"Aw, go ahead. You deserve it. I'll tell Mother you won't be home for dinner."

"Thanks, Sis!"

"You're welcome. Just don't be too late. We have to pack."

"I won't," Diz said, as Frannie grabbed her hand and dragged her in the opposite direction.

❦❦

"Where is everyone else?" Diz asked, when they were in the car.

Frannie checked her lipstick in the mirror and fussed with her hair. "There isn't anyone else."

"There isn't?" Diz's brow furrowed. "But I thought you said—"

"I just said that so your sister would let you go." Frannie turned toward Diz. "You don't mind, do you?"

"No. I just—"

"I didn't think Elsie would be too happy with us spending time together by ourselves."

"Why wouldn't she be?" Nothing was making any sense to Diz.

"I don't know. I just wanted you to myself for once, is that such a crime?"

"Gee, no. I mean, why would it be? But I still don't understand why you thought Elsie would care."

"How about if we go grab a burger and take a drive?"

"Okay, but I still don't see why you thought Elsie would care one way or the other."

"I heard you the first time, Diz. Just drop it, okay?" Frannie started the car and put it in gear.

"Sure. You don't have to get sore about it."

After a few minutes of stony silence, Diz decided to break the ice. She desperately wanted to be in Frannie's good graces, and it felt like they'd already gotten off to a rocky start. "So, what do you want to talk about?"

Frannie glanced at her for a second and her face instantly brightened. A smile played on her lips. Diz's stomach fluttered.

"You. I want to talk about you."

"Me?"

"Yes, you."

Diz's palms got moist and she wiped them on her shorts. Why on Earth would Frannie want to talk about her? "There's nothing interesting to say."

"I don't believe that for a second, Theodora Hosler."

Something about the way Frannie said her name made Diz's skin tingle.

"Why did your parents name you Theodora?"

"My father was hoping for a boy. They were going to call him Teddy."

"So they named you Theodora as a consolation prize? That's horrible."

"It's not as bad as it sounds. I mean, my dad and I do lots of stuff together. He's the one who taught me to play ball."

"Well, that's one good thing."

"And what's wrong with Theodora, anyway?" It was true that Diz wasn't overly fond of the name, but to have someone else, especially Frannie, speak disparagingly of it, well, that was another matter.

"There's nothing wrong with the name, silly. Just with your parents' reason for giving it to you."

"Oh."

They pulled into the parking lot of a burger joint, forestalling further conversation as they went inside and got seated at a booth.

The vinyl seat squeaked in protest when Diz plopped down. She looked around. Although the place was hopping, she didn't recognize anyone.

When they had ordered, Frannie asked, "What do you like to do when you're not playing ball?"

Diz leaned forward and raised her voice to be heard over the din of people talking and laughing and dishes clattering. "Swim, play basketball, read books, go to the movies. But really, I like to play ball more than anything in the world. So when we're not playing, I'm practicing."

Frannie leaned forward too. She had her chin in her hands.

"Why are you looking at me like that?" Diz fidgeted in her seat.

"Like what?"

"I don't know." Diz shrugged. "Like the fate of the world hinges on my answers to your questions."

"Maybe it does."

Frannie winked, and Diz felt her face grow hot. That seemed to happen a lot when she was around Frannie.

"Very funny."

"How is it possible that we've been playing on the same team all season long, almost forty games, and I hardly know anything about you? How is it possible that this is the first time we're really getting to spend any time alone together?"

"I don't know." Diz grabbed a paper napkin from the dispenser and began to shred it. Frannie reached over and stilled her hands, and Diz's heart tripped.

"Are you nervous?"

"No." Diz knew she sounded defensive.

"I think you are nervous. How adorable is that?"

Yet another blush crept up Diz's neck. She wasn't feeling very adorable, just embarrassed. She quickly withdrew her hands and folded them in her lap.

"Why are you—"

"Here you go, girls. Two burgers, one well, one rare, fries with both, and a vanilla milk shake with two straws."

Diz grabbed the Heinz bottle and poured ketchup on her hamburger.

"Are you planning to have any burger with all that ketchup?"

"Huh?"

Frannie pointed to the ketchup oozing out of the sides of Diz's hamburger bun.

"Oh. I like ketchup."

"I can see that."

Diz busied herself with eating, grateful for the distraction from the previous conversation, which had her feeling off-balance.

When they'd finished and split the bill, Frannie asked, "You still up for a drive?"

"Sure, I guess."

"If you don't want to…"

"No. I do."

"Okay, then. Let's go."

CHAPTER FOUR

Phoenix, 1941

The sun was near setting as they left the hubbub of the city behind. Diz wasn't sure where they were headed, but she didn't really care. Her belly was full, she'd made the roster for the championships, and she was with Frannie, who finally seemed to be satisfied with a comfortable silence, although Diz had no illusions that the quiet would last.

Sammy Kaye's "Daddy" was blaring from the radio, and Frannie was tapping her fingers on the steering wheel in time to the music.

Diz studied her. She was... What was she? Different, Diz decided. Frannie was different from any other girl Diz knew, not that she knew that many. Frannie laughed easily, didn't seem to care what other girls thought, she was popular... *And pretty. Don't forget pretty.* Boy, was she.

"A penny for your thoughts?"

Diz jumped. "Thoughts? I'm not thinking." She shifted in the seat as warmth spread through her. That seemed to happen often around Frannie too.

"Could have fooled me. There was most certainly something going on in that noggin. The scenery just isn't that interesting."

Diz opted to change the subject to something safer. "Where are we going?"

"Nowhere, really. I just thought it would be nice to go somewhere quiet."

The road ahead was completely devoid of vehicles. Diz swiveled in the seat and glanced behind them. There wasn't a car in sight in that direction either. "I'd say you found it."

"I'd say so too," Frannie agreed, as she turned onto a dirt road so overgrown by vegetation that it was hardly visible from the main road.

They bounced along on the uneven surface for half a mile before rolling to a stop at the top of a rise. In front of them, the sun was a huge orange ball and the sky was streaked with pinks and reds.

"Spectacular, isn't it?" Frannie asked. She put the car in park.

"It's like a painting," Diz said in awe.

Frannie shook her head.

"What?"

"You continue to surprise me, that's what."

"What did I do now?"

"You waxed poetic about a sunset."

"I did not." Diz stared at the dashboard and willed her face not to redden in embarrassment again. Why did Frannie have to scrutinize everything she said?

"No? Then what do you call it?"

"I don't know. I just said what I felt."

"Exactly!" Frannie scooted closer to Diz on the seat. "You see things other people miss. But you're so quiet and shy, it's like pulling teeth to get you to open up and say anything."

Diz scoffed. "I say plenty."

"Yeah? When?"

"I don't know. Lots of times."

Frannie threw her head back and laughed. That was the last straw. Diz fumbled with the handle, threw open the door, and stomped away. Why did Frannie constantly feel the need to challenge her?

She hadn't gotten five paces before Frannie caught up to her and wrapped her arms around her from behind. "What's the matter?"

"Nothing." Diz squirmed away.

"Nothing?"

Diz jutted her chin out. "Why do you always have to make me feel…"

Frannie moved closer again. "Why do I always have to make you feel…what?"

"I don't know." Diz threw her hands up. "I get so confused around you. It's like I can never say anything right."

"What do you mean? I think you say lots of things right. When you say things."

"See? You did it again." Diz pointed a finger accusingly.

"Did what? I swear to God, Diz. I have no idea what you're going on about."

"When you say things." Diz mimed quotation marks with her fingers. "Why'd you have to add that?"

"I don't know." Frannie waved a hand dismissively. "What does it matter?"

"It matters to me," Diz huffed.

"Okay, then." Frannie held up her hands in surrender. "I'm sorry. I didn't mean anything by it."

"Okay, then."

"Good." Frannie lowered her hands.

The two girls stood almost toe-to-toe. Diz could see the pulse beating in Frannie's neck and a drop of sweat as it trickled down into her shirt.

"Do you know how to dance?"

"What?" Diz blinked.

"I asked if you know how to dance? You know…" Frannie twirled around, holding an imaginary partner.

"I've never tried."

"Well, we need to fix that." Frannie ran to the car and turned up the radio. Tommy Dorsey and his orchestra were playing "Let's Get Away From It All." She came back and stepped even closer to Diz than she was before.

Diz didn't move. She didn't breathe.

"Here." Frannie put her left arm around Diz's waist. "Put your right arm around my shoulders."

Diz did as instructed.

"Excellent. Now, put your left hand in mine." Frannie held up her free hand and Diz entwined their fingers. Frannie began to turn them in a circle.

Diz, who was several inches shorter than Frannie, couldn't figure out where to put her head.

Frannie must have recognized Diz's dilemma, because she unclasped their hands and guided Diz's cheek to her shoulder. "Better?" She took Diz's hand again.

Diz closed her eyes. "Fine." Diz's body tingled every place it came into contact with Frannie. She concentrated on not stepping on Frannie's feet.

"Relax," Frannie said, and tugged on Diz's hand. "You're going to squeeze my hand to death."

"Oh. Sorry." Diz eased her grip.

"You're doing great."

Diz could feel Frannie's words as a vibration against her ear. She tried to think of something to say so she could feel that again and again, but nothing came to her. And then the song ended.

Diz started to pull away, but Frannie held her fast. "Let's keep going, shall we?"

"S-sure." Diz's heart tripped happily.

They danced through Artie Shaw, Harry James, and Glenn Miller.

"Mm. This is nice," Frannie said.

"Mm-hmm."

"Are you enjoying yourself?"

Oh, yes.

"Diz?"

Belatedly, Diz realized she hadn't answered the question out loud. "Uh-huh."

"I'm glad."

When the last notes died away on The Andrews Sisters' "I'll Be With You in Apple Blossom Time," Frannie brought them to a halt.

Slowly, reluctantly, Diz opened her eyes and turned her head. Frannie was watching her from inches away. As if in a dream, Frannie leaned in and softly touched her lips to Diz's lips. The moment was so brief, Diz wondered if it had really happened at all.

And then Frannie leaned in again. This time, the contact was prolonged, Frannie's lips soft but firm on Diz's mouth. Diz's heart hammered in her chest. Her blood seemed to pump straight out of her head, traveling downward to her belly and beyond. She thought maybe she should object. Were girls supposed to kiss other girls? And why was her body doing the fox-trot?

When Frannie pulled back, Diz stayed stock still, her eyes firmly closed. She could still taste Frannie's mouth. Whatever she was supposed to think, all she knew was that she wanted more.

"Was that okay?"

Was it ever. Diz opened her eyes and tried to wrestle her body under control. "Uh-huh." It came out as a squeak.

"You're sure?"

Diz nodded, not trusting her voice this time. Whenever she had daydreamed about her first kiss, she pictured it being in a romantic restaurant, over a candlelit dinner, like they did in the movies. But this, this was nothing like anything she'd expected. It was...perfect. Frannie's lips were so soft. Diz let out a dreamy sigh.

"Hello, Diz?"

"Huh?" Frannie was watching her with an intensity that made Diz squirm.

"Have you ever been kissed by a girl before?"

Diz shook her head.

"Never?"

She shook her head again. Idly, she wondered what kissing a boy would feel like. Would it feel different than kissing a girl?

"Have you ever been kissed before, period?"

Diz's heart thumped. Was Frannie reading her mind? She probably shouldn't be thinking about kissing a boy when she had just finished kissing Frannie. She dropped her gaze to the ground and shook her head one last time.

Frannie squeezed their joined hands and Diz looked up without making eye contact. "It's okay. You're a really good kisser."

"T-thank you."

"How old are you, Diz?"

"I'm sixteen. Almost seventeen." Finally, Diz met Frannie's eyes. "How old are you?"

"Nineteen."

"Oh." Diz frowned. She'd known Frannie was older, just not how much older. "Do you mind that I'm younger?"

"Not at all. I think you're the sweetest thing."

Something occurred to Diz. "Have you kissed other girls before?" She wasn't sure why, but the answer seemed desperately important to her.

"Once or twice."

"Which was it? Once? Or twice?" Diz felt a surge of jealousy.

Frannie huffed out a breath. "It was twice, but the second one didn't count."

"Why not?"

"Because I only did it on a bet. I didn't really mean it."

"Oh." Diz kicked at a pebble on the ground at her feet. "Did you mean it just now with me?"

Frannie let go of one of Diz's hands and lifted her chin with two fingers. She was staring at Diz's lips and Diz swallowed hard.

"Oh, yes. I definitely, definitely meant it." Frannie lowered her head and captured Diz's lips once again.

When they separated, Diz was light-headed. Surely this was better than kissing a boy ever could be.

"Do you believe me?" Frannie asked.

"Uh-huh."

"Are you ever going to answer me with something more than two syllables?"

"Uh-huh."

"Good." Frannie laughed and tugged on Diz's hand. "We'd better get going before it gets full dark out here. I'm sure your folks will wonder where you are."

"Oh, my gosh!" In all the excitement, Diz had completely forgotten about the clock. "What time is it?"

"Not too late, yet. But we really should get a move on."

With no traffic, they made good time. Several times, Frannie took one hand off the steering wheel and briefly held Diz's hand. Each time, Diz's heart happily pitter-pattered.

When they reached Van Buren Street, Frannie turned.

"What are you doing? I live—"

"I know where you live. There's something I want to do, first."

Diz started to protest, but Frannie pulled into the now-deserted parking lot at University Stadium. "Why are you taking me back to the ball park?"

"You'll see."

They giggled as they stumbled their way to the third base dugout.

"What are we doing here?" Diz whispered.

Frannie removed her belt. "I want us to remember this date always." She felt her way along the bench until she was at the end, then laid down on the dugout floor so she was looking up at the underside of the bench, the sharp point of the belt buckle in her hand.

Diz couldn't really see what she was doing because her arm was in the way. When Frannie was finished, she tugged on Diz's hand.

"Come see."

Diz lowered herself to the floor and looked up. There, in neat handwriting, was a date. 8/24/41.

∽≼∙≽∾

Phoenix, 2014

"Oh, that's so romantic." Julie clasped her hands over her heart. "I'm so glad this bench is still here."

"I can't believe it is," Diz said. She blew her nose.

Julie laid a hand gently on Diz's knee. "You must miss her so much."

Diz nodded. "It's been almost nine years now, and I still miss her every day. I talk to her, and I imagine she hears me, but it isn't the same."

"I don't see how it could be. Sixty-four years together is a long time."

"It is," Diz agreed. "Don't get me wrong, we had our ups and downs, but I can't imagine being with anyone else. She was it for me." Diz yawned. "I'm sorry. Bringing all this up seems to have worn me out."

Julie looked at her watch. It was almost two o'clock. "Oh, good heavens. I've kept you out much longer than I intended." She jumped up. "I've got to get you home."

Diz tucked the tissue in the pocket of her shorts. "Now the trick is going to be getting me back up those stairs." She chuckled. "Whose bright idea was it to come down here, anyway?"

Julie laughed with her. "I'm pretty sure it was yours."

"So it was." Diz placed her hands palm down on the bench and pushed. Her bottom barely lifted off the bench before she plunked back down.

"Well, that isn't going to work." She motioned to Julie. "If you could just help me get my legs under me, I think I can make it the rest of the way."

After much pushing and pulling, Diz was on her feet and shuffling to the bottom of the stairs. "Okay, here we go," Diz said.

Julie supported her under her right arm, and Diz used the railing to lift herself up the steps, resting between each step.

"Wait here." Julie released the brakes on the chair, maneuvered it to where Diz was standing, and positioned it behind Diz's knees. She reset the brakes and held the chair as Diz gracelessly dropped down into it.

"Well, that was fun," Diz deadpanned. "Remind me not to try a damned-fool stunt like that again."

Julie shook her head. "I'm pretty sure I told you that before you got out of the chair this time."

"So you did. You're a smart girl." Diz winked.

"And you're a determined girl."

"Thank you for not saying that I'm stubborn. Frannie would've called me pig-headed. She always did."

"I'm waiting until I know you better."

"I imagine by the time I'm done answering all of your questions, you'll know more about me than I know about myself."

"Somehow I doubt that."

As Julie rolled Diz toward the parking lot, Diz twisted around in the chair and looked back at the field.

"Do you want me to stop and turn you around?"

"That's sweet. No. That's not necessary. I just wanted to see it one more time. Lots of memories here."

"I bet."

"Speaking of which, you'd best tell me what you're going to want to know next so I can get started thinking about it."

"I'd like to pick up right where we left off today. I mean, here you'd just been kissed for the first time, and it was the night before you left for the 1941 National Championships."

Phoenix, August 24-25, 1941

Diz knew she should be asleep. It would be daylight soon enough and they were getting an early start on the road. But sleep would not come. She kept replaying the day's events over and over again in her mind.

The national championships. She was going to Detroit as a member of the reigning world champs. And, best of all, Frannie was going too.

Frannie. Diz let out a dreamy sigh and touched her lips reverently with her fingertips. She'd spent an extra fifteen minutes in the bathroom after she got home, checking to see if her lips looked any different now that she'd been kissed for the first time. They looked the same to her, but she certainly felt different.

When she thought of Frannie now, her heart pounded and her whole body was alive with sensation.

She closed her eyes and she was in Frannie's arms again, turning in circles on a bluff in the middle of nowhere.

How had Frannie found that spot? Did she know about it beforehand? Was that where she'd taken the other girls to kiss them? Diz's stomach lurched at the very idea of that. Surely she was not like the other girls Frannie had kissed. No, surely she was special. Wasn't she?

Diz desperately wanted to know. Maybe she could get Frannie alone and ask her; she resolved to try. And who were the other girls? Diz sorted through the friends who often attended the Ramblers' games to root for Frannie. They were the same girls Diz had seen Frannie get in the car with that very first day they'd met. Were any of those girls the ones Frannie had kissed?

"You have got to stop thinking about this and get some rest. You're going to be dead on your feet in the morning," Diz mumbled to herself.

But it was no use. She simply was incapable of getting her brain to shut off. She turned over and yanked the pillow over her head.

She revisited getting out of Frannie's car in front of the house. More than anything, Diz had wanted to give Frannie a kiss goodbye—to tell her what the evening had meant to her.

But she imagined her mother, or Elsie, looking out the window, waiting for her. Or worse yet, coming out on the front porch. What would they think if they saw her and Frannie together, kissing?

A rush of heat warmed Diz's cheeks. What was it her mother had said to Elsie when she'd learned that Diz made the team?

"Now, you watch over your little sister. She's a lot more naïve than you are. Make sure she doesn't fall in with the wrong crowd."

"What wrong crowd would that be, Mother?"

"You know…those odd girls. The queer ones."

"Oh, Mother. There are no queer girls on the Ramblers. You worry too much."

Diz groaned. Were there any queer girls on the Ramblers? Frannie had kissed Diz. Did that make Frannie queer? Did the fact that Diz let herself be kissed, the fact that she enjoyed the kiss and let it happen more than once, did that make *her* queer? It was all so confusing.

Diz wished she had someone to talk to about it. She thought about going next door and waking Elsie, and immediately dismissed the idea. Not only would Elsie be sore about being awakened in the middle of the night, but what if Elsie told their mother what Diz and Frannie had been up to? What if Elsie disapproved?

No, Diz would just have to keep quiet about it and try to figure it out herself. At least, in a few hours, she'd be seeing Frannie again, even if it would be in a crowd.

Diz pictured Frannie one more time, in that split second right before the first kiss, her lips parted and moist, her breath sweet, and her arm around Diz's waist. Finally, she drifted off to sleep.

CHAPTER FIVE

Phoenix, 1941

Diz barely waited for the car to come to a stop before grabbing her bag and hopping out.

"Ouch! What's your hurry? Watch where you're going," Elsie grumbled, as she collected her own bag.

Diz hardly noticed. Frannie was standing with some of the other girls and the mere sight of her made Diz's heart leap.

"Young lady. Aren't you forgetting something?"

Diz skidded to a stop, turned around, and walked back to the car. "Yes, Mother?"

"You give me a proper kiss goodbye."

Dutifully, Diz complied.

"Be a good girl. Don't give Mr. Hoffman any trouble."

"Yes, Mother."

"Remember to wash be—"

"Mother! I'll be fine. I promise."

"Okay then. Have a good time."

Diz already was halfway across the parking lot. *Look up, look up, look up.* She slowed her steps the closer she got to Frannie.

But Frannie didn't look up. In fact, she didn't seem to notice Diz at all. Stung, Diz changed directions and joined the girls who were loading the suitcases on the trailer behind Dot Wilkinson's car.

They would take two cars to Detroit, caravan-style, seven people in each car. It would be cramped, but maybe Diz could arrange to sit next to Frannie. That would be dreamy.

"Are you going to give me that bag, or are you just going to stand there?"

"What?" Diz blinked.

"The bag," Dot said. "Give me the bag."

"Oh. Sure." Diz handed the bag to Dot.

"Here's mine, Dot."

Diz heard Frannie's voice before she saw her and her stomach did a little flip. Frannie passed her bag to Dot as she put her free arm around Diz.

"Hiya, Diz. Nice day for a drive, don't you think?"

"H-hi." Diz's shoulders tightened even as warmth spread through her. Could Dot tell how she and Frannie felt about each other?

Mr. Hoffman whistled. "Gather 'round, everybody."

To Diz's surprise, Frannie kept her arm right where it was as they turned and walked to where the coach was waiting.

"What's the matter? You seem a little tense."

"Nothing's the matter. But what if…"

"What if, what?" Frannie asked.

"Do you think anybody can tell?" Diz whispered.

"Tell what?"

"You know…"

Frannie brought her mouth so close to Diz's ear that Diz could practically feel her lips. "That we kissed?"

The word vibrated against Diz's ear-drum and sent shivers down her spine. Her eyes darted right and left. Was anybody watching them? Was anybody close enough to hear?

"You need to relax. It's not like it's written on our foreheads or anything. Just act natural."

"Natural," Diz repeated.

Frannie put pressure on Diz's shoulder to slow them down. "Have I ever put my arm around you before in public?"

"Sure, but—"

"Then don't you think it would be more suspicious if I didn't put my arm around you now?"

Diz thought about it. "I don't know."

"Listen. The only thing that could give it away is you being so jumpy. Calm down. Everything is fine."

"Okay, everybody. It's going to be a tight squeeze, as you know, so let's make the best of it," Mr. Hoffman was saying.

"Rookies on the hump for this first leg," Dot said. "Diz, you're with me. Frannie, you go with Mr. Hoffman."

Diz wanted to object. She didn't care that she'd be perched on top of the drive train, but why couldn't she and Frannie ride in the same car?

Her dejection must have shown, because when they broke to go to their respective assigned cars, Dot said to her, "Sorry, kid. Rookies always get the short end of the stick."

"That's all right, Dot. I'm just glad to be here." That was true, after all. But having to stare at the car ahead of them all day, knowing Frannie was in there, was going to be torture.

≪⧫≫

By the time they stopped in Albuquerque, New Mexico to stretch their legs and find a spot to eat the lunches they'd packed, Diz's legs were so cramped she wasn't sure she could stand up.

She waited until the other three girls in the back seat had all piled out. Then slowly, carefully, she uncurled herself and slid across the seat.

"Can I help?" Frannie reached into the car, her hand outstretched.

As their palms touched, goose flesh crawled up Diz's arms. Frannie's hand was callused from swinging the bat, but her touch was gentle.

"Thanks." Diz knew she was grinning like a fool just at the sight of Frannie, but she didn't care. And when Frannie winked at her as they stood toe-to-toe, it was all Diz could do not to reach forward and...

"Okay, everybody," Mr. Hoffman said. "Sorry it was too wet in Gallup to get a workout in. I'm sure your legs are stiff. Do your best to stretch. Otherwise, you've got half an hour to eat up and whatever else you need to do before we get on the road again. I want to be in Amarillo and settled before nightfall."

Frannie stepped back. "Lunch time," she said lightly. "I brought a sandwich and an apple. What do you have?"

"A sandwich and a pear."

"Well, that all sounds pretty boring, doesn't it?" Frannie turned Diz around and pointed across the street. "Do you see what I see?"

The sign read, "The Iceberg Café." In smaller letters on the big glass window, the café advertised that it sold ice cream. "I can't afford—"

"My treat," Frannie said. She grabbed Diz's hand and dragged her across the street. "Besides, I need to go potty and I bet they have a nice bathroom in there."

It was hard to argue with that, so Diz allowed herself to be led toward the restaurant.

"Where are you guys going?" Elsie asked.

"To get some ice cream," Frannie said. "Want to come along?"

Elsie shook her head. "Diz, you know Mother wouldn't approve. You haven't even eaten your sandwich yet."

"Well, Mother isn't here, now is she?" Diz knew she sounded churlish, but she couldn't seem to help herself. For hours and hours, she'd been stuck in the most uncomfortable position she could imagine, listening to Amelina, Marjorie, and Elsie gossip about boys. Virginia "Dobbie" Dobson sat next to Dot in the front seat, and Kathleen "Peanuts" Eldridge was wedged against the front passenger door. The three of them were having their own conversation. So, left to her own devices, Diz spent her time wondering what Frannie was up to in the other car.

Was she wondering what Diz was thinking about? Was she reliving their kisses? Was she wishing they were sitting together too?

"That was a little harsh, don't you think?" Frannie asked as she pushed open the door to the café. "Your sister was only trying to look out for you."

"I suppose." Diz frowned. "I'll apologize to her. I just didn't feel like being nagged."

"What can I get you girls?" the soda jerk asked.

"Two chocolate ice cream cones to go, please." Frannie plopped down on one of the stools at the counter and took the change for the ice cream out of her pocket. "What were they talking about in your car?"

"Boys." Diz sat down. "You?"

"Same."

"I wish we could be in the same car."

"Me too." Frannie batted her eyelashes at Diz. "What do you suppose we'd talk about?"

Diz's palms started to sweat. "Um…"

Frannie laughed and patted Diz's knee. "Stay here and wait for the ice cream. I'll be right back." She plunked the change down on the counter as she walked away.

Diz watched as Frannie wove her way past the tables and to the back of the restaurant where a sign indicated there were restrooms. Maybe it was better that they weren't in the same car, after all.

Dusk painted the sky a spectacular array of blues, oranges, and reds as the team pulled into a small motel on the main drag in Amarillo, Texas.

Everyone waited in the cars as Mr. Hoffman went into the office to see about rooms for them. When he came back, he had three keys in his hand. He handed one key to Dot, one to Marjorie, and one to Elsie.

Diz's heart sank as she did the math. Two double beds per room, plus one cot. Five in a room. Surely she'd be bunking in with Elsie's group and she'd be stuck on the cot. She was a rookie, after all. That meant that Frannie most likely would be either with Dot's group or with Marjorie's group, also on a cot.

"I'm sorry, girls, but they only had one cot." Mr. Hoffman put one beefy hand on Diz's shoulder, and the other on Frannie's shoulder. "You two can choose who gets stuck on the floor."

"I'll—" Diz started to say.

"I've got an idea," Frannie broke in. "Diz is small and I don't move much in my sleep. What if we slept three in one of the beds? Elsie and Diz are sisters, so they're used to each other, and I don't mind being close to the edge. The three of us could be in one bed. That way, nobody would have to sleep on the floor."

Dot was saying something, but the buzzing in Diz's ears made it hard for her to hear. Surely Frannie didn't just suggest that the two of them sleep together…with her sister?

"I'll take the cot tonight," Jessie Glasscock said, "but only if Frannie irons my uniform in return."

"Deal." Frannie stuck her hand out for Jessie to shake.

"Okay. Sounds like you've got it all worked out," Mr. Hoffman said. "Let's unload only what you need for the night first and then get some dinner. The manager tells me there's a restaurant a few blocks away that serves a good steak."

⤜⤛

"Are you going to eat those potatoes?"

"What?"

"The potatoes?" Dot poked her fork in the direction of Diz's plate. "Are you planning to eat them?"

"No. Go ahead." Diz slid the plate closer to Dot.

"What's wrong with you, kid? You haven't said two words all meal."

"Nothing's wrong," Diz said. "Just not that hungry, I guess." As casually as she could, Diz shifted in her seat to get a better view of Frannie. She was sitting all the way at the other end of the table and seemed to be having a grand time chatting with Louise Curtis and Marjorie. Was Frannie as nervous as she was about sleeping in the same bed? She didn't appear to be.

"Well, you really ought to eat something. Put some meat on those bones," Dot said.

Diz speared a piece of broccoli and shoved it in her mouth. "Better?" she asked, when she finished chewing.

"Better would be you finishing off that ribeye."

Diz picked up the knife, cut the steak into cubes, and took a bite, savoring the flavor.

"Now that's more like it." Dot leaned over and stabbed another potato. "It's understandable that you're nervous, you know."

Diz's eyes got wide. "W-what?"

"I was nervous too the first time."

Diz's hand froze midway to her mouth. "Y-you were?"

"Heck, yeah. There I was, just a young kid, away from home for the first time, sleeping in a hotel, surrounded by girls who were older than me."

66

Diz lowered the fork. "What happened?"

"I got over it. When we walked out of that tunnel at Soldier Field in Chicago in 1934 in front of all those fans, I got goose bumps. But once the first batter stepped to the plate, it was just another game."

Diz blew out a breath she didn't know she was holding. *Softball.* Dot was talking about softball.

They finished eating and all walked back to the motel together. Everyone was in high spirits.

"How about a game of cards?" Louise asked.

Everyone agreed that they would meet in Marjorie's room.

"Don't stay up too late, girls. We've got an early start in the morning. I'd like us to work out in Oklahoma City and have plenty of time to get to the hotel in Tulsa and settle in before tomorrow night's game," Mr. Hoffman said.

Diz yawned and struggled to keep her eyes open. The all-day car trip, combined with too-little sleep last night, was taking its toll.

Finally, after Dobbie won for the third time, Diz stood up. "I hate to be a party pooper, but I'm exhausted. I'm going to go get some shut-eye."

"Little Sis is right," Elsie said, getting up too. "It's getting late. You heard what Mr. Hoffman said. It'll be rise and shine at six o'clock."

Reluctantly, all the girls agreed and went to their respective rooms.

Elsie, Amelina, and Louise collected their toiletries and towels for the trip down the hall to the bathroom.

"Rookies last," Louise said, as Diz picked up her towel too.

Diz sat back down on the bed. Louise's laughter echoed down the hall.

"I thought we'd never be alone." Frannie sat down so close to Diz that their thighs were touching.

"We were alone when we got the ice cream." Diz smoothed the crease in her Levis. The heat of Frannie's bare leg where her shorts ended sent waves of warmth through Diz's body.

"No," Frannie disagreed. She ran her fingers through Diz's curly hair, settling an errant strand back into place. "There were lots of strangers around."

Diz swallowed hard. Frannie's eyes were so...*green. They're so green. And soft. And close. And her mouth...* Diz gasped when Frannie leaned forward and touched their lips together. It was barely a whisper, but...

"No!" Diz jumped back, shaking her head. "No. They could come back any second now."

Frannie pursued her, scooting closer yet again. "Relax. They only just left." She cupped Diz's cheek and leaned in again.

Diz closed her eyes. Frannie's touch felt like the sun kissing her face at first light.

"...And then Donald said..."

Diz's eyes popped open and she stood up so fast she practically fell over. She tugged at her blouse to settle it.

Elsie, Louise, and Amelina came bursting through the door.

"What did he say?" Elsie asked. "Come on, you've got to tell us now."

Diz pretended to check something in her bag.

"Well, he said I had the nicest smile he'd ever laid eyes on," Louise said. "Can you imagine?"

"Your turn, rookies," Amelina said, as she stowed her toilet kit.

"Y-you..." Diz cleared her throat. "You go first, Frannie."

"We could go together."

Diz glared at Frannie. How could she be so flip at a time like this? They'd almost gotten caught. "No. I'll wait until you come back."

"Suit yourself." Frannie breezed out the door.

When she returned ten minutes later, Diz barely waited until she'd cleared the door to make her exit.

"Reckless," Diz muttered, as she hurried along the hall. "Crazy. That was just crazy."

As she brushed her teeth, she checked herself in the mirror. Her face was flushed and her pupils were dilated. She ran a hand through her hair where Frannie's fingers had been. God, that had felt so good.

Stop it. Just...stop it. How are you going to get through the night lying right next to her?

Diz considered her options. What if she just said the mattress was too uncomfortable and she wanted to sleep on the floor? She frowned. Frannie would probably be really hurt if Diz did that. No, she didn't want to upset Frannie. She would just have to make the best of it and hope that Frannie behaved.

When Diz got back to the room, everybody was in bed except for Frannie. She was sitting on the edge of the bed, facing the door—facing Diz. She was wearing a worn old t-shirt and a pair of beat up old shorts.

Oh, my. It's going to be a really, really long night.

Frannie smiled, and Diz could have sworn she gave her a ghost of a wink. "I thought I'd wait until you got back to get under the covers. That way you don't have to climb over me to claim your spot."

Diz swallowed hard as the image of climbing over those bare legs flitted across her mind.

"Turn off the light, will you Diz?" Amelina asked. She rolled over and faced the opposite wall, pulling the covers over her head.

Diz slid her toilet kit back in her bag and turned off the light. The room turned pitch black. "Great." How was she supposed to find her way to the bed without tripping?

A hand reached out and grabbed her, and she swallowed a scream.

"The bed's over here," Frannie said.

She pulled Diz toward her and Diz was suddenly glad for the cover of darkness.

"Thanks," she said, as she slid under the covers that Frannie held up for her and scooted over until she was right next to Elsie, as far away from Frannie as she could get.

"Hey. Give me some space, will you?" Elsie elbowed Diz. "Move over. Frannie won't bite you. Will you, Frannie?"

"No. I'm safe as can be."

Diz rolled her eyes. *Not by a long shot.* She shifted as Elsie requested and held her breath when she felt the mattress dip from Frannie's weight.

When Frannie's hand brushed against the side of her leg, Diz nearly levitated off the bed.

"Sorry," Frannie whispered. The covers rustled.

"What are you doing?"

"I'm taking my shorts off. I hate sleeping in them—too constricting."

Diz groaned as warmth spread through her limbs. Frannie was less than a foot away from her, lying there in just her panties and an old, ripped t-shirt.

"Shh." Elsie pounded on her pillow and fluffed it up again. Within a minute, she was snoring loudly.

Oh, this is just perfect. I'm in Purgatory. Diz lay on her back, her hands stiff at her sides, afraid to move in either direction. She concentrated, listening to hear if Frannie was asleep.

The answer came several minutes later when Frannie's fingertips grazed hers and she interlaced their fingers.

Diz's heart leapt. She should object. It was too risky. What if they got caught? What if Elsie could feel that on the other side of the bed?

As if reading her thoughts, Frannie ran her thumb over the back of Diz's hand, then let go.

Diz exhaled in relief. *I'll never be able to sleep.*

And yet, somehow, she must have, because she awoke in the middle of the night, horrified to realize that she was lying on her side, her arm thrown over Frannie's middle. Carefully, cautiously, she withdrew her arm and rolled onto her back.

She tried to envision what it would be like if it was only her and Frannie in the bed, and if they were in a room all by themselves. Would they sleep wrapped around each other? Holding hands? She decided they would. The thought made her smile, and she fell into a deep sleep to the sound of Frannie breathing steadily beside her.

CHAPTER SIX

Phoenix, 1941

U p and at 'em, Sleepyhead."
Diz sprang up at the sound of Frannie's voice close to her ear. She immediately took stock of the room and its inhabitants. Amelina and Louise were putting their pajamas away. Louise's hair was wet, like she'd just gotten out of the shower.

Elsie was nowhere to be found, so Diz assumed she was in the bathroom. Frannie was sitting on the side of the bed. Now her shorts were back on.

Thank God.

"You're next in the bathroom, since I went before you last night," Frannie said.

Diz yawned, nodded, and stretched. "Okay."

Everyone seemed to be acting normally. Louise and Amelina weren't paying either her or Frannie any mind, and if Frannie was aware that Diz had put her arm around her in the middle of the night, she gave no sign.

Elsie burst through the door, a towel turban on her head, pretending to be Ethel Merman and singing "Anything Goes."

Diz threw a pillow at her on her way out the door.

An hour later, after a hastily consumed breakfast, they were all loading the bags back on the trailer and scrambling into their respective cars.

Today, Diz didn't mind that she and Frannie were separated. The close call in the motel room when Frannie kissed her still had her shaken. Who knows what would have happened if Louise hadn't been telling a story? Diz and Frannie might not have heard them right outside the room, and Elsie might have witnessed the kiss. Of course, she would have told their mother...

Diz shuddered. Given the admonishment her mother had given Elsie about watching the company Diz kept, surely finding out about the kiss would result in her mother demanding that Diz quit the team. Playing for the Ramblers was everything Diz had dreamed of since she was old enough to hold a softball.

Then there was the matter of waking up in the middle of the night with her arm firmly wrapped around Frannie's waist... Diz's pulse increased at the memory. Thank goodness she woke up when she did and shifted positions.

Unbidden, the image of Frannie sitting on the bed, her bare legs dangling over the edge, popped into Diz's head. She stifled a moan. No, it was just as well that they were in separate cars. She could only imagine what it would be like if the two of them were forced to sit thigh-to-thigh in the backseat of the Chrysler.

She closed her eyes and said a quick prayer. *Please, God, please let there be two cots at the hotel in Tulsa tonight.*

❧❧

By the time they reached Oklahoma City shortly after noon, Diz was more than ready for a break. If she had to listen to one more six-part, off-key rendition of Jimmie Davis's "You Are My Sunshine," she thought she might be sick.

The girls tumbled out of the cars, dragged their equipment off the trailer, and jogged to the empty field where Mr. Hoffman was waiting for them.

"We've got an hour to work out. Let's make it count. Ten minutes of throwing, then we'll take some batting practice and infield after that."

Diz and Frannie paired off to toss the ball back and forth. Diz stopped at a place she thought would be good, but Frannie apparently had other ideas.

"Let's give ourselves some room. This is a big field, there's no reason for all of us to be on top of each other."

So they kept walking, until they were at least fifty yards from anyone else.

"So, how did you sleep?" Frannie asked.

She playfully bumped hips with Diz, who looked back to see if anyone was watching.

"Good Lord, you worry too much." Frannie sighed in exasperation and pulled Diz up short. "Look, no one is paying any attention to what we're doing. But if you keep looking like a kid who got caught with a hand in the cookie jar, we're done for."

Diz hung her head. "I'm sorry. I've never done anything like this before, you know. I'm nervous."

"It's not like I do this kind of thing every day, either," Frannie said. She started walking again.

"Don't be sore."

"I'm not."

"You are."

"Go out there so we can do what we're supposed to be doing." Frannie nudged Diz.

"I said I was sorry."

"I heard you. It's fine. Go on."

Reluctantly, Diz jogged far enough away so they could have a catch. She knew Frannie was lying. She obviously was peeved. What Diz couldn't figure out was what she was supposed to do about it.

Tulsa, Oklahoma, August 30, 1941

Diz laced up her cleats and glanced down the bench. Frannie was busy tightening the knots on her glove and never looked up.

They hadn't had a minute alone together since the workout in Oklahoma City. Tonight, they would sleep in separate rooms on cots. Diz had gotten her wish. So why was she feeling so miserable?

Mr. Hoffman whistled, and the girls huddled up. "All right. This is just an exhibition game. The main objective is to make enough money to get us to the championships. You know I want to win, but I don't want anyone getting hurt." He pointed at Dot. "That means you."

"I never get hurt."

"But you don't know how to do anything halfway."

"Tulsa is a good team. I don't want them thinking they can manhandle us in the tournament."

"You let me worry about that," Mr. Hoffman said. "Here's the lineup…"

Because she was the fastest girl on the team, Diz led off.

"Strike her out, Tiger!"

"No batter, no batter."

Diz squinted. The sun was setting right over pitcher Nina Korgan's right shoulder, making it next to impossible to see the ball. The first pitch sailed by her before she could get the bat off her shoulder.

"Steee-rike one!"

Diz tightened her grip on the handle. From the dugout, she heard her teammates shouting encouragement. On the mound, Korgan was getting set to hurl again.

"Time!" Diz held a hand up, and the umpire granted her time out. She stepped out of the batter's box and took a practice swing.

"C'mon, Diz. Show her where you live!" Frannie's voice was unmistakable. Diz breathed a sigh of relief. Despite her protestations to the contrary, Diz was sure Frannie was miffed. After all, she'd avoided Diz ever since the workout in Oklahoma City. Maybe this was a sign that she was over it.

"Steee-rike two!"

Diz shook her head to clear it. "Pay attention. Geez." She sucked in a deep breath and blew it out, staring down the pitcher.

The ball was fat and right down the middle. This time, Diz swung hard. But the bottom dropped out of the ball at the last second, and she missed it badly. She trudged dejectedly back to the bench.

"Don't worry about it," Elsie said. "You'll get her next time."

But Diz didn't get her next time, or the time after that, or the time after that. In fact, she was oh-for-four. And she wasn't alone. Frannie, too, put up big zeros for the game, as did most of the rest of the team. In all, the Ramblers managed only five hits for the game, and they got skunked, five-to-nothing.

After the game, the team had a quiet dinner at a local restaurant and returned to the hotel. They were all tired from the early workout, the drive, and the game. Tomorrow, they would start the day with another early workout before getting on the road to Chicago, where they were scheduled to play five more exhibition games.

"Anybody up for cards?" Peanuts asked as they entered the hotel lobby.

Elsie yawned. "I'm bushed. I'll pass."

Diz, who was practically falling asleep on her feet, was grateful she wouldn't have to be the first one to put a damper on the party.

In the end, the girls collectively decided to call it an early night.

"Rookies last," was still the order of things, so Diz sat cross-legged on her cot, pounding a ball into the pocket of her glove, waiting patiently for the other four girls to finish getting ready for bed. When her turn finally came, Diz dashed out the door. If she were lucky, maybe she'd run into Frannie.

Alas, much to her disappointment, she reached the bathroom without encountering a soul. Once inside, she stripped off her uniform and ran the water for a bath. She took stock of her body. One scrape on her left shin that she couldn't remember how she'd gotten, and one black-and-blue circle on her right thigh…it was an easy night.

The water was more tepid than hot, but it felt good just the same. Diz washed herself, and then sank down under the bubbles and leaned her head back against the tub. Because she apparently was the last one to get ready, she figured she could take her time. She closed her eyes.

Bam, bam, bam!

Diz started, her heart pounding in time with the pounding on the door. "Occupied," she called.

"Are you going to stay in there all night?"

Oh, my God. It was Frannie. And Diz was naked.

"Um… Just a sec." Diz jumped up and grabbed her towel, hastily dried herself, and stepped into her pajama bottoms. She threw on the matching top, quickly ran a comb through her hair, and unlocked and opened the door.

There was Frannie, casually leaning against the doorjamb, still in her uniform. "I thought maybe you drowned in there. I was worried." Frannie made a show of looking Diz up and down. "Good to know you're okay." She winked.

Diz blushed and moved to her right to get around Frannie. "I'm fine, thanks."

"Where are you going?" Frannie put out an arm, effectively stopping Diz.

"Back to the room." Diz took a step forward.

"Not so fast."

The tone of Frannie's voice sent a shiver down Diz's spine and the hair on her arms stood at attention. How was it that the sound of three simple words, said that way, by this girl, could have such an effect her?

"Come in here. I haven't gotten to kiss you all day." Frannie grabbed Diz's arm and tried to coax her back into the bathroom.

Diz resisted. She looked down the hall in both directions.

"Here we go again." Frannie threw up her hands.

"What?"

"You're scared of your own shadow, that's what. You make me so frustrated!"

"I'm just being practical."

"You're just being a scaredy-cat." Frannie let go of Diz. "I've got to get ready for bed." She moved Diz out of the way and slammed the bathroom door.

Diz stood in the hallway. Why did it seem like every interaction between her and Frannie went sideways? She raised her hand to knock on the door, then changed her mind. What could she say that would make things better? It wasn't like she was going to change her mind about taking a chance on the two of them being discovered in the bathroom together. Slowly, dejectedly, she walked back to her room, wishing all the while that she could somehow make Frannie see things her way.

Hours later, Diz still lay awake staring at the ceiling, trying to make sense of her feelings for Frannie. The few times they were alone together always seemed to end either with them kissing or fighting. Diz hated confrontation. She abhorred that Frannie went to bed mad at her; it made her stomach hurt just thinking about it.

She touched her lips. Frannie had kissed those lips, and the memory of it sent a signal of an entirely different kind to Diz's belly and below. She squeezed her eyes shut, willing her body to calm down. If only what she and Frannie shared didn't feel so good.

෯෧

Diz dragged her way through the workout the next morning. Frannie barely gave her the time of day. She tried to catch Frannie's eye before they piled into the cars for the long trip to Chicago, but Frannie somehow always seemed to have her back turned.

"This is ridiculous," Diz muttered, as she squeezed into her now-customary spot over the drive-train.

"What is?" Elsie asked.

"Um… How tired I am. It's ridiculous how tired I am."

"Well, that cot certainly didn't look all that comfortable. I'm surprised you could sleep a wink."

"I didn't." At least in that remark, Diz was telling the truth.

"Why don't you get some shuteye now?" Marjorie handed Diz the blanket that was sitting on the seat.

"Margie's right," Dobbie added from the front seat. "We'll probably drive clear to St. Louis before we stop for lunch. You might as well take a snooze."

Diz accepted the blanket and tried to get comfortable. The seat was stiff and creaked and squeaked with every rut in the pavement. Dust swirled on the breeze as they drove through countryside dotted with fields in dire need of water. At first, Diz simply stared past Elsie out the window and let the conversation flow over her.

After a while, her eyelids began to droop. Eventually, Diz rested her forehead on her folded arms and fell asleep.

In the end, she was so exhausted that she apparently slept through an impromptu stop at a roadside fruit stand and a potty break, only waking when Elsie shook her to tell her that they had arrived in St. Louis, where they would be eating a late lunch.

Diz's neck was sore and her legs were cramped from staying in one position for so long. She got out of the car, straightened up, and almost immediately doubled over as a spasm seized her back.

"Are you okay?"

Diz moaned in pleasure as Frannie's sure hands kneaded the knots out of her back.

"Better now."

"Why are you so tense?" Frannie lowered her hands.

Carefully, Diz stretched until she was fully upright. "I fell asleep all hunched over."

"How long were you like that?"

"Most of the way here from Tulsa."

"Ouch."

"You can say that again."

"If we'd been in the same car, you could've leaned on me instead."

"I wish," Diz said.

"Me too."

The sun was high in the sky, and Diz used a hand to shade her eyes. Most of the girls were headed toward a restaurant diagonally across the street, while a few others were gawking at some dresses in a nearby store window. None of them was in earshot.

Diz turned to face Frannie. "I'm sorry about last night."

"S'okay. I know you're not comfortable with me yet."

"It isn't that," Diz said. "It's just..." She sighed. What was it? "It's just..."

"Don't worry about it." Frannie waved a hand dismissively.

But Diz was worried about it; she could tell that Frannie was hurt. "Look, I'm not used to being kissed. I don't know how I'm supposed to feel, or how I'm supposed to act."

"You're obviously just too young—"

"I'm not a kid!" Diz looked around and lowered her voice. "I'm not a kid. It isn't that."

"No? Then what is it?"

"Don't"—simply unable to think clearly with Frannie looking at her like that, Diz lowered her gaze—"don't you worry about getting caught? About what people will say? They might think we're queer or something."

Frannie barked out a short laugh. "Well, we can't have that, can we?" She started to walk away.

"Wait." Diz put a hand on her arm, but Frannie kept moving. "Please. Please, wait. I didn't mean that the way it sounded."

"No?" Frannie rounded on Diz. "Just exactly how did you mean it, Theodora?"

Diz recoiled as if she'd been slapped. The way Frannie said her name sounded like something distasteful, something dirty. "I... I only meant that if anybody accused us of that, we could get kicked off the team."

Frannie shook her head sadly. "That's not what you meant, and you know it. You said exactly what you meant."

"But..."

"Don't worry about it." Frannie started moving again. "You won't have that problem anymore."

Diz felt panic well up in her throat. "No. No, Frannie. Please."

"Please, what?" Frannie refused to look at her. "It's obvious you don't feel the same way I do, so I won't bother you anymore. After all, I wouldn't want anyone thinking you were like me."

"Like..."

Frannie stopped short. "Queer, Theodora. I wouldn't want anyone thinking you were queer."

The pain in Frannie's expression took Diz's breath away. She opened her mouth to say something, anything. But nothing came out. Instead, she watched in silence as Frannie ran down the street.

Phoenix, 2014

"Oh, no." Julie gasped and held a hand to her heart.

"Oh, yes," Diz said. "It wasn't my finest moment." She picked up a tortilla chip and dipped it in the spinach and artichoke mixture. It was mid-afternoon, and today the restaurant was quiet. She pointed the loaded chip at Julie. "Are you going to eat any more of these or are you going to make me eat them all myself? They're not good for my girlish figure, you know."

Julie shook her head. "How can you eat at a time like this?"

"It was a long time ago, dear," Diz said kindly. "Time heals all wounds."

"But Frannie... You loved her. How could you...?"

"I don't have a good answer for you. I wish I did." Diz's tone was quiet and contemplative. "The truth is, I was sixteen years old and confused about who I was and what I was doing. I had no idea what I was saying."

"Poor Frannie."

Diz nodded. "She took it pretty hard. But then, I wasn't in too good shape myself." For a minute, Diz stared off into space, her mind obviously focused elsewhere.

"Are you okay?"

"Huh?" Diz refocused on Julie. "Oh, yeah. But I wasn't back then, I'll tell you." Diz bit into the chip and some of the dip dripped onto her napkin.

"What happened?"

"What happened?" Diz finished swallowing. "Well, for one thing, the Ramblers lost all but two exhibition games on that trip, including three in a row to Garden City."

"You did? But you were the defending world champs."

"Yep. We were," Diz agreed. She loaded another chip with dip and munched on it until it was gone. "But on that trip, we just didn't have it. And believe me when I tell you, neither Frannie nor I hit worth a lick. We made mistakes in the field—mental mistakes. We were both so distracted, I don't think we knew whether we were coming or going."

Julie consulted her notebook. "Tulsa won the championship that year."

"Don't remind me," Diz said.

"Was that the same Tulsa team that beat you in the exhibition game the night Frannie tried to pull you into the bathroom?"

"One and the same."

Julie scanned down the page. "But it doesn't look like you lost to them in the tournament."

"Nope. We lost in the first round, if you can believe it." Diz shook her head. "Only time that ever happened."

"Because you'd played so poorly in the exhibition games?" Julie asked.

"That was probably part of it," Diz agreed. "But mostly it was the luck of the draw. In '41, it was a single-elimination tournament. We drew the damned New Orleans Jax Brewers. They nicked Amelina for three hits in the first inning, we committed one infield error that scored a runner, and that was all she wrote."

"So you went all that way to Detroit and got knocked out of the tournament on the first day?"

Diz paused with a chip midway to her mouth. "We did. We packed up our stuff early the next morning and left for home."

"All those exhibition games just to play one game in the national tournament?"

"Yep."

"I can't even imagine what that trip home must've been like for you."

"There wasn't much in the way of conversation or fun, I can tell you that."

"What happened between you and Frannie? I mean, obviously you made up."

"Not right away we didn't. In fact, that didn't happen for a long time."

CHAPTER SEVEN

Phoenix, December 7, 1941

H ey, Diz. A bunch of us are going up to South Mountain to have a picnic. Why don't you come?" Jessie bounced a basketball on the pavement.

The weekend city recreational basketball league was in full swing, and most of the Ramblers had just finished playing a game against their archrivals, the Queens.

"I don't think so," Diz said. "My dad is coming home tonight and I'm supposed to cut the grass before he gets here." While what she said was true, it wasn't the real reason Diz declined Jessie's invitation. As casually as she could, Diz glanced behind her, where Frannie was chatting with Louise and Marjorie. As always happened when she saw Frannie these days, her throat tightened and her heart ached.

Frannie, no doubt, would be among the picnickers today, and being around her was just too painful. No matter how many times over the last three months Diz had tried to apologize, no matter how many times she had tried to explain, Frannie would have none of it. While she was always polite to Diz, she rarely smiled at her, and there was no warmth in her eyes.

Diz never saw Frannie with another girl—not in the way they had been together—but she worried constantly that someone would make a play for Frannie, or worse, vice versa. Diz shuddered at the thought. She dug her hands in the pockets of her Levis.

"I'll see you guys later," she said to the group in general.

Several of the girls acknowledged her with a wave or a word, but not Frannie, and that made Diz even more miserable.

All the way home, as she walked along through the orange groves, she practiced what she would say to Frannie, if only Frannie would give her the chance.

"I didn't mean that there was anything wrong with being queer, just that other people might look at us funny." Diz shook her head. No, that wouldn't win Frannie back.

"I really want to go back to kissing you. I just don't want anyone to know about it?" Definitely not.

"Nothing I've ever done has felt as good as kissing you. Can't we please make up?" That one had potential.

Diz was still thinking about it as she yanked open the screen door and waltzed inside. The door slammed shut behind her and she winced, awaiting the inevitable rebuke from her mother.

But the scolding never came. Diz scrunched up her face. "Mother? Are you here?" Diz checked the kitchen. It was empty, yet she could smell something cooking. "Mother?" Diz continued to walk through the house, checking rooms as she went.

When she reached the parlor, a cold chill ran up her spine. There was her mother, her hair mussed, her lipstick smeared, and mascara running down her face.

"Mother! What's wrong?"

But her mother didn't answer. Instead, she waved a hand vaguely in the direction of the radio. Then she blew her nose in the hanky she was holding.

Diz ran to the radio and turned up the volume. A reporter from the NBC News Network was saying something about bombs, and American casualties at a place called Pearl Harbor.

Diz knelt in front of her mother. "Mother, where is Pearl Harbor? Is that far from here?"

"Hawaii." Her mother's voice shook. "The Japanese attacked us."

"Oh." Diz tried to process the information. Hawaii was someplace exotic and far away.

"We're going to have to join the war now."

"Well, that's good, right? Now we can give those bullies what for and how come!" Diz punched the air.

Diz's mother blinked, seeming to see her for the first time. "Good?" She put her head in her hands. "You don't understand."

"What don't I understand, Mother?"

Diz's mother began to sob and rock back and forth. Diz had never seen her mother like this. Panic welled up in her. "What is it? What did I say?" Diz, never one to be overly affectionate with her mother, threw her arms around her now as her mother cried huge, wracking sobs.

When the crying subsided into hiccups, Diz started to stand up. "I'll go get you a fresh hanky."

"No!" Diz's mother clutched at her. "Don't go yet."

Diz resumed her crouch. "Okay. I'm right here." Diz took her mother's hands. Never had her mother shown such vulnerability. She was always so sure, so in command.

They stayed like that for several minutes as Diz's mother stared off into space, the tears rolling down her cheeks.

Finally unable to stand it anymore, Diz said, "Mother? Please, tell me what has you upset? I mean, Hawaii is a long way away. We'll be safe here, won't we?"

Diz's mother sniffled and looked down at her. "Don't you see?"

Diz shook her head. She most certainly did not see, and the fact that her mother was beside herself forced a bubble of fear up into Diz's throat.

"The Japanese bombed our naval fleet. Their planes bombed our battleships. They also attacked the airfields. Many of our planes and pilots were lost today."

At the words "planes" and "pilots," the light began to dawn for Diz. "You're worried about Daddy. But Daddy's in San Francisco. That's not near Hawaii."

"You don't understand." Fresh tears flowed down her cheeks. "Your father will want to be part of it. He's going to want to enlist. We'll lose him to the war."

Diz sat down heavily on the floor. Was that true? Surely Daddy wouldn't leave Mother and them to fend for themselves? How would they survive? "He won't leave us."

"Yes, he will." Diz's mother wrung the handkerchief in her hands. "He'll go. It's his duty." Her voice was hollow.

"But what are we supposed to do? How will we get money for food and the house?"

"Your father will no doubt take a pay cut in the service. We'll have to work. I can take in laundry and sewing, and you girls can get jobs."

"But I don't graduate high school until June. And Elsie is in college."

"We'll have to find a way."

A thought suddenly occurred to Diz. "What about softball? What about the Ramblers?"

"How can you think about something so trivial at a time like this?" her mother chided.

The words felt like a cold, hard slap across the face. Trivial? Softball and the Ramblers were everything to Diz. Trivial? It might be less important than having to keep the household going without her father at home, but it certainly wasn't trivial. Her teammates were her only friends. Her teammates... *Oh, my God! Frannie. I'd have to give up seeing Frannie.*

The idea of not at least being able to see Frannie, even if it was only on the softball field, was more than Diz could bear. She jumped up and ran, shoved open the screen door, and burst outside. She kept running. At first, she wasn't sure where she was going, but one single thought, one word, one name, coalesced in Diz's mind. Frannie. She had to get to Frannie.

Diz didn't stop running until she reached the picnic area where the girls always hung out at South Mountain.

There they were, lounging on the rocks, eating and laughing. How could they laugh at a time like this? She searched the faces until she found the only one that truly mattered.

"Frannie!" Diz ran over and grabbed Frannie by the hand, pulling at her, nearly unbalancing her.

"Hey! What on Earth are you doing?"

"Please. I have to talk to you." When Frannie didn't immediately move, Diz tugged harder. "Please. It's important."

"Geez. Okay. Just don't knock me over." Frannie disentangled their hands and made a helpless gesture to a girl she was talking to. Idly, Diz registered that she didn't know the girl.

When they were far enough away not to be heard, Diz said, "You have to forgive me. I might never see you again. You have to forgive me."

Frannie's eyes grew wide. "What are you talking about? Are you going away somewhere?"

Diz shook her head. "No. The Japs bombed Hawaii today. My mother is a mess. She says Daddy will be going to war now and I'm going to have to go to work. I might have to give up the Ramblers." Diz looked at Frannie beseechingly. "But I can't give up you. I just can't. Please. Please don't make me do that." To her horror, Diz felt tears sting her eyes. Angrily, she wiped them away. Crying was for sissies. She wouldn't cry.

"You're talking nonsense." But Frannie's voice wavered. "America's not in the war."

"We will be now. My mother's sure of it. And they were talking about it on the radio. The Japs took out a lot of planes, and a lot of American pilots died. My dad is a great pilot. They're going to need him."

"What does that have to do with the Ramblers and me?"

Diz groaned in exasperation. "If I have to get a job after school, I might not have time for softball. I'll never get to see you anymore."

"Then you wouldn't have to worry about people thinking anything funny was going on between us, would you?"

Frannie's eyes were hard, but her voice still betrayed months-old hurt.

"Please." Diz grabbed her hands. "I'm begging you to forget what I said that night. I was scared. I…" She cleared her throat, tight with emotion. "When my mother said I might have to give up the Ramblers, all I could think was that softball means everything to me. And my next thought was that I couldn't live without you, without seeing you, and talking to you. I've hated these past few months. I've hated how we are with each other. I miss you, Frannie. Please, please let bygones be bygones."

Frannie uncoupled their hands and seemed to consider. "I see that I still come second to softball."

"Argh! You and softball go hand in hand." Diz searched for what she wanted to say. "The game means everything to me. But the game is nothing without you in it."

"So, you're not afraid of people thinking you're queer?"

Diz wanted to scream. Why couldn't Frannie see how she felt?

Frannie started to walk back toward her friend. "You *are* still scared."

"Don't go. Don't keep walking away from me." Diz crossed her arms, virtually hugging herself. "I'm less afraid of people thinking I'm queer than I am of never getting to kiss you again," she blurted.

Frannie turned to face Diz. Her eyes popped open wide in surprise.

"Is that so?"

Diz stood up straighter. "It is."

Although Frannie stared at her, Diz refused to look away or blink.

"Okay, then."

"O-okay, what?"

Frannie shrugged. "Okay then, we can try kissing again and see what happens."

"Oh. Okay, then." Suddenly, Diz didn't know what to do. She looked around, really taking stock of their surroundings for the first time. "Well, when do you want to start?"

Frannie threw back her head and laughed. "You're something, Theodora Hosler."

Diz blushed.

"How about if I pick you up Tuesday night and we go to a movie?"

"Really?" Diz loved the movies, but she didn't get to go very often.

"Really. Will your parents let you go on a school night?"

"S-sure."

"You don't sound sure," Frannie said.

"Sure," Diz said, with more authority this time.

"Okay then, it's a date."

࿔࿔

When Diz arrived home again, her mother was in the kitchen, apron on, a grim expression on her face. She and Elsie were fixing a salad.

"Where have you been, young lady?"

"I went to tell the girls the news." Well, Diz reasoned, that was true—at least she went to tell one girl the news.

"Your father will be home soon. Go get cleaned up. We're going to have a nice dinner on the table for him tonight."

Diz heard the car door slam just as she was putting on a fresh blouse. She pulled the curtain aside and peeked out the window. Her mother ran out to greet her father, clinging to him as if for dear life. Although she opened the window, Diz couldn't hear the conversation.

She walked into the kitchen just as they were coming back inside.

"Hey there, sport." Diz's father ruffled her hair. "How's my favorite youngest daughter?" He threw an arm around her shoulder.

"I'm your only youngest daughter."

"That's why you're my favorite one." Her father winked.

If he was upset by the news of the bombing, he didn't show it. Maybe her mother was wrong. Maybe everything would stay just the same for them.

But the dinner conversation disabused Diz of that notion.

"Kids," her father began as he stabbed a piece of steak, "I know you heard today's news about the bombing at Pearl Harbor."

Both Elsie and Diz nodded. "Yes, Daddy."

"Well, that means that America is going to jump into the fray now. No more sitting on the sidelines." He made eye contact with each of them. "That goes for me too. No more sitting on the sidelines." He put his fork down. "Tomorrow, I suspect President Roosevelt will ask Congress to declare war on Japan, and Congress will most definitely approve. As soon as that happens, I'm going to go right down to the recruitment center and sign up."

Diz's mother bit back a sob, and her father reached out and patted her hand. "Beverly, you know I have to do this. They need skilled pilots."

"They can have other skilled pilots. I don't want them to have you." Diz's mother threw her napkin on the table. "Excuse me." She shoved back her chair and ran from the room.

Diz's father cleared his throat. "Don't you worry your pretty little heads about your mama. She'll be all right. She's just a little overwrought right now." He picked up his fork. "Eat your food before it gets cold."

❦

Just as her father had predicted, President Roosevelt asked the Congress to declare war the next day, and Congress agreed. Diz's mother stayed in her bedroom all day, not even coming out to eat.

Diz's stomach was tied in knots too, especially when her father came back from the recruitment office and announced that he'd been accepted into the military and would likely be getting his orders soon.

The following day, Tuesday, he went back to work and flew to San Francisco as usual, but Diz's mother continued to sequester herself in her bedroom.

Diz arrived home from school and hurried to get her homework done. At half past four, she knocked on her mother's bedroom door.

"Mother?" Diz waited, but got no response. "Mother? Are you hungry? I can make you a sandwich."

"No. I'm not hungry. You and Elsie fix something for yourselves."

"Well, actually…" Diz shifted from foot to foot. "I was going to ask if I could go out for a little while. *The Maltese Falcon* is playing down at the theater and I was going to go with a friend." Diz held her breath, waiting for the reply.

"Honestly, Theodora, I have no idea how you could even think of going to the movies at a time like this, but go if you want to."

"Thank you, Mother!"

"Just make sure you're back before ten o'clock."

90

"I will be, Mother."

"Do you need the eleven cents for the movie?"

"I've got it. Thanks." Diz scrambled out the door before her mother could change her mind.

She stood down at the corner where she had arranged for Frannie to pick her up. She didn't have to wait long.

Frannie looked beautiful in a nice pair of tan slacks and a forest green checkered blouse that accentuated the color of her eyes. Her lipstick and makeup were expertly applied.

Diz felt underdressed in her standard Levis and a clean, collared shirt.

"Are you going to stand there all night? Get in."

Diz did as she was told. "Gosh, you look so pretty tonight."

Frannie turned to her. Her eyes were sparkling. "Why, thank you, Diz. I didn't know you were such a flatterer."

Diz's face flushed. "I'm not. I'm just telling the truth."

"Still, that was very sweet."

Frannie put the car in gear and pulled away from the curb. "Are you hungry? I thought maybe we'd get a burger first."

Diz's face grew even hotter as she thought about the way their last trip to the burger joint had ended up.

"I bet I can guess what you're thinking," Frannie sang.

Diz squirmed.

Frannie brushed her fingers tantalizingly along Diz's arm. "I really am famished and we really are going to get something to eat."

"I-I know."

"Uh-huh."

They shared a chocolate malted and French fries with their burgers, and when they were done, they both sat back, completely stuffed.

"That was really good," Diz said.

"It was," Frannie agreed. "And we have just enough time to get to the movie."

They paid the bill and decided to walk the two blocks to the theater.

"I'm really excited to see this one. I loved the book."

Frannie looked at her oddly.

"What?"

"You like to read?"

"Are you kidding me? I love to read." Diz paused. "Don't you?"

"I'm more of a visual kind of girl. I prefer the movies," Frannie said.

"Well, I like them too."

An awkward silence ensued, and Diz searched for something to say. "I think Humphrey Bogart will make a dashing Sam Spade."

"For eleven cents, I certainly hope so." Frannie opened the lobby door. "Let's get a popcorn." She pulled Diz into the refreshments line.

"We just finished that big dinner. Where are we going to put the popcorn? I'm full."

"There's always room for popcorn."

"Where do you like to sit?" Diz asked once they were inside the theater.

"Let's sit in the back." Frannie led them to the very last row.

The lights dimmed and the movie started. Diz got lost in the action on the screen. She nearly jumped out of her seat half an hour later when Frannie took her hand.

Diz swallowed her instinct to pull away, afraid that if she did so, she might lose Frannie all over again. Besides, holding hands with Frannie felt really, really good. She checked all around them, but nobody seemed to be paying any attention to them.

Frannie disentangled their interlocked fingers as the closing credits scrolled on the screen.

"Did you enjoy that?" she asked as they exited the theater.

"It was super," Diz said. "I thought the movie was almost as good as the book."

Frannie laughed.

"What?"

She leaned over and whispered in Diz's ear. "I wasn't talking just about the movie, silly."

"O-oh." Recognition dawned for Diz. "Um… Yeah, that was super too." She grinned.

"Good. Because I have another surprise for you."

"You do?" Diz's pulse picked up at the sultry quality of Frannie's voice.

"Mm-hmm. Come with me."

They got back in the car and Frannie drove north and east.

"Where are we going?"

"You'll see."

A short while later, Frannie stopped the car. "Don't the stars look amazing tonight?"

Diz glanced up at the sky. "They're spectacular." Although Diz thought she'd been paying attention on the drive, she had no idea where they were. She glanced around. "There aren't even any cars out here."

"That's the point," Frannie said, her voice pitched low. She turned off the car and slid across the seat toward Diz.

"O-oh."

CHAPTER EIGHT

Phoenix, 2014

I'm so glad you and Frannie worked it out," Julie said. "I mean, I knew you must have."

"You did, eh?" Diz raised an eyebrow.

"Well, I… What I meant to say was…"

"No need to get flustered, dear. It's okay. I know full well that Ricki's wasn't the only obituary you've been carrying around." Diz winked. "I thought about it a long time before I wrote in that article that we were long-time companions, knowing it was going out there for all the world to see."

"I bet you did," Julie said. "Was that the first time you ever talked about it? Publicly, I mean?"

Diz nodded. "I outed myself at age eighty. Who would have thought?" She shook her head in wonder. "It's not like Frannie and I were hiding or anything. But you need to remember, we come from a very different generation. We just never talked about things like that."

"I understand."

"Can I get you ladies more coffee? And can I clear this for you?" The server pointed to the mostly eaten chips and dip.

"Are you doing all right, Diz? Do you want to stop?"

"No. I'm good. We can keep talking for a while longer if you want."

"I do."

"In that case, I'll take another cup of coffee, please," Julie said to the server. "Diz?"

"What the heck. Why not? Sure. I'll have another cup."

The server disappeared.

"Now, where were we?" Diz asked.

"You were saying that times were different and you never talked about being gay."

"No. Not openly like you folks do today. But it just felt wrong when Frannie died not to speak up about who she was to me and what our relationship was. I knew it would've made her smile to see me acknowledge our status openly. She probably laughed her ass off in Heaven. In fact, she's probably tickled to death about me talking to you like this." Diz paused. "Hey, I made a pun there, did you catch it? Frannie being tickled to death? Morbid, but funny." Her eyes twinkled. "Don't laugh now. Nope, don't laugh."

Julie stifled a chuckle.

"Ha! I knew you couldn't do it."

"I'm sorry."

"Don't be. I miss Frannie every day. More than you can imagine. I ache to feel her next to me at night. But laughter is good. It's what she would want."

Diz leaned back as the server filled their coffee cups and left them alone again.

"She'll be gone nine years next week." Diz's eyes filmed over and she sniffled. "I talk to her all the time, you know. You might think I'm crazy for this, but I believe she can hear me. And sometimes, it almost feels like she's lying down at night next to me. At least, I like to think so."

"That's beautiful," Julie said. "I'm sure you're right."

"You have a nice smile, you know—kind. Reminds me a little of Frannie's. You ought to smile more. Especially when it reaches your eyes."

"Oh...um... Thank you." Julie lowered her head and consulted her notes.

"I'm sorry," Diz said. "I've embarrassed you again, haven't I?"

"Maybe a little," Julie allowed. "Can we get back to talking about you, please?"

"Sure. But, for the record, you're cute when you're out of sorts."

96

"So," Julie said, drawing out the word, "you had your second date on December 9, 1941, two days after Pearl Harbor. What happened after that?"

Diz picked up the coffee cup and blew on the steaming liquid. Carefully, she raised the cup to her lips and took a small sip. "Ouch. That's hot."

"Yes. You might want to wait a minute to let it cool down."

Diz set the cup back down and stared at a point over Julie's shoulder, seemingly lost in the past. "After that, our whole world changed. On December 11, 1941, Germany and Italy declared war on us, and we reciprocated. The war consumed everybody. We all knew someone who had gone to war or was about to go, and we all had to do our part at home. We were busier than bees in a hive."

"Did your dad get shipped out right away?"

"No. We were lucky in that way. Because he was such an experienced pilot and flight instructor, he was initially stationed at Williams Field, right here in Chandler, where he trained other pilots for the Army Air Forces Advanced Flying School."

"So you got to stay in school and keep playing ball."

"I did that year." Diz picked up the coffee cup again, tested to see if it was still too hot, and took a cautious sip.

"What do you mean by, 'that year'?"

"Eventually, when the European Theater of Operations opened, my father was assigned to the famous 354th Fighter Group. They flew out of the Boxted Airdrome in Essexshire, England." Diz paused. "Are you sure you want to hear about this? It's going to mess with your timeline. We're getting ahead of ourselves."

Julie eagerly leaned forward. "You can't just leave me hanging like that. Tell me more about your dad. We'll go backwards and fill in the blanks afterward."

"If you're sure," Diz said. When Julie nodded enthusiastically, Diz said, "Would you like to see a picture?"

"Would I? Sure!"

Diz twisted to her left and extended her misshapen fingers toward a bag hanging off the back of her wheelchair. Her fingertips brushed the nylon material, but came away empty.

"Let me help you," Julie said. She stood and moved the wheelchair closer to Diz so that the bag was within easy reach.

"Thank you, dear." Diz reached her hand inside and felt around. "Ah, there it is." She pulled out a worn leather wallet and opened it, thumbing through until she found what she was looking for. "Damned arthritis," she said, as she fumbled with the plastic sleeve in which a dog-eared, sepia-toned photo was encased. "Sorry. Too many years of ball playing for these old fingers." As she finally liberated the picture, she ran a thumb tenderly across its surface before passing it across to Julie.

"Oh, my. He's so handsome." Julie angled the picture in order to cut down the glare from the nearby window. The man in the photograph was of average height, thin, with a moustache, and a hat jauntily perched on his head at an angle. He was posed in front of an airplane. "He reminds me of a shorter Clark Gable."

Diz smiled. "He'd like that comparison." She pointed at the aircraft. "That's a P-51 Mustang. It was his favorite plane. He and his men flew them as escorts for the big, heavy bombers."

"He must have had some great stories to tell when he got h-home." Julie's voice faltered on the last word when she caught sight of the expression on Diz's face. "Diz?"

Diz shook her head. "He never came home. His plane took fire as he was protecting the bombers during a critical raid on February 11, 1944. His squadron mates said he continued to fly and fight, even though he was critically wounded. He managed to get the plane back to the base, where he crash-landed. He didn't survive his wounds, but he saved his men and kept the plane from falling into enemy hands."

"I'm so, so sorry, Diz. I didn't know," Julie said.

"Yeah, well..." Diz waved a hand, as if she was waving away a painful memory. "It was forever ago. The men he commanded stayed in touch with my family for a long time after the war. They had a lot of respect for him, and that meant a lot to us."

Julie was still jotting notes when Diz finished talking.

"Can I make a recommendation?" Diz asked.

"Of course." Julie finished writing and took a long swallow of coffee.

"I think we should stop for today and start fresh next time. You can get your notes in order in the interim, and I promise to fill in the major missing blanks for you between the declaration of war in '41 and my father's death in '44. There are some important milestones you're not going to want to miss."

"I'm sure."

"Next time, I'll tell you what happened when Elsie went to Sweetwater, Texas, and joined the WASPs in 1943."

"The what?"

"The Women Air Force Service Pilots."

Julie wrote the name down. "I can see I have some research to do before next week. I'll look forward to that." She put the notebook away. "But what about you and Frannie and the 1942 season?"

"Oh." Diz waved a hand. "It was more of the same. Not much changed on the Ramblers front that year. We played ball, hung out at South Mountain with the girls sometimes, finagled time to be alone and stole kisses when we could, won the Pacific Coast regional tournament, and lost in the semifinals of the national tournament. That was the start of the dominance of the blasted New Orleans Jax. By that time, they'd picked up Nina Korgan from Tulsa. Damned if she didn't beat us a second year in a row with another one-to-nothing shutout. Then she went on to beat Chicago in the finals. That's pretty much all there is to tell about that."

Julie dragged her notebook back out and made a notation, then checked her watch. "Geez. I did it again. I kept you way too long."

"No, dear. You're fine. But I am fading and I don't want to leave out anything that might be important to your story."

"No worries there," Julie said. "You've been fantastic. I can't believe the level of detail you remember."

"Good to know I still have my marbles, if not my wheels," Diz joked. She picked up the tab on the table, reached back into the wallet, and removed some bills. She counted out enough for the bill, plus twenty percent tip, and slid it under her coffee cup. "There. That ought to do it."

"Diz, I should be the one paying."

"We'll alternate. I'll feel better about that arrangement." She replaced the wallet in the bag and motioned to Julie to help her transfer from the seat into her wheelchair.

"You make it hard to argue with you."

"Good. That's the idea."

"So you want to jump right to 1943 next time?" Julie asked.

"It was a big year. I think you'll find it very interesting."

"Okay, then. I'll have to trust you on that."

"You will, at that," Diz agreed.

Phoenix, 1943

"You're late. Mother will be furious."

"Then don't tell on me, Sis," Elsie said. She yanked a floral-print cotton dress off the line and dropped the clothes-pins in the bucket at her feet.

"Where were you?" Diz asked. "I got home from work an hour ago. You should've been here before me."

"I went over to the hangar and took Daddy's Piper out for a spin."

"You were flying? Oh, my God. Mother will have a cow."

"Like I said, she won't know if you don't tell her." Elsie looked toward the house. "Where is she, anyway?"

"Inside, sewing her fingers off, where do you think? She's fixing Mrs. Price's dress for the fundraiser."

"Oh."

They were silent for a moment. Nettie Price's husband, Nigel, was reported killed in action in the Pacific Theater. He was the first of their family's acquaintances and friends to lose his life in the war. Their friends were banding together to raise money to help with the funeral expenses.

"Do you think Daddy's okay?" Diz asked.

"Mother got a letter from him just the other day. He says his group is leaving New Jersey for England soon and he's itching to get into the action. He misses us like crazy. You should ask

Mother to read you the letter. He talks about you and your new job."

"He does?"

"Yep."

"What does he say?"

Elsie playfully threw a tee-shirt at Diz. "Ask Mother, why don't you?"

"Hey!" Diz caught the shirt, folded it, and put it in the laundry basket. She and Elsie worked in companionable silence for a few minutes, making short work of the rest of the clothes on the line. Diz picked up the basket and turned toward the house.

"Wait," Elsie said.

Diz lowered the basket. "If we don't get in there, Mother's going to go on the warpath."

"I need to tell you something." Elsie lowered her voice.

"You and Joe are getting back together?" Joe was the Arizona State University classmate Elsie had been dating off-and-on for the past year. Presently, they were "off."

"No. I caught him making out with MaryLou at the 902 the other night, when he said he was going to be studying for the chemistry test. Jerk."

"MaryLou? Eww."

Elsie folded her arms across her chest. "I know. Jerk."

"Is that what you wanted to tell me?"

"Huh?"

"Is that what you were going to tell me? That Joe was a no-good bum? I already knew that."

"Oh. No." Elsie stepped closer to Diz. "I need you to keep a secret."

"What kind of secret?"

"The secret kind, all right?" Elsie snapped.

"Geez. Okay. What's the big deal?"

"The reason I went to the airfield was to meet with someone."

"A boy?"

"What? No! Why is that all you can think about?"

Diz didn't want to address the irony of that question. She was momentarily distracted by thoughts of her and Frannie, dancing cheek-to-cheek in their special hideaway the night before.

"…in August."

Diz blinked, tuning back in. "Say that again?"

"I said, this woman named Jackie Cochran is recruiting experienced girl pilots to ferry military planes to bases all over the country. She wants me. Me! Can you imagine? I said yes, of course. I start training at a place called Avenger Field in Sweetwater, Texas, in August."

Completely taken aback, Diz nearly dropped the laundry basket and all the clean clothes on the ground. "You can't."

"What are you talking about?"

Diz struggled for breath as her throat constricted. Her future was slipping away right before her eyes. She was supposed to be able to quit her job at the Goodyear factory and go to college when Elsie started earning money. If Elsie left now…

"What about Mother?" Diz asked, appealing to her sister's sense of family duty. "She needs us both. You're supposed to get a swell teaching job after you graduate next month. You promised that if Mother and Daddy let you go to college, you'd help out."

"Why aren't you excited for me? Cripes! I'll get a job when I get back. Don't you see, Diz? This is my chance to contribute—to make a real difference in the war effort. Why would you want to begrudge me that?"

"What about making a difference here at home? What about me? I'm supposed to start at ASU in the fall. With you gone, I'll have to stay at Goodyear running a stupid drill press and making airplane parts for the rest of my life."

"Ah. Now we're getting somewhere. This is really about you. Don't be so dramatic, and for God's sake, don't be so…so…selfish! It will only be 'til the end of the war. That'll be any day now, if you listen to the radio reports."

"Yeah? Well, what about softball? That's the middle of the Ramblers' season. We've got a real shot at getting back the title. I thought you were like the rest of us, Ramblers first and foremost. We're a team, a family."

"Of course we are, but this is different. They need me, Diz. My country needs me. There aren't that many girls like me with lots of flying under their belts."

"Only 'til the end of the war." Diz mimicked Elsie. "Well, good luck when you tell Mother. And wait until Daddy hears."

Elsie straightened up defiantly. "He'll be proud of me."

"He'll be proud of you for abandoning Mother and me? I don't think so." Diz stalked away.

She went into the house, dropped the laundry basket on the sofa in the parlor, and marched directly to her room, where she flopped down onto the bed. She grabbed a pillow and hugged it to her chest, wishing with all her heart that it was Frannie in her arms.

Frannie would know just the right thing to say. Frannie would calm her down. She would see the positive in this situation. There must be one.

For the moment, all Diz could think about was that she wouldn't get the chance to go to college, get a degree, and get a good enough paying job that her mother would stop pestering her to find a nice boy to date so he could eventually marry and support her.

ی‌‌ی

"What do you hear from Elsie?" Frannie asked. She fired the ball back to Diz as they warmed up their arms before the seventh and deciding game of the Arizona State Championships against their archrivals, the Queens.

Diz shoved aside the anger blooming in her chest at the thought of her sister, off living the glamorous life, while she was stuck here working two jobs. She should have started her freshman year at ASU by now.

Diz caught the ball effortlessly and winged it back. "She's been in Sweetwater for a month, training and checking out on all kinds of planes. You know I don't know much about flying or airplanes. Something about an AT-6 and a BT-13. She says the instructors are men who mostly resent teaching girls to fly."

"I bet." Frannie held the ball. "You're still sore about her leaving."

Diz noted that it wasn't a question. She regretted, once again, pouring her heart out to Frannie. If she'd kept her feelings about

Elsie and the WASPs to herself, they wouldn't be having the discussion she was sure they were about to have.

"I know what you're going to say. You're going to tell me that everything is going to be all right in the end, and I should be proud of Elsie."

"I can't tell you how to feel, but, yes. I think you should be. She's doing an important job—a necessary job." Frannie tossed the ball to Diz.

"I know. I'm trying to look at her side of it. I really am."

"Then I'm proud of you."

Diz brightened. "Elsie has met some nice girls and made some friends. She even said in her last letter that she met a couple of girls who reminded her of us."

"Really? Are they…"

Even from twenty feet away, and even though Frannie didn't finish the sentence, Diz blushed. "Stop it. How should I know? And I'm sure Elsie doesn't know either."

"Did she send you a picture?"

"Yes. As a matter of fact, she did."

"I suppose it's too much to hope for that you have the letter on you?"

"It's in my bag. I brought it because Elsie sent a message for the team. I was going to read it to everybody after warm-ups."

"Well, show me and let's see if we can tell." Frannie jogged toward Diz and together they headed for the dugout.

Diz rummaged through her game bag until she found Elsie's letter. She slid it out of the envelope, and carefully unfolded the pages. The photographs were inside the fold.

Frannie peeked over her shoulder. "I bet she means those two." She pointed at a pair of young women in leather bomber jackets and fly suits. They were standing in front of a plane, laughing together. One of the girls was tall, and the other was tiny.

Diz turned over the picture. "The handwriting on the back says their names are Jessie Keaton and Claudia Sherwood."

"Notice the way they're looking at each other? Those girls are in love. I'm sure of it," Frannie said.

Before Diz could answer, the rest of the team piled into the dugout.

"Whatcha got there, Diz?" Jessie asked.

"It's a letter from Elsie."

Everyone gathered around, all chattering at once, wanting to know how Diz's sister was doing.

"She sent a message for all of us," Diz said. "She says, 'If you lot don't beat the blasted Queens in the tournament, I swear I'm going to jump in one of these planes and buzz right over your heads.'"

"Sounds like Elsie," Jessie said.

Mr. Hoffman, who had been standing off to the side, stepped forward. "I strongly suggest you ladies do as Miss Hosler says. We've let the Queens hang around in these games long enough. Let's get out there and finish this. Oh, and by the way, I've already bought our train tickets to Detroit and the national championships. So, now you *have* to win."

All the girls put their hands in the middle of their tight circle. Dot Wilkinson said, "Okay, on the count of three, 'Let's go Ramblers.' Ready? One, two, three…"

CHAPTER NINE

Phoenix, 1943

It was the bottom of the seventh inning and the game was still scoreless. Dobbie was at the plate with one out, and Dot was in the on-deck circle. Diz and Frannie stood together on the dugout steps, cheering along with the Ramblers and half of the fans at the Phoenix Softball Park. The remainder of the fans, of course, were Queens fans. They were busy jeering the Ramblers' batters.

"C'mon, Dobbie. Give it a ride!" Frannie screamed.

"Hey, Dobbie. Hey, Dobbie. It's all you, girl!" Diz called.

"Strike her out. She's no batter! My mother could hit better than her!" The taunt came from the stands behind home plate.

Dot took a menacing step toward the fan, brandishing the bat in her hands. Before she could get there, some nearby Ramblers' fans pounced on the man, pummeling him and starting a melee.

The racket caught the attention of the umpire, who called time. He whirled around and pointed at the main combatants. "Knock it off. One more outburst and I'll toss all of you."

Fights during games between the Ramblers and the Queens were commonplace. On more than one occasion, Diz and her teammates had followed Dot into the stands to teach a lesson to a heckler. The umpire no doubt had this in mind when he stopped the game and dealt with the situation before it got out of control.

After several moments, the crowd sorted itself out and everyone returned to their seats. Dot walked back to the on-deck circle, a smile on her face. Diz had never seen anyone scrappier than Dot. And every girl on the team would've walked through fire right alongside her.

"Play ball," the umpire shouted.

Dobbie stepped back to the plate and stared down the pitcher. After taking the first pitch for a strike, she slapped a single up the middle.

"Woo! Way to go, Dobbie! Smack her in, Dot!" Frannie moved into the on-deck circle as Dot rubbed a handful of dirt on her bat and took a practice swing.

The first pitch was a rise ball. Dobbie took off for second base, as the catcher came up from her squat and let loose with a strike to the shortstop covering the bag.

"Out!"

"She was safe!" Dot yelled at the second base umpire who made the call. "She slid under the tag!" He completely ignored her. Dot pleaded her case to the home plate umpire, who was the head of the umpiring crew.

He turned his back to her and dusted off home plate as if he hadn't heard her.

"C'mon, Bob. Get in the game. She was safe and you know it." Dot took a step toward the umpire.

"One more step and I'll toss you out of the game, Dot."

Dot opened her mouth to say something more, then obviously thought better of it. Instead, she kicked at the ground, no doubt intentionally dirtying up the plate the umpire just swept off.

Diz shook her head. Dot always liked to shake things up, especially where the umpires were concerned. "Take it out on the ball, Dot!" Diz called.

Sure enough, Dot caught the next pitch on the sweet spot of the bat and lashed a double to right-center field. She popped up on the bag in a cloud of dust and immediately shouted at the umpire, "That should've been a game-winning hit and you know it!"

The umpire, well used to Dot's antics, waved a hand as if to dismiss her.

"Let's go, Frannie. It's your show," Diz said, as she came alongside Frannie in the on-deck circle.

Frannie winked at her and walked to home plate.

"Time!" the Queens' manager called. He walked to the mound and, after a short discussion with the pitcher, catcher, and the infielders, retreated to the dugout.

When the catcher returned behind home plate, she stood wide of home plate, setting up a target for an intentional walk. Diz's heart thumped hard. The Queens were intentionally walking Frannie to get to her. They didn't think she could beat them.

After the fourth ball thrown to her, Frannie dropped the bat and trotted to first base. "You've got this, Diz. Make 'em pay!"

Diz took in a deep breath, trying to calm her nerves. This was the biggest game of the year so far; the state championship was on the line, and they were down to their last out. It wasn't that she'd never been in pressure situations before, but this was by far the most important at-bat of her career to date.

"Time!" Coach Hoffman called. He motioned to Diz to meet him halfway up the third-base line. "Listen, Theodora. I don't need you to do anything heroic up there. I just need you to find a hole. The reason I put you in the number six slot instead of leading off tonight was because I knew we were going to get to a moment like this where we needed a contact hitter who could leg-out a hit. Dot and Frannie are both fast enough to advance if you find a hole. Then we'll leave the rest for Amelina to clean up, okay?"

Diz nodded glumly. Even the coach didn't expect her to be able to win the game for them at the plate. She trotted back to home with her head down, thinking about all the things that could go wrong, and how horrible it would feel to make the last out the only time they'd really been threatening to score all night.

Then she remembered that pep talk Elsie gave her the day she and Frannie were vying for a spot on the team. Elsie believed in her. Diz reached home plate and stepped into the batter's box. She surveyed the field, scouting for an open spot to place the ball. Out of the corner of her eye, she saw Frannie standing on the bag at first.

Frannie put her fingers to her mouth and whistled. When Diz turned fully to face her, Frannie shook a fist at her in exhortation. "You've got this, Diz!"

Frannie believed in her, Elsie believed in her, and, as she became aware of the cheers from the stands and the dugout, Diz realized that everyone in the stadium was on their feet—for her—little Theodora Hosler.

She held her hand up to the umpire, indicating that she wasn't yet ready and settled. After a practice swing, she screwed her cleats into the dirt, trying to get comfortable with her stance. There was a huge gap in left-center field. It was no wonder—Diz was a dead-pull hitter and a lefty—so nine times out of ten, she hit to right field. But if she could just get the perfect outside pitch, maybe, just maybe...

"Steee-rike one!"

Diz blinked. The pitch went past her before she even had time to decide whether to swing or not. She sucked in a deep breath and blew it out. "Focus, Diz. Focus."

The next pitch was so far inside that Diz had to dive out of the way. She picked herself up and brushed off the dirt, staring down the pitcher. If she was trying to get Diz to back off the plate, it wasn't going to work.

Diz stepped into the box again and waited for the next delivery. She watched the ball, a change-up, all the way into the catcher's mitt.

"Ball. Two balls, one strike," the umpire announced.

"Here we go, Diz. Here we go!"

"Whack it, Diz!"

"No batter, no batter. She's a lightweight."

"Easy out!"

"Like you can, kid!"

Diz allowed all the noise to fade into the background and zoned in on the pitcher and the ball. She followed the wind-up. The pitch was a flat fastball. Diz swung hard and made solid contact.

"Foul ball!" The umpire swiped both hands dramatically to the right, indicating the ball was fouled to the right side of the first base line. "Two and two."

"One more, Pitch! Finish her!"

"No batter, no batter!"

"She's afraid up there. Strike her out!"

"Show 'em, Diz! Show 'em what you've got!"

"They're afraid of you, Diz!"

Diz stepped out of the box. It seemed like every single person in the stadium was standing and screaming; and all of that attention was focused squarely on her.

"Now or never, Diz. Now or never," she muttered. When she stepped back in the bucket this time, she wiggled her shoulders and stood up a little taller in her stance.

The pitcher went into her wind-up, released the ball at her hip, and the white blur hurtled toward home plate, low and outside. Diz cocked the bat, stepped with her right leg, and shifted her hips forward as she swung. The contact reverberated through the bat and into Diz's hands. She watched the ball off the bat and followed through with everything she had.

Dot, who had been on the move with the crack of the bat, paused and ducked on her way from second base to third, as the ball sailed almost directly at her head. The shortstop reached for the ball, her glove arm fully extended…and came up with an empty glove. The line drive landed in shallow left center field and skidded all the way to the fence before the left fielder corralled it and threw it back in.

The throw was on target.

"Let it go!" someone on the Queens infield yelled, alerting the cut off to let the ball go all the way to the catcher.

The catcher snatched the ball and turned to make the tag at home on a sliding Dot.

"Safe! She's safe!" The umpire made the signal emphatically, crouched over the play.

Diz, who had been running as hard as she could, turned around after safely touching the bag at first, and was promptly mobbed by her teammates.

"You did it! I knew you could do it!" Dobbie said.

Dot, her blue eyes twinkling, ruffled Diz's hair. "Way to go, kid. Way to go."

"Woo-hoo! That's what I'm talking about," Amelina said.

"Nicely done, Miss Hosler," Mr. Hoffman said. He was beaming from ear-to-ear.

Amid the hubbub, Diz spotted Frannie. She was standing a little off to the side. Her smile was dazzling enough to light up the night sky. Frannie nodded and mouthed, "I'm so proud of you," and Diz's heart soared.

Before she knew it, Diz found herself hoisted up on her teammates' shoulders. They marched her around the field before finally setting her down in the outfield and tackling her to the ground, covering her in a pile of bodies.

"Let her up. Let her breathe," Mr. Hoffman admonished.

The players untangled themselves and Frannie reached down and helped Diz to her feet. For a long moment, Diz simply stood there, basking in the love and adoration she saw in Frannie's eyes. It was a look unlike any other that had ever passed between them, and Diz's breath caught in her throat.

"Sportsmanship, ladies," Mr. Hoffman reminded them. "Go shake hands and be gracious winners, please."

Frannie broke eye contact, and the moment was over.

"Meet you all at the 902," Jessie yelled, as the team finished shaking the opponents' hands. "Time to party!"

The 902—so named because its address was 902 West Van Buren Street near University—was the Phoenix bar where the girls hung out after the games.

"You coming, Diz?" Peanuts asked. "We'll sneak you a beer, won't we, Dot?"

"Uh-huh."

Diz looked to Frannie and raised an eyebrow. As was their habit, they had driven to the game together. Oftentimes, they used the excuse that Diz was underage to skip the bar so they could go for a drive and make out.

"Sure we're going. We have to celebrate!" Frannie picked Diz up and twirled her around.

Diz's face grew hot. Would Peanuts and Dot figure out they were more than best friends? "Put me down. I'm dizzy."

Frannie threw back her head and laughed. "Of course you are. That's your name."

"Put me down," Diz said quietly.

Apparently understanding the underlying message, Frannie did as asked and backed away.

"Okay," Dot said. "Meet you there."

If she had noticed anything odd, she didn't show it.

"C'mon girls, let's go!" Marjorie and Dobbie each threw an arm around Diz and propelled her forward toward the parking lot.

Diz looked over her shoulder to see Frannie following a short distance behind. Her expression was inscrutable.

≼›∂∾

"Are you mad at me?" Diz asked, when she and Frannie had driven a couple of blocks.

"Why would I be mad?"

"Because I told you to put me down."

"You're a big girl, Diz. You have a right to tell someone to put you down if you don't want to be picked up and twirled around."

"But you're not just someone, and you know it."

They were silent for another block.

"I was just a little worried about Dot and Peanuts, that's all," Diz said.

"What about Dot and Peanuts?"

"You know... That they might figure it out."

Frannie sighed. "Because we were all excited and celebrating and I treated you like everyone else treats you?"

The edge in Frannie's voice made Diz wince. "But you're not like everyone else. That's the point."

"Exactly. When we're in public, you don't let me be like everyone else. Everyone else is chummy and affectionate and playful. If I try to be that with you, you get stiff as a board and can't wait to get away from me. I keep waiting for you to get over it, but you never do."

"Please, Frannie. Please, let's not fight. Not tonight. We just won the state championship. We're going to the nationals again."

"I'm not fighting with you, Diz. I'm simply stating the facts."

"You're angry."

Frannie slammed on the brakes at the intersection and turned in the seat to face Diz. "Of course I'm angry. It's been two years. Two years I've been doing this dance with you, hoping you'll get more comfortable with us"—Frannie indicated the two of them— "but you never do. I don't know, maybe you never will and I'm just fooling myself."

"No," Diz said. "I am comfortable with us. It's just—"

"It's just that you're so afraid of anyone knowing we're sweet on each other, that you go out of your way to ignore me unless we're alone together. How do you think that makes me feel?"

Diz frowned. "Haven't you heard the rumors about the girls from the Jax team? You know, the Savona sisters?"

"What about them?"

"Everybody says they're freaks because of the way they act, and the way they look. The newspapers are hinting that they're queers. Some people say they shouldn't be allowed to play if they are."

"We're not them," Frannie said.

"I know that. But if people start talking about us being queer… It scares me. I'm sorry. I don't mean to be that way. I'm trying, I really am."

"Well, you wouldn't know it from the way you act." Frannie hit the accelerator and the car lurched forward.

They were only a block from the bar. Diz knew she had to do something, anything, to fix this before they arrived at the 902. "Turn there." She pointed to a darkened side street.

"Why? There's nothing down there but the backs of the buildings on Van Buren."

"Please, just do it for me?"

Frannie did as Diz asked.

When they were halfway down the street, Diz checked her surroundings. "Stop the car and turn off the lights."

"What?"

"Put the car in park and turn off the lights. Please?"

Again, Frannie did as she was instructed.

Diz reached out in the dark and found Frannie's hand. She tugged until Frannie reluctantly gave in and moved toward her on the seat.

Diz used her fingertips to trace Frannie's forehead, her cheek bones, her jaw line, and finally, her lips. "You are so beautiful."

"Sweet talking will not change—"

Whatever Frannie meant to say was swallowed by Diz's kiss. When Diz teased Frannie's lips open with her tongue and deepened the contact, Frannie moaned.

114

Diz tilted her head to the side, pulling Frannie in deeper. When Frannie would have broken contact, Diz pursued her until they were both panting and breathless.

"Damn you, Theodora, for being able to turn me inside out like that."

Diz touched her lips to Frannie's once more, before pulling back. "I know you don't believe me, but I love you, Frannie. I love you more than anything in this world."

"Yeah. Well, you have a funny way of showing it." But Frannie leaned in for another kiss.

"Mmm. How would you like me to show it?"

Frannie laughed, the sound low and seductive. "Not here, shy girl." She slid back behind the wheel. "And if we don't show up at the bar soon, people really *will* start to talk."

⤚⥰⤙

By the time Diz and Frannie got inside, the party was in full swing.

"There she is, the woman of the hour!" Peanuts proclaimed.

Within seconds, Diz was surrounded by the entire team. They were all holding up their beer bottles and chanting her name.

"Geez, guys. It's not like we won the national championship yet or anything," Diz said.

"True," Majorie said, "but we might not have had another shot at it if you hadn't clobbered that ball."

"Here you go, kid. This one's on me." Peanuts shoved a cold beer bottle into Diz's hand and winked.

"Thanks."

"Must feel pretty good, all this attention."

Diz turned to see a pretty blonde standing a little too close for comfort. She backed up half a step, but the girl pursued her. "Yeah, well. It takes a team to win a game." Where was Frannie? Diz stood on her tiptoes and craned her neck, trying to find her in the crowd, to no avail.

"I was at the game. Nice hit."

"Thanks." Diz backed up, and bumped into the solid mahogany bar. The girl's perfume was so overpowering it made Diz's nose itch.

"Hurry up and drink your beer so I can buy you another."

Diz considered herself fairly dense and naïve, but if she didn't know better...

"Diz. There you are."

Diz's knees practically buckled in relief when Frannie insinuated herself between Diz and the girl. "Hi." She hoped she sounded as grateful as she felt.

"C'mon. Let's dance." Frannie grabbed Diz's hand.

Diz barely had time to put the beer on the bar before Frannie dragged her toward the dance floor. Several of their teammates already were dancing, some with boys, and some with each other.

"That girl was flirting with you!" Frannie shouted to be heard over the music.

Diz didn't know what to say to that, so she said nothing.

"If she so much as lays a well-manicured finger on you..."

Diz opened her eyes wide. "It wasn't like that. I don't even know her name."

"Well, she obviously knew yours."

"She was at the game."

"I don't care. If she thinks she can make a move on you..."

This was a new side of Frannie and Diz wasn't sure what to do with it. Was Frannie really jealous? Of a girl who wore too much perfume?

"Her perfume was too strong."

"Well, that's something."

"Surely you don't think I cared about her?"

"I hope not."

Diz couldn't believe it. She moved closer so that she wouldn't be overheard. "You're the only one for me. I could never care about another girl."

"Good thing."

There was that look again, the one Frannie gave her earlier today. Diz's pulse skyrocketed.

"Have we been here long enough yet? It's getting hot in here. I think we should go for a drive," Frannie said.

Diz nodded. She didn't trust her voice.

CHAPTER TEN

Phoenix, 1943

The temperature had finally cooled off by the time they parked the car in their usual spot. The stars were shining brightly in the late night sky, and Diz was snuggled securely in Frannie's arms, her head nestled on Frannie's chest.

"I love being here with you like this," Diz said.

"Me too."

"It's like no place else exists in the world, except in your arms."

"I like the sound of that."

"Can I ask you something?"

"Mm-hmm." Frannie's voice vibrated against Diz's ear.

"How come I don't know anything about your life outside of softball? I mean, I've never seen your house, or met your parents, or—"

"Your house is closer to the field. It makes more sense for me to pick you up."

Frannie's answer was too fast, and Diz could feel the instantaneous tension in the arms wrapped around her. Still, there were questions she'd been asking herself for too long, and tonight, she was going to get answers.

"Okay. But that doesn't explain why you've never invited me to your house, or talked about your work, or…anything, really."

"You know where I work."

Diz sat up and turned to face Frannie, surprised to see something akin to fear there. "I know that you've been working at

119

Korrick's, in the stationery department, since I met you. I know that you look and smell really nice when you're at work. But I want to know so much more. I want to know everything about you."

"You know everything you need to know. You know everything that matters."

Diz could've sworn she heard a quaver in Frannie's voice. She took Frannie's hands in hers and ran her thumbs over the soft skin in the vee between her thumbs and forefingers. "Why won't you share anything personal with me? Don't you love me?"

"Of course I love you. I wouldn't be here if I didn't."

Diz recoiled at the sharp edge in Frannie's voice. "Please, don't be mad."

"Why all these questions now? We're celebrating a big win, having a grand time, and I just want to enjoy the moment."

She wanted to push harder, she wanted to know—but more than anything, Diz wanted to be right here, alone with her sweetheart. She leaned forward and kissed Frannie softly. "You're right." *Time to get back on safe ground.* "We were really something tonight, weren't we?"

"We sure were." Frannie pulled Diz back in to snuggle. "I was so proud of you out there, I could've burst a button."

"Yeah, well, that was only the states. We still have to win the nationals."

"True. But did you see how relieved Mr. Hoffman was that we were going to need those train tickets, after all?"

"I wonder why he bought them in advance? I mean, he could've lost all that money."

Frannie squeezed Diz. "I think it was because he knew you were going to come to bat in the bottom of the seventh inning and win the game for us."

"Mm-hmm. I'm sure that was it." Diz felt a bubble of happiness well up in her chest and she smiled. She, Theodora Hosler, won the final game of the 1943 Arizona State Softball Championship for the Phoenix Ramblers, the only team she'd ever wanted to play for. It was like something out of a movie. And now, here she was, gazing at the stars, in the arms of the woman she loved. Life was just about perfect.

ఌఌ

Phoenix, 2014

"Wow, Diz. Sounds like you were really hitting your stride," Julie said.

"Yes, well, in some ways, I was."

Diz squinted into the morning sun and fumbled in the side pocket of the wheelchair for her sunglasses. It was a picture-perfect March morning. The hummingbirds were singing, the wildflowers were blooming, and the temperatures were moderate and pleasant.

"It sounds like there was a 'but...' in there."

"Huh?"

Julie continued to push Diz's wheelchair forward. "It sounded like you were about to correct me about 1943 being a banner year for you."

"Oh." Diz removed her foot from the foot rest and put it out to use as a brake.

"Hey! You'll get hurt," Julie said.

"Sorry." Diz returned her foot to the footrest. "I don't think I'll ever get used to being in this damned chair. Stop here, please." Diz waited for Julie to set the brake. "Hold these for a second, will you?" She picked up the bouquet of red roses from her lap, handed them to Julie, and pushed herself up on shaky arms. She stood still for a moment, her hands gripping the armrests, as she steadied herself. "Frannie's right over there."

Diz slowly shuffled forward until she was standing in front of a large headstone. Etched into the granite was: "Francine Louise Hainey, February 19, 1923 – March 18, 2005, Always & Forever, Diz."

"This is a beautiful spot," Julie said.

"We picked it out together a lot of years ago. We liked that you could see our special spot from here." Diz pointed toward the foothills off in the distance. "That's why we installed a bench. So that whoever was left of the two of us could sit and feel like we were looking at our place together."

Diz took the flowers from Julie and lovingly placed them on the grave. "These are for you, my love—your favorites, from your forever valentine."

"You probably want some privacy, so I'll just—"

"No. You're fine. I'm sure Frannie is enjoying our times together. She's probably adding in her two cents from up in Heaven, telling you how stubborn and pig-headed I was and that I always leave out the best parts. I think she's happy that you're keeping me company."

"I sure hope so."

"Why don't we sit down for a spell and I'll tell you more about my girl. This seems like an appropriate place for it, where she can correct me when I get it wrong."

Diz moved to the nearby bench and plopped down on it. Julie joined her.

"So, you had a question about 1943?"

"You made it sound earlier like I'd gotten it wrong when I said that 1943 was when everything seemed to fall into place for you."

"Yes and no. I certainly grew up plenty and came into my own that year, both on the field and off. You know what happened in the state championship. Then, we took the train to Detroit and lost in the finals of the national tournament. The Jax thumped us, seven-to-nothing."

"They'd beaten you in '42, as well, right?"

Diz nodded. "They beat us too many times in the '40s. They were just that good. They had the Savona sisters and Nina Korgan, and that was pretty much all they needed." Diz shook her head. "That was one thing about the Jax—if somebody beat them, they would turn around and hire that player to work for the brewery and put them on the roster. We were always proud that we never did that on the Ramblers. All of our players were home-grown."

"So," Julie prompted, "everything was coming up aces for you on the team. With the game-winning hit, you solidified a place in the starting lineup, right?"

"Oh, I'd pretty much already done that by the time we won that game." Diz waved a hand. "But things at home were...complicated. With Elsie and Daddy gone, I had a lot more responsibility. In addition to my job at the Goodyear factory, I took a part-time job at Woolworth's to help out. And, of course, I was spending as much time as I could with Frannie."

"Did you ever get your questions answered?" Julie asked.

"About Frannie and her home life, you mean?"

"Yes." Julie poised a pen over her notebook.

"As a matter of fact, I did, but not because she came out and told me. I got tired of her being so secretive about it, so I followed her as she was walking home from work one day."

∽§∖৵~

Phoenix, 1943

Diz's heart was pounding. What if Frannie spied her? She dropped farther back and tried to blend in with the crowds on the sidewalk. Would Frannie be upset that she was trailing her?

"You know she will be," Diz muttered to herself. "If she wanted you to know, she wouldn't have been dodging the questions for the past three months."

It wasn't that Diz was insensitive to Frannie's right to privacy, but after being together for two years, surely she had a reasonable expectation that she would know more about her girl than she did.

Frannie crossed the street and disappeared into an orange grove.

"How am I supposed to follow you now without being spotted?" Diz waited a full minute, then ran in the direction Frannie had headed. She pulled branches aside, dodged fallen fruit, and skidded to a stop at the edge of the grove, where it fell away to reveal a dilapidated old farmhouse.

Whatever Diz had been expecting, this wasn't it. She ducked behind the fattest tree trunk and watched as Frannie chatted quietly—too quietly for Diz to hear—with a harried-looking, older woman in a housedress.

Just as Frannie started to walk away, a wiry, disheveled man stumbled out of the house, very nearly falling down the porch stairs. He pointed a finger at Frannie.

"Don't you move, girl." His words were slurred and loud enough for Diz to hear. "I ain't given you permission to go nowhere yet."

Frannie froze in her tracks, and from her hiding place, Diz watched in horror as the man approached and slapped Frannie hard across the face.

"You need to learn better manners."

"I'm tired, Uncle Walter. I worked a long shift today, and I just want to get cleaned up and—"

"Are you talkin' back to me?" He raised a hand to Frannie again.

In that moment, Diz knew beyond a shadow of a doubt how much she truly loved Frannie, and that she would willingly stand in the way of a madman in order to protect her.

She charged forward, covering the ground quickly, barely registering the shock on Frannie's face as she grabbed the man's upraised arm with one hand, and shoved him hard in the chest with the other. "Don't you touch her!"

Walter twisted out of Diz's grasp. "Well, well. Whadda we have here?"

Diz lifted her chin and stood in front of Frannie. "I'm Theodora Hosler, Frannie's gir—a friend of Frannie's. And if you ever touch her again—"

"That girl there is my kin. I'll do anything I bleeding well please. Took her in when she had no one, didn't I? Gave her a roof over her head and food to eat."

Diz's nostrils flared. "I don't care what the circumstances are, you have no right to—"

"Stop, Diz." Frannie put a hand on Diz's shoulder. There was an edge of panic in her voice. "This isn't your business."

"Girl's right. It ain't your business." Walter glared at Diz. His fists were clenched menacingly by his sides.

"It's my business if you think you can bully her."

Walter turned a steely-eyed glare to Frannie. "You best control your lap dog afore I kick her inta next week."

"Come on, Diz." Frannie squeezed the shoulder she was touching.

Diz didn't budge. She crossed her arms over her chest, feeling bolder than she ever had in her life. "I'm not going anywhere until he apologizes to you and promises never to lay a finger on you again."

"Please, Theodora." Frannie pleaded.

"You best be listening to her, little girl."

"I'm not afraid of you. Anyone who hits a girl is a coward."

Walter lunged forward and took a swing at Diz. She ducked, and the punch sailed over her head, hitting Frannie with a glancing blow to the arm.

Diz lowered her shoulder and threw all of her weight forward, slamming the man in the chest and knocking him backward. He fell hard on his hip.

The haggard-looking woman, who up until this point had been standing off to the side, finally spoke in a quavering voice. "Francine, you best take your friend and get on out of here. Right now. And don't come back for a while, neither. You know how he gets."

Frannie didn't say a word. Instead, she grabbed Diz by the arm and began to run.

Bewildered, Diz let herself be pulled along. When they turned the corner, she realized there was another building—a small barn—several hundred feet behind the house.

Frannie dragged her inside and hurried past some empty horse stalls to a room in the rear of the barn. The place smelled faintly of hay and horses, and Diz wondered why they were in here.

When they crossed the threshold to the back room, Diz realized with a shock that this was Frannie's bedroom—here—inside a horse barn. Her girl lived in a barn?

Frantically, Frannie snatched a suitcase from a makeshift closet and began throwing clothes into it.

"What's going on?" Diz finally asked. "What are you doing?"

Frannie continued to grab jeans, shirts, dresses, shoes, and toiletries, and throw them haphazardly into the suitcase.

"Frannie?"

When Frannie looked up, the expression on her face was a mixture of anger, fear, and something else Diz couldn't quite identify.

"He has a gun, Diz. A shotgun. And he won't be afraid to use it. Not now." She closed the suitcase and secured the latches. "Grab my softball bag and let's go. We have about five seconds before he comes after us."

Diz wanted to argue, wanted to take Frannie's hand, sit her on the bed, and talk about what was going on. She wanted to understand.

But Frannie was all motion. She already was at the door, suitcase in hand. Her eyes swept the room once more, she stopped to grab something off the dresser, and then she led the way out of the barn via a side door Diz previously had failed to notice.

Frannie's car was parked outside, and she threw the suitcase in the trunk, grabbed the softball bag from Diz and tossed that in as well, slammed the trunk, and jumped into the driver's seat.

Diz was barely in the passenger's seat when Frannie gunned the engine and peeled out. As the house receded behind them, Diz swiveled around and caught a glimpse of Walter, standing out on the porch, a shotgun raised and pointed in their direction. She shivered. What kind of man was he?

They drove for several miles before Frannie turned onto a deserted street, slammed on the brakes, and put the car in park. She whipped around on the seat to face Diz. She was visibly shaking. "What in the world were you thinking?"

"What do you mean? He was hurting you. I had to stop him." Diz moved toward Frannie, who stopped her with a raised hand. Sullenly, Diz crossed her arms.

"It wasn't your place. You shouldn't even have been there." Frannie faced forward and pounded her palms on the steering wheel. "Damn it, Diz!" She rested her forehead against the backs of her hands and closed her eyes.

Diz could see that Frannie's hands were still trembling. She couldn't stand it anymore. She scooted closer and covered Frannie's hands with her own.

Frannie jerked her hands away and shrunk toward the driver's door, and Diz's heart broke just a little at the rejection.

"How did you find me? Were you spying on me?"

"N-no." Diz squirmed as Frannie stared stonily at her. "I mean… I just wanted to know where you lived."

"Well, now you know. Feel better?"

Frannie's tone was like ice and Diz swallowed hard as guilt crept in. Even as she had convinced herself otherwise, she had invaded Frannie's privacy, and there was no getting around that. Belatedly, it occurred to her that what she'd seen in Frannie's eyes while they were packing was shame. She was ashamed of where she lived—of how she lived. That was why she'd been so secretive, that was why she never invited Diz over.

Diz felt miserable. "Not really," she said quietly. "I'm sorry I showed up uninvited. I shouldn't have."

"No, you shouldn't have."

"But I'm not sorry I stopped that bastard." Diz unconsciously made a fist. Maybe Frannie would forgive her, maybe she wouldn't, but if she had it to do all over again, Diz knew that she would've made the same choice.

"Who are those people, Frannie? What did that man mean when he said he 'took you in when you had no one?' Where are your parents?"

For a long time, Frannie said nothing, and, as the sun set in a blaze of colors in the western sky, Diz wondered if she would continue to shut her out.

"My mom and dad are both gone, lost when our house caught fire." Frannie's voice was so soft, Diz had to strain to hear her. "I was fourteen and sleeping at a friend's place when it happened."

"Oh, my God. I'm so, so sorry. I-I didn't know." Poor, poor Frannie. Diz felt even worse now about pestering her to talk about her family.

Frannie shook her head sadly. She seemed a million miles away. "Maybe if I'd been there, I could've gotten them out, and then..."

"And then you wouldn't be living in a barn at the mercy of that rat bastard," Diz finished for her.

"He's not that bad when he's sober. And he wasn't always that way. My mother was Uncle Walter's best friend. They were fraternal twins. I remember lots of times, when I was little, Uncle Walter would take me out and play catch with me." Frannie smiled wistfully. "He's the one who taught me to hit a change-up."

"Well, he got one thing right. No one hits a change-up better than you."

"When Mama died, there wasn't anywhere else for me to go. My father's parents were already dead. My mother's mom was gone, too, and my grandfather was too busy to take care of a teenage girl. So Uncle Walter and Aunt Martha took me in. It worked okay for a little while."

"It must've been so hard for you, losing your folks like that."

Frannie nodded. "I was inconsolable for a long time. I would go outside and sit in my parents' car—this car—and cry for hours. I could still smell my father's aftershave in the upholstery." Frannie ran her fingers lovingly over the back of the seat. "My aunt and uncle didn't know what to do with me."

"I can tell you what they shouldn't be doing to you." Diz muttered.

"I wasn't the only one struggling, Diz. Uncle Walter took my mother's death hard." Frannie stared out the windshield, seemingly once again transported back in time. "He stopped going to work consistently, started drinking more and more, and got fired from his job as a construction foreman. We got evicted from the house we were living in when he couldn't pay the mortgage."

"What is that place you're living in now?"

"It belonged to my grandparents. My granddad was a proud farmer—he owned horses, cattle, and a local farm stand. He dropped dead of a heart attack not long after the fire and left the family farm to Uncle Walter.

"At first, Walter didn't have time to keep up the farm because he was busy working, himself. And after he lost his job and started drinking so heavily, he had to sell the horses and cattle for the money. A few months ago, he lost the farm stand too."

"Let me guess," Diz said, "that's when things really started to go downhill."

Frannie nodded. "He started blaming me for ruining his life, and, well, you can see what happens when he's been drinking."

"Why do you stay? I mean, you're old enough to be on your own now."

Frannie seemed surprised by the question. "Uncle Walter and Aunt Martha are the only family I have. They didn't have to take me in, but they did. What I make at Korrick's puts food on their table. It's my way of repaying them for their kindness."

"Kindness?" Diz scoffed.

"Yes, kindness. Because of them, I was able to finish high school. Because of them, I had clothes on my back and a full stomach. Because of them, I could play softball. Don't you see?" Frannie finally made eye contact. "I owe them everything."

In truth, Diz didn't "see" at all. This Frannie was completely different from the self-confident, independent, devil-may-care girl she knew. "Her" Frannie would never allow herself to be manhandled by a drunk bully. Diz wanted to tell her so, but somehow, this didn't seem like the right time. Instead, she opted for talking about more immediate concerns.

"Your aunt said you shouldn't come back for a while. What did she mean?"

Frannie sighed. "She meant exactly what you heard her say. I can't go back there now. Maybe not ever. We'll see."

"But where will you go?"

"I don't know. Sometimes, when he gets like this, I sleep in my car for a few days until it blows over, and then it's fine again. But this time..." Frannie looked pointedly at Diz. "Thanks to you, this time is different."

"I couldn't just let him hurt you." Diz's voice broke on a sob. "I couldn't. I love you, Frannie. I'm never going to let anyone hurt you, ever again."

"I can take care of myself, thank you."

"But you weren't... Taking care of yourself, I mean. I know you could've taken him, yet you didn't lift a finger."

"He's sick, Diz. Alcohol is a sickness for him. He doesn't even know what he's doing. After he sobers up, he doesn't remember a thing."

"That's no excuse!"

Frannie pinched the bridge of her nose between her thumb and forefinger. "Can we please not talk about this now? I have to figure out where I'm going to sleep. And it's getting late." Frannie raised an eyebrow. "Speaking of which, where does your mother think you are?"

Diz frowned. With everything that had happened, she'd completely lost track of time. She should've been home hours ago.

Frannie must've divined that from Diz's expression, because she said, "Yeah. That's what I thought. I'm going to drive you home right now."

"And then what?"

"I just told you, I don't know."

"I do," Diz said, as a plan began to take shape in her mind. "You're going to stay with me tonight."

"I beg your pardon? You? You, who is afraid of being discovered? You want me to share your bed with you, in your mother's house?"

Frannie had a point... "You can sleep in Elsie's room. I know my mother will approve." The more she thought about it, the more Diz liked the plan. "That's what we'll do. You can have Elsie's room for now."

"How are you going to explain it to your mother? She's barely even met me outside of a wave here and there at a softball game or when I pick you up or drop you off."

"I'll just tell her you need a place to stay for a little while. It will be fine. You'll see." Diz didn't know if that was true or not, but there was no way she was going to allow Frannie either to go back to that place, or to sleep in her car. The temperature would be dipping into the thirties tonight.

Frannie was silent.

"I'm not going to take no for an answer."

Frannie shook her head, but said, "Fine. Just for tonight, though, and then I'll figure something else out."

CHAPTER ELEVEN

Phoenix, 2014

The midday sun was high in the sky when the echoes of Diz's story died on the faint breeze. For several minutes, she watched as Julie furiously took notes.

"I don't know that Frannie would much like me telling you the sordid details of her home life, but, the truth is, if you're going to tell the full story, it was a big part of what made her tick."

"How so?"

"Like all of us, Frannie's personal experiences shaped her. All she'd ever known was that the people she loved left or hurt her." Diz shifted positions. "How about if we change locations and I'll go on with the story? After sitting so long, this old body and this hard bench are having a disagreement. Do you feel like a burger? My treat."

"It's my turn to buy," Julie said.

"Fair enough. How about a burger on your dime?"

Julie laughed. "Sounds perfect." She helped Diz stand and continued to support her until she stopped swaying.

"Just let me have a moment with my girl." Diz toddled back to the headstone and laid a hand on it, as if doing so would bring her closer to Frannie. "I hope you don't mind, sweetheart. I agreed to help this girl out. In order to do that, I have to give her the straight skinny. I know you know that, even if the details are a bit messy at times. Don't worry, I think it will all work out fine."

She leaned over and planted a soft kiss on the granite. "I love you, Francine Louise Hainey. I keep thinking this will get easier

131

with time, but I miss you more every day. Somehow, though, telling Julie our story has been liberating. It's almost like you're right here, telling it with me. Anyway, enough of the nonsense. I hope you like the flowers." Diz fussed with the roses one more time. "I'll see you as soon as I can. Do try to stay out of trouble until then."

ക്കൈ

Phoenix, 1944

"Francine, would you be a dear and fetch me that platter on the top shelf? I can never quite reach it, and Theodora, of course, is no help there."

Frannie stood on tiptoes and pulled down the heavy china platter. "Here you go, Mrs. Hosler."

"Thank you, dear." Diz's mother set the platter on the counter and swept an errant lock of hair off her face. "It's been such a pleasure having you here and getting to know you these past few weeks. Why, Theodora never talks about any of her friends. We hardly knew she had any. It's so nice to know she's spending time with a nice girl like you."

Across the room, Diz nearly spit out the lemonade she had in her mouth. A quick glance at Frannie confirmed that she, too, was having difficulty keeping a straight face. If her mother only knew!

The first night Frannie spent in their house, Diz had been the one to go to Frannie's bed. She wanted to be sure that Frannie was okay, especially after everything that had happened with her uncle, and their discussion in the car afterward.

Although Frannie had allowed her to climb into the bed, they didn't speak, and barely touched. Shortly before dawn, Diz kissed Frannie gently on the forehead, and crept back to her own room. She made no other overtures, sensing that Frannie needed time and space to adjust to her new surroundings, and to decide if she was going to forgive Diz for following her home.

It was a full week before Diz heard the creak of the floorboards, and watched the diffused light from the hallway spill through, as the door eased open and Frannie came to her. With her mother's room right down the hall, they didn't dare do more than steal a few kisses and hold each other, but it was enough. And so it had been every night since.

"Mother, Frannie and I are meeting some of the other girls out at Blue Point for a picnic. I don't know if we'll be home for supper, so please don't make us anything."

"I swear, between the basketball games, the picnics, and your jobs, I never see you. I thought softball season was bad, but I didn't imagine the winter would be so busy."

Diz dutifully went and gave her mother a kiss on the cheek. "I cut the grass already, and all the clothes are in off the line. Frannie and I went over to Mrs. Haverly's for you and picked up the lettuce, tomatoes, cucumbers, celery, potatoes, and onion from her Victory Garden, just like you asked. Everything is done."

"You girls be careful out there."

"We will be, Mother."

Diz grabbed the picnic basket off the table. "We won't be too late. We both have to work tomorrow."

"Bye, Mrs. Hosler."

"Goodbye, girls."

"Do you think she has any idea that we spend every night together?" Diz asked, breaking the comfortable silence they'd been enjoying on the car ride.

"Gosh, I sure hope not," Frannie said. "I imagine if she did, she'd have put a stop to it by now."

"Yeah, you're right. My mother isn't exactly subtle."

Frannie glanced away from the road momentarily to look at Diz. "I'm really, really glad you've finally gotten over being so paranoid about getting caught. I like the new, more relaxed Diz." Frannie slid her hand across the seat and interlaced their fingers.

"Well, now that we have so much more time alone together, we don't have to sneak around when we're on the road or spending time with our friends."

"True."

"Maybe..." Diz took a deep breath. *Now's as good a time as any.* She started over. "I've been thinking. Everybody has been really swell about you staying at my house."

"Mm."

"I mean, Jessie, Dot, Dobbie, Peanuts, Jean, Marjorie... None of them asked a question or raised an eyebrow. You said you'd been living with your aunt and uncle, they needed the space back, and you had nowhere to go, and everybody thought it was the most natural thing that you would come stay with me."

"Diz?"

"Mm-hmm?"

"You're rambling. You only do that when you're nervous. Spill. Whatever you're working yourself up about, you've got about five minutes to tell me before we pull into the parking lot."

"Right. Well, the thing is, what if, when we've saved up enough, I mean... What if we got a place together?"

"What?" Frannie disentangled their hands.

"You can't go back to that awful place," Diz rushed on, "and Daddy and Elsie eventually are going to come home. Our friends are already used to us staying in the same place, so it would seem natural for us to keep doing that."

She finally dared a peek at Frannie. "Why are you looking at me like that?"

"I can't figure you out." Frannie shook her head in bewilderment. "All this time, you've been crazy worried that anyone might think we were queer—that something was going on between us—and now you want to get a place together? How does that figure?"

Diz cleared her throat. "It's just..." She threw up her hands. "I love having you next to me at night. I'm worried about what will happen when the war ends and everything goes back to normal. I'm not planning to live at home forever. Sooner or later I'm going to move out on my own. I don't make enough right now to do it, but when I go to ASU and get my teaching certificate, I will. So, I thought, maybe even before that, if we pooled our money, we could afford a place together."

As the silence stretched between them, Diz squirmed. She probably shouldn't have said anything. She knew better. Springing this on Frannie, on the way to meet their friends... What could she have been thinking?

Frannie parked the car, and morosely, Diz reached for the door handle. "I'm sorry. It was probably a bad idea," she said. "I shouldn't have brought it up."

"Diz?"

"Yeah."

"I just need some time to think about it, okay?"

"Sure."

"You know I'm still sore about you spying on me, right?"

Diz nodded.

"If you hadn't done that, I'd still be living where I was."

"You weren't happy there!"

"Whether I was happy or not is beside the point. You spied on me. You violated my privacy and now I'm homeless."

"Are not."

"Excuse me?"

"You have a home with me." Diz crossed her arms over her chest and hugged herself. "Don't you like getting to snuggle every night? Don't you enjoy me falling asleep in your arms?"

"Of course I do, don't be silly. It isn't that."

"Then what is it?"

"It's...complicated."

"It seems pretty simple from where I'm sitting." The last word died on Diz's lips as Jessie, Marjorie, Amelina, and Louise bounded over to the car.

Marjorie opened the passenger door. "Hi, girls. Glad you could make it," Marjorie said, apparently oblivious to the tension between Diz and Frannie. "What'd you bring?" She lifted the lid of the picnic basket in the back seat. "Oh, how on earth did you ever manage to get enough cheese for sandwiches, Diz?"

"Mother traded ration coupons with Mrs. Haverly—cheese in exchange for bacon this month," Diz answered.

Marjorie continued to rummage in the basket. "And crackers with homemade jam. It's a feast!"

Dot, Peanuts, and Dobbie pulled up just then, followed in another car by Jean Hutsell, Delores Low, Shirley Wade, and Zada Boles.

"Hail, hail, the gang's all here. Let's get this party started!" Louise proclaimed.

"What's the latest from Elsie, Diz?" Jessie asked, once they'd gotten all the blankets spread out on the rocks and the picnic baskets arranged.

"Mother and I got a letter just the other day," Diz said, biting into a cheese sandwich. The mention of Elsie and her absence no longer angered Diz. After all, the war was going well, and she'd be coming home soon enough. "She says she and some of the other girls have been towing targets for the infantry boys on the ground to shoot at. She said—and I quote—'If this is the best Uncle Sam can do, we're in trouble. Some of these boys can't hit the broad side of a barn.'"

The girls all laughed.

"One of the boys apparently shot up Elsie's plane instead of the target she was towing."

"Oh, my goodness. That sounds positively harrowing," Marjorie said.

"She was in good spirits. Seems like she's made some lifelong friends and gotten to fly some bigger planes," Diz said. "Of course, Mother wasn't happy with the infantry-shooting-at-her part of the letter."

"I can imagine," Amelina said. "Pass me one of those crackers and some jam, will you, Frannie?"

Frannie did as requested.

"I admire her," Louise said, taking a bite of her Spam sandwich. "She's doing something important for the war effort."

"Speaking of which, has anyone heard from Navy Specialist First Class Ford Hoffman lately?"

Everyone looked to Dot.

"Last time I talked to him, he said to make sure we were all keeping in shape and avoiding any jammed fingers on the basketball court," Dot said.

"Sounds just like him," Marjorie said.

"I liked that last picture of him in his uniform," Frannie said. "He looked pretty sharp."

The girls talked, ate, skimmed stones in the water, gossiped about boys and the latest headlines from the warfront, sang songs, and ate some more until the sun was low in the western sky and the comfortable temperatures of the daytime made way for the cooler temperatures of the evening.

"I hate to be a party pooper, but Mother is home all alone and will be expecting us," Diz finally said.

"I bet she misses your dad, especially with Elsie gone," Dobbie said.

"Yeah, she's pretty lonely."

"It's great that she's gained another daughter in Frannie, though," Marjorie said.

Diz smiled. She hoped that Frannie was thinking the same thing she was—the girls thought her being part of Diz's family was completely natural. "Are you kidding me? My mother loves Frannie more than she loves me."

"That's only because I can reach the items on the top shelf in the cupboard."

"True," Diz agreed, playfully elbowing Frannie. It was the closest she'd felt to her all day. "Anyway, we've got to get going.

The ride home was a quiet affair. Although Diz badly wanted to pick up the discussion where they'd left off when they arrived at Blue Point, it was clear to her that Frannie didn't want any part of it right now.

By the time they walked through the screen door and into the house, it was almost nine o'clock. Diz already had begun to trudge up the stairs when she realized that something was amiss—the lights were still on in every room.

She froze in mid-step, stopping short so quickly that Frannie, who was behind her, ran into her back. The memory of coming home to find her mother crying on the morning Pearl Harbor was attacked, burned brightly in Diz's mind.

"Mother?" she called, tentatively. Diz turned, scooted around Frannie, and retraced her steps. "Mother?" She checked the kitchen, the dining room, and, finally, the parlor. "Mother!"

The sound of Diz's voice must've alarmed Frannie, because in an instant, she appeared at Diz's side.

"Mother? What's going on?" Diz knelt in front of her mother, who sat motionless in her father's favorite chair, a dazed expression on her face. She held something loosely in her hands, and Diz took it from her and began to read.

"The Secretary of War asks that I extend his deepest sympathy in the loss of your husband..." Diz dropped the telegram to the floor and clamped a hand over her mouth. Her whole body shook. "Mother?" Tears rolled down her cheeks. "Mother? That's a m-mistake, right? They've got the wrong guy, right? They can't be talking about Daddy. Mother? Say something!"

Diz's mother remained unmoving in the chair. If she heard Diz, she made no sign of it.

Diz picked up the telegram off the floor and shoved it beseechingly at Frannie. "You read it. It's a mistake."

Frannie read it silently. When she was done, she folded it and put it on the small table beside the chair.

"Did you read it?" Diz asked Frannie.

"The whole thing." Frannie's voice was soft, low, and somber.

"I read it wrong, didn't I?"

Frannie shook her head sadly. "I'm afraid not."

"But Daddy was the best pilot there ever was."

"I'm sure he was. It's a war, hon. Lots of good men are dying over there."

Diz wrapped her arms around herself. "But not my father. Not Daddy."

"I told you not to go."

Diz and Frannie both turned at the hollow sound of Mrs. Hosler's voice. "Did you say something, Mother?"

"I told you it was too dangerous; I told you you'd never come back to me alive. I told you I couldn't lose you. I begged you not to leave me. Not to leave me and our girls."

Diz and Frannie exchanged a glance. "Who is she talking to?" Frannie asked.

Mrs. Hosler continued to stare straight ahead. "Your duty as a man, and as an American, to go? You had a bigger responsibility to us. God, I hated arguing with you. You said I was being selfish." She lifted a hand and let it fall back into her lap.

"What about now, Ted? Am I being selfish, now that I'm a widow? Now that you've left me to raise our girls all by myself? What about now?" The last word broke on a sob, and Diz's mother buried her face in her hands.

Diz climbed onto the arm of the chair and enveloped her mother in a hug. The two of them rocked back and forth for a very long time.

"Diz? I'm going to go upstairs now and give you two some privacy."

Diz blinked and focused her bleary eyes on Frannie. "Don't. Please don't go." She stood up and smoothed her wrinkled shirt with both hands. "I need you."

Frannie smiled wistfully. "Your mother needs you. You need each other."

"Mother, please. You're scaring Frannie and me," Diz pleaded. "We need you."

For a long moment, Diz thought her mother hadn't heard her. Then, Mrs. Hosler took a deep breath in and focused on Diz's face. She seemed to regain some of her composure.

"I'm sorry. I need to pull myself together for you girls." She turned her attention to Frannie. "It's all right, Frannie dear. You're part of our family now." She blew her nose on the handkerchief she had up her sleeve. "I'm sorry I'm such a mess."

"I'm the one who's sorry, Mrs. Hosler. I wish there was something more I could do."

"You're a good friend to Theodora. That's important to me. Ted was always better with her than I was. He always knew just what to say." She dabbed at her eyes with the hankie.

"You're a great mother," Diz protested.

Her mother ignored her and continued talking to Frannie. "As a little girl, Elsie would drag the step stool over to the counter whenever I was baking a pie. She was fascinated by the process— the rolling of the dough, the mixing of the ingredients—she always wanted to help.

"Theodora, on the other hand, only wanted to know when she could be dismissed, so that she could go outside and play ball. She would sit at the end of the driveway and wait for Mr. Hosler to come home from work so she could badger him into teaching her how to throw a fastball like Dizzy Dean."

Diz smiled at the memory.

"Daddy, Daddy, Daddy! I've got your glove and the ball right here already. Can we play? I've been practicing. I think I can throw it faster now."

"Yeah, sport?" Diz's father ruffled her hair. "Let me just get out of this monkey suit and I'll be right out."

"Hurry, Daddy. It'll be dark soon."

Fresh tears flowed down Diz's cheeks. How was it possible that she would never hear his shouts of encouragement at a game anymore? That she would never feel the warmth of his hug when he came home from work? Or shy away from the scruffiness of his five o'clock shadow at the end of a long day, when he rubbed his cheek against hers?

Diz grabbed the telegram off the table and unfolded it. This time, she would read it all the way through and discover the mistake in identity, for surely there was one.

"The Secretary of War asks that I extend his deepest sympathy in the loss of your husband, Major Theodore V. Hosler. Report just received states he died February 11, 1944, at airbase Boxted, Essexshire, England, from injuries suffered during a sortie over Germany. Confirming letter follows. Edward F. Witsell, Acting the Adjutant General of the Army."

Diz read it twice. There was no mistake. She would never throw her father a fastball again, and Elsie would never again soar with him in the skies above Phoenix.

"Elsie! How are we going to tell Elsie?"

Diz's mother rubbed her eyes. "I have a phone number somewhere from the last letter she sent."

"We can't just call her up and tell her, Mother."

"We have to."

"No." Diz looked to Frannie. "Frannie and I will go get her and tell her in person. She's only at the Las Vegas Army Airfield."

"We don't have enough gas ration coupons for a trip that long. No, I'll call the air base in the morning and ask if they can have her fly to Kingman, or Luke out in Goodyear. Then you can drive over there and pick her up. Or maybe she can take a bus home."

The grandfather clock in the corner chimed ten o'clock, and Diz's mother rose slowly from the chair, tracing her fingertips over the armrest, pausing at a spot worn thin by her husband's elbows. "It's late, girls. I think it's best we all try to get some rest."

"Are you going to be okay, Mother?"

"We could stay with you, Mrs. Hosler."

"That's very sweet of you two, but I'll be all right. Why don't you two bunk together for tonight? I think Theodora could use your company, Frannie. That is, if you don't mind?"

"I'd be happy to," Frannie said, "assuming that's what Diz wants."

Diz, still reeling from the news of her father's death, nodded dumbly. Somewhere beyond the fog of grief, she registered that her mother had just sanctioned her sleeping with Frannie. Surely, this all must be a surreal dream.

CHAPTER TWELVE

Phoenix, 1944

The next few days and nights went by like a blur. Diz could never remember being hugged and kissed by so many people she didn't know. Food magically appeared in the kitchen—casseroles, pies, Spam meatloaves—and Diz couldn't bear to look at any of it.

Frannie stayed by her side throughout, and her touch was the only thing Diz could feel through the numbness.

"She's over there, in the corner, with the minister and his wife," Frannie said.

"Hmm?"

"You were keeping an eye out for your mother, right?"

"How did you know that?"

"Because I know you. You've been watching her like a hawk."

"I'm worried about her. She's okay when people are here, like now, but when the house is empty, she just sits in Daddy's chair and stares off into space. And every night she cries herself to sleep in her room."

"I know. I can hear her too."

"I know you can." Since the night they learned of her father's death, Frannie had spent every night in Diz's bed, not even sneaking out before dawn, holding her, comforting her, and wiping away her tears. They didn't talk much—after all, what was there to say? Frannie had suffered the same kind of loss, and Diz couldn't begin to imagine how she had handled losing both of her parents all at once.

"Does the pain ever go away?" Diz asked.

"Honestly?" Frannie shook her head. "I wish I could tell you it did. That feeling of shock, like none of this is real, that goes away after all the attention fades. But then you're left with this huge, gaping hole in your life where your parents used to be. It's like a never-ending nightmare of loneliness."

"I don't know how you did it, all by yourself, like you did."

"I didn't have a choice."

"I wish I'd known you then."

Frannie offered a pained smile. "I wish you had too."

"I would've taken care of you, just like you're taking care of me." Diz laced their fingers together, squeezed, then let go. "Thank you for being here. It means the world to me."

"I'm not going to lie. This is hard for me. It reminds me..." Frannie cleared her throat. "Well, that doesn't matter now. What matters is that I'm here for you, and there's nowhere else I'd rather be," Frannie said.

"I haven't exactly been the life of the party."

"Diz, no one expects you to be. You just lost your father. Everyone understands—"

"Not really," Diz interrupted. "But you do. I'm so lucky."

A shadow crossed Frannie's face, and Diz asked, "Are you sure you're okay with all this?"

The shrill ringing of the telephone cut through the din in the parlor and interrupted their conversation. Diz ran to the kitchen to answer it. "Hello?"

"Diz?"

Diz strained to hear through all the noise in the house, and the noise on the other end of the line. "Elsie? Is that you?"

"Yes. Sorry it's so hard to hear. The phone is in the office right next to the main hangar," Elsie shouted. "What's going on there? I just got back from doing a three-day ferry run and my CO gave me a message that I needed to call home right away. Are you okay? Is Mother okay?"

Diz didn't mean to cry. She tried her hardest not to, but hearing Elsie's voice broke something deep inside her, and Diz slid down the wall she'd been leaning against, sobbing uncontrollably.

"Sis? Are you there? H-hello? Diz?"

Diz tried to catch her breath. "I-I'm h-here." She hiccupped. "W-where are you? A-are you in L-Las Vegas?"

"Yes. Diz? What's going on? What's wrong?"

Diz compulsively wrapped the long phone cord around her finger, unwrapped it, and wrapped it again. "Y-you need to come home. Right away."

"Why?"

"I'll tell you when you get here. Can you get a plane to Luke? Or Kingman?"

"I don't know. I don't think so. Just tell me what's going on. I know something's wrong." Alarm colored Elsie's tone. "Tell me. Is it Mother? Has something happened to her?"

Diz closed her eyes tightly. She didn't want to tell Elsie over the phone. She imagined how she'd feel if it was her, learning news like that so far from home.

"Sis?"

Diz sighed. "It's D-Daddy."

Silence.

"What about Daddy?" Elsie's voice was wary, tight.

Diz clamped her teeth together, squeezed her eyes shut, and shook her head, as a fresh wave of pain and grief swamped her.

"Theodora Hosler, you're scaring me. What about Daddy?"

"H-he's gone. Oh, Elsie. Daddy is gone." Diz pulled her knees up to her chest and circled them with her free arm. "He's gone," she whispered.

For a long time, the only sound on the other end of the phone was keening. Eventually, a strange voice came on the line. "Hello? This is Elsie's friend, Annabelle. Who's this?"

"I'm Elsie's sister, Diz."

"What's happened?"

Diz didn't think she had it in her to repeat the news. Just then, the phone was lifted from her hand.

"This is Diz's friend, Frannie."

Diz looked up, startled to see Frannie standing above her. Of course Frannie would've come looking for her when she didn't return right away.

"Mm-hmm," Frannie was saying. "Yes, that's probably best... Mm-hmm, I agree... Right. Okay, well, I'll tell Mrs. Hosler to expect her then… Mm-hmm. Thank you for looking after Elsie… Very good. Goodbye." Frannie hung up the phone and sat down next to Diz.

"I couldn't…" Diz started, her voice trailing off. The two of them sat silently side-by-side for a few minutes. "I didn't want to tell Elsie over the phone, but she kept pressuring me."

"It's okay. You did what you had to do." Frannie rubbed Diz's back. "Elsie's friend, Annabelle, is going to see to it that Elsie gets on the next bus home. She says she thinks there's one first thing tomorrow morning."

"Oh."

"I told her that would be best, since I overheard your mother talking to the minister about having the memorial service day after tomorrow."

"How can she think about having the service so soon? We don't have Daddy's body yet."

Frannie shrugged.

"There you girls are." The puffiness underneath Mrs. Hosler's carefully applied makeup underscored her exhaustion. "The minister and his wife are leaving, and I wanted you to meet them, Theodora."

Diz stood up and walked with her mother.

"Who was on the phone?"

"It was Elsie."

Mrs. Hosler stopped walking. "Did you tell her?"

Diz nodded, not trusting her voice.

"How did she take it?"

Diz shook her head.

"Is she all right?"

Again, Diz nodded.

"Speak to me, Theodora."

"She's going to try to get a bus tomorrow morning if she can."

"Good."

"Are you planning to have the funeral day after tomorrow?"

"Yes."

"But, we don't have a body to bury," Diz protested. "We don't even really know what happened yet."

Her mother tenderly pushed a lock of hair off of Diz's forehead. "Not having a service won't bring your father back, sweetheart. We have to face that he's gone."

Diz's bottom lip quivered and again tears welled in her eyes.

"I've decided to have the memorial service now, and a proper funeral when we have something to bury."

The word "something" hit Diz like a fist in the heart. She'd been trying so hard not to envision what might have befallen her father—how he might have died. Was he shot? Burned alive in his plane? "Injuries suffered in a sortie over Germany..." What did that mean?

"Ah, Reverend Faulkner. I wanted you to meet Theodora, my youngest daughter."

Diz shook the reverend's outstretched hand. He had kind eyes, and exuded an air of compassionate warmth.

"I'm so sorry for your loss, Miss Hosler."

"Thank you."

"My wife and I need to be going, Beverly. I just wanted to say goodbye for now. Don't worry about the service. We can talk about that more at length tomorrow."

"Thank you, Reverend."

Diz waited until he walked away. There were still half a dozen ladies chatting amongst themselves in the parlor. "Is it okay if I go out for a little while, Mother? I won't be gone long. I just need some air."

"Of course. Take Frannie with you, please. And don't go too far. I don't want to be worrying about you."

Diz found her girl upstairs sitting on the bed. For a brief second, she thought she saw tears in Frannie's eyes. Then Frannie blinked and they were gone.

Diz insinuated herself in between Frannie's legs and took her hands. "Thank you."

"For what?"

"Everything. For being here, for being so understanding, for talking on the phone for me when I couldn't, for being so patient with my mother and all these people coming in and out of the house."

"It's okay."

But Diz could see that it wasn't. "Want to get out of here for a little while?"

"Sure. Where do you want to go?"

"Anywhere that isn't here."

"What do you say to a movie?"

"I can't take a war movie right now," Diz said.

"I was thinking more of a musical comedy. Mickey Rooney and Judy Garland's new movie, 'Girl Crazy,' is playing downtown."

Diz hesitated. She felt guilty for skipping out on her mother for the length of a movie, but being cooped up in the house was making her stir crazy.

As if reading her mind, Frannie added, "It'll only be a couple of hours. Those old biddies down there will be talking at least that long."

"You're probably right."

"My treat for the movie? I'll even spring for the Coca Colas and popcorn."

"Oh, big spender, eh?" Diz already felt better and they hadn't even left the house yet.

⤴⤵

The movie proved an excellent distraction. Diz and Frannie left the theater walking side-by-side and humming "Embraceable You."

Frannie started the car. "Can I tempt you with an ice cream?"

Diz put a hand over her midsection. "I don't think my stomach could handle that right now, but you're sweet to ask."

As they pulled away from the curb, Diz stared out the passenger window at the stars twinkling in the night sky. "But there is something I'd like to do."

"Name it."

"Are our softball bags still in the trunk?"

"Mm-hmm."

"Let's go have a catch."

Frannie glanced at Diz. "You know it's pitch black outside, right?"

148

"The ball park has lights."

"You want to break into the stadium, turn on the lights, and play catch?"

For once in her life, Diz felt like throwing caution to the wind. "Technically, it wouldn't be breaking in if we hopped over the fence."

"You don't think anyone would notice those bright lights? You can see them halfway across town."

"Since when did you get to be such a scaredy-cat? I thought that was my job." The more Diz thought about it, the more desperate she was to do this. "Please? To honor all those games of catch I played with my father. I always felt closest to him when we were spending time together on a ball field."

"This is crazy. You know this is crazy," Frannie said. She was standing in left field.

"I do. Thank you for indulging me." Diz jogged out to right-center field and stretched her throwing arm.

"Yeah, well. When the police come, I'm going to tell them it was all your cockamamie idea."

"Relax. We're not going to be here that long." Diz tossed the ball to Frannie. She took in a deep breath of the crisp, February air, and for the first time in days, she felt alive.

"Speaking of not being anywhere that long, what are we going to do now that Elsie is coming back home?"

Diz's heart stuttered. "What do you mean?" She caught Frannie's throw and fired the ball back again.

"When I agreed to come stay with you and your mother, it was only supposed to be for a short while, until I figured something else out. We always knew that when Elsie came home, I was going to have to leave."

"B-but everything's changed now," Diz said.

"Has your house magically gained another bedroom?"

Frannie's throw was a little wide, and Diz ranged to her right to snag it. "No, but you're already sleeping with me. Mother gave you permission."

"She gave me permission because she didn't want you to be alone in your grief." Frannie leaped to snare Diz's high fastball.

149

"Now that you're officially staying in my room, you can just keep staying there." The tightness in Diz's chest made it suddenly hard to breathe.

Frannie shook her head. "You, Elsie, and your mother are going to need time alone together to adjust, without me under foot. This is about family, and I… I'm not part of one anymore."

Diz's pulse hammered in her ears. "Mother considers you part of our family now. You're another daughter to her. She needs you too." Diz threw the ball even harder this time. The popping noise it made when it landed in Frannie's glove sounded like a firecracker in the still of the night.

Diz's shoulders slumped. Instead of throwing the ball back, Frannie trotted over to her and put an arm around her. Diz shrugged her off. Frannie persisted. Diz no longer had the strength to protest.

"I love you, Diz. You know that, right?"

Diz took a shaky breath in and slowly shook her head. "If you loved me, you wouldn't be trying to find a way out."

"This isn't about you, sweetheart. I just need to find different living arrangements."

"No, you don't."

Frannie let out a deep sigh. "We don't have to settle this tonight. What do you say we skedaddle before we get caught?"

Reluctantly, Diz allowed herself to be led off the field. She stood by silently as Frannie killed the lights, and followed when Frannie climbed the fence and dropped over the other side. She couldn't take one more heartache right now. She simply…couldn't.

When they arrived back at the house, Diz wordlessly got out of the car, climbed the steps to the front porch, and went inside. She heard Frannie come in after her and lock the door. Inside, all the lights were off, save for a single lamp in the parlor. That's where Diz found her mother, sitting in her father's chair. Her eyes were closed.

"Mother?" Diz gently shook her. "Mother? You should get up and go to bed. You're exhausted."

"Is that you, Ted? Why are you so late?"

The air rushed out of Diz's lungs. She swallowed hard. "No, mother. It's me, Theodora."

Mrs. Hosler opened her eyes and straightened up in the chair. "Oh, of course." She cleared her throat and touched her fingers to her hair. "Did you girls have fun?"

"Sure, Mother. Why don't you go to sleep? It's been a long day. Elsie will be home tomorrow."

"That's right. She will be, won't she?"

"Yes, she will."

"Okay, then." Mrs. Hosler stood up and stretched. She glanced around the room. "I really should straighten this place up."

"Don't worry. I'll take care of it. You go to bed." Diz gave her mother a gentle push in the direction of her bedroom.

"If you're sure." Mrs. Hosler yawned.

"I am."

"Where's Frannie?"

Diz tried to ignore the pang in her heart. "I think she went upstairs already. Go to bed, Mother. It's been a long day, and I'm sure tomorrow will be even longer."

"Good night, dear. You're a good daughter. I know you miss your dad as much as I do, and you've done a good job of looking after me these past few days. I just want you to know I noticed, and I appreciate it."

"You're welcome. Now, go on."

After Mrs. Hosler went to bed, Diz spent a few minutes cleaning up the dirty glasses and plates visitors had left on the dining room table. She was surprised, and not a little hurt, that Frannie wasn't down here helping her.

She pushed in the chairs, shook out the tablecloth, and washed the dishes in the sink. When she was satisfied that the place was as orderly as she could make it, she turned out the lights and trudged upstairs to get ready for bed.

Frannie was lying on her side, facing the other way, when Diz slipped under the covers. Everything seemed to be spinning out of control. She snuggled up against Frannie's back, wrapped an arm around her middle, and stifled a sob.

How could she ever go back to sleeping all by herself? How could she give up the feeling of Frannie breathing next to her, and the gentle sound of her snoring?

Frannie rolled onto her back and pulled Diz into her arms. "I love you, Theodora Dizzy Hosler." She kissed Diz on the nose.

"I love you too."

"Everything's going to be all right, I promise. Get some sleep."

"Mm-kay." Diz listened to the rhythmic beating of Frannie's heart, her head rising and falling with Frannie's chest. Her eyelids grew heavy, and she slipped into an exhausted slumber.

CHAPTER THIRTEEN

Phoenix, 1944

Diz sorted through the mail as she walked back up the driveway. She stopped dead when she got to an official-looking envelope with the raised seal of the War Department, Adjutant General's Office. Although it was addressed to her mother, Diz reasoned that the letter was for her, as well.

She walked up onto the porch, sat down heavily on the steps, and opened the letter to read.

Dear Mrs. Hosler:

It is with deep regret that I am writing to confirm my telegram of 27 February, 1944, in which it was my sad duty to inform you of the death of your husband, Major Theodore V. Hosler.

A casualty message just received in this office states he died 11 February, 1944, at an Allied airbase, Boxted Airdrome, Essexshire, England, from injuries suffered during a sortie over Germany. Your husband was buried with dignity and with full military honors. Details of his interment and any wishes the family may have regarding relocation of the remains will be handled under separate cover.

I know that added distress is caused by failure to receive more information, so I have included herein a letter from one of your husband's squadron members, who was eyewitness to the events surrounding Major Hosler's unfortunate demise.

I sincerely regret that this message must bring so much sorrow into your home and my deepest sympathy is with you in your bereavement.

Sincerely yours,

Edward F. Witsell
Acting The Adjutant General of the Army

Diz wiped her eyes on her shirt sleeve, set the letter aside and removed the other piece of paper from the envelope.

My Dear Mrs. Hosler:

You have no doubt by now received notification of the death of your husband, Major Theodore V. Hosler, who perished of injuries sustained in combat on February 11, 1944. Confident that this announcement came as a great shock to you, I am writing these few lines to let you know the circumstances surrounding his death, and to let you know that I was with him upon the occasion of his passing.

Major Hosler was one of the finest fliers I ever knew, and I was proud to serve with him. On February 11th, we were on a mission to protect the big, heavy bombers during a critical raid over

```
Germany. Major Hosler's plane caught fire
during   a   firefight.   Impossibly,   your
husband continued to fly and fight, even
though   he   was   critically   wounded.   He
managed to wrestle the plane back to the
base   at   Boxted,   where   he   crash-landed.
Although your husband did not survive his
wounds,   he   saved   his   fellow   squadron
members, including yours truly, and kept
the plane from falling into enemy hands.

     I was, as I said, very proud to serve
with   your   husband.   He   was   a   masterful
pilot.  More  than  that,  he  was  a  great
team  leader,  and  a  good  man.  The  whole
squadron attended his burial at Boxted. I
am  certain  the  Army  will  inform  you  of
the details of his burial so that you can
have  his  remains  returned  to  the  States
for final disposition.

     I extend to you my deepest sympathy on
the loss of your husband, who was a hero
to us all.

     Sincerely,

     First Lieutenant Scott T. Richardson
```

Diz's throat was tight with emotion. Her father was a war hero. It was confirmed right here, in this letter. "I'm so proud of you, Daddy."

"Elsie should be here any…"

Diz quickly wiped away more tears at the sound of her girl's voice. It seemed all she'd been doing for the past few days was crying. It was no wonder Frannie didn't want to stick around.

"What's up?" Frannie sat down next to Diz and put an arm around her. She peeked over Diz's shoulder to see the letter. "Oh, baby, I'm so, so sorry." She pulled Diz's head onto her shoulder and kissed the top of her head.

Diz didn't even have the strength to worry about who would see them this way. To anyone watching, it would simply appear like two best friends consoling one another. So she leaned into Frannie's comforting embrace and allowed the love to wash over her like a balm. After several minutes, she straightened up, although she continued to stay in the circle of Frannie's arm.

"I'm sorry. All I do is cry these days."

"It's okay. I get it."

"But I'm driving you away."

"What?"

"You want to leave because I'm so depressing to be around."

Frannie turned to face her. "That has nothing to do with anything. What in the world makes you think that?"

"You said as much last night."

"That's not what I said at all. I just said I was going to need to find someplace else to live with Elsie coming home, and that your mother needs to have things be as normal as possible. It's going to be a period of adjustment for all of you. I'm not part of that."

"You're part of me," Diz reasoned. "That makes you part of everything that happens in my life."

"I'm not leaving your life, Diz. You can't get rid of me that easily."

"Good." Diz smiled wanly. "Because I'm not letting you go anywhere."

"Sis! Oh, my God."

Diz scooted a respectable distance away from Frannie as Elsie ran up the driveway, duffle bag slung over one shoulder. She dropped the bag on the porch and lifted Diz into a tight embrace.

"You look...different," Diz said, when she disentangled herself. She smoothed the letter that had crumpled between them and put it back in the envelope.

"You got a new hairdo," Frannie said.

"Oh, good Lord. Where are my manners?" Elsie stepped forward and gave Frannie a hug. "Hi, Frannie. In her last letter, Mother said that you were staying in my room. I'm so glad you were here to keep Mother and Diz company."

"You'd better get inside and see Mother. She's been waiting for you all morning."

156

"How is she?"

"Not good," Diz said. "She spends most of her time staring off into space. Last night, she fell asleep in Daddy's chair. When I went to wake her, she thought I was him."

"Oh, no."

"You should probably be the one to give this to her." Diz handed the letter to Elsie. "And you might want to read it first."

"What is it?" She turned it over in her hands.

"The letter with the details of what happened to Daddy."

"Oh." Elsie walked over and sat down on the porch swing. Tears streamed down her face as she finished reading. "At Sweetwater, we would hear a lot of stories of our boys getting shot down and killed over there. Heck, I flew my share of planes whose engines had to be rebuilt, or their wings repaired, or the controls replaced, because they'd been shot up. But somehow it never seemed so personal to me. I guess that's because I didn't know any of the pilots."

"Did you get to fly a P-51? The plane Daddy was flying?"

"Yep. She's a honey. Knowing Daddy, he must've loved flying that bird." Elsie sniffled and dried her eyes. "I miss him so much. I always imagined that he might be flying one of the planes I tested after it was fixed up."

"Who knows, maybe he did," Frannie said.

"Maybe," Elsie agreed.

"Theodora? Who are you talking to?"

Diz picked up Elsie's bag and motioned her sister to open the screen door. "Elsie's here, Mother."

Elsie ran to her mother and the two women clung to each other. "Oh, Mother. I'm so sorry I wasn't home when you got the news."

"You're here now, and that's all that matters." Mrs. Hosler leaned back. "Let me look at you… Something's different."

"Frannie thinks it's her hairdo," Diz said. "But I think there's something else."

Elsie blushed. "Can we talk about it later? Right now, all that matters is Daddy." Elsie handed her mother the letter.

"When did this arrive?" Mrs. Hosler's voice quavered. She looked from Elsie to Diz.

"This morning's mail," Diz answered.

Mrs. Hosler slumped into the closest chair, and withdrew the letter from the envelope. She started to unfold the pages, then stopped. For a long time, she simply held it in her lap without reading it.

"Do you want me to read it to you, Mother?" Elsie offered.

Mrs. Hosler shook her head. "I'm perfectly capable of reading it myself. The truth is, whatever it says," she said dully, "it can't bring my husband back."

"But, Mother, it says he was a hero," Diz said. "Don't you want to know that?"

"I already knew that. Anyone who spent any time with your father knew that."

"Hello? Anybody home?"

"That sounds like Dot," Elsie said. "It's open," she called.

Seconds later, most of the Ramblers team filed in.

As if by agreement, Dot stepped forward to speak for the group. "Mrs. Hosler, Diz, Elsie, we just wanted to come by to express our sympathy and to extend our condolences. We're sorry for your loss."

"Aren't you just the sweetest group of girls," Mrs. Hosler said. "Theodora, why don't you get out some of the sandwiches Mrs. Haverly brought over yesterday? I'm sure your friends are hungry."

"That's okay, Mrs. Hosler," Peanuts said. "We just wanted to pay our respects."

"I insist that you stay and have something to eat."

The girls all looked at each other. "Okay. But just for a little bit," Dot said.

Diz went and got the sandwiches and placed them on the dining room table, along with some plates and napkins.

Before long, the house was filled with the noise of her teammates and friends.

"Hey, Elsie," Amelina said, "is that a ring on your finger?"

All conversation ceased and everyone turned their attention to Elsie, who was blushing a deep shade of crimson.

"Sis?" Diz grabbed her sister's left hand and examined her ring finger. "Are you engaged?"

"That's what's different!" Frannie exclaimed.

"Elsie?" Mrs. Hosler, who had been sitting off by herself, rose slowly and made her way over. "Is that true? You never said a word about any boys."

Elsie squirmed. "This is hardly the time—"

"Elsie Marie Hosler, you answer the question this very minute."

"Yes."

"I'm sorry, I didn't hear you?"

Elsie narrowed her eyes and stuck out her tongue at Marjorie. "I said, yes. Yes! I met a fella while I was at Sweetwater. He's a flight instructor. He's just...dreamy."

"Why is this the first time your father and I are hearing about this?"

The room went silent, as everyone looked at Mrs. Hosler.

"I mean..." Her eyes filled with tears and she put trembling fingers to her mouth. "I'm..."

"It's okay, Mother." Elsie put an arm around her. "It's natural. It's just habit."

"It's not okay." Mrs. Hosler stepped back. "And it never will be. Excuse me, girls." She ran from the room.

Diz heard the bedroom door slam shut. She started to go after her.

"Don't," Frannie said. She put a hand on Diz's shoulder. "Let her go. Give her some privacy and some time to digest everything."

"Frannie's right," Dobbie said. "It's a lot to take in at once. She'll be all right."

"This is all my fault," Elsie said. She plopped down into the nearest chair. "I was going to bring Pete home to meet Mother and Daddy. I was just waiting for the right time."

"Of course you were," Jessie said.

"And then, when Diz told me that Daddy was gone, well, that hardly seemed the right moment, now did it? I wasn't going to say anything. I wasn't."

"I'm sorry I brought it up," Amelina said.

"No, it's not your fault. I should have taken the ring off before I got here."

"Excuse us for a minute, guys." Diz grabbed Elsie by the hand and pulled her into the kitchen. "Who is this guy?" All of the pent up anger Diz thought she'd resolved, came flooding back. "When are you planning to get married? Is he local? Where will you live?"

"What is wrong with you? Why are you being so hostile?" Elsie asked. "I told you, his name is Pete—Peter Redondo. He's a flight instructor at Avenger Field. He's from Dallas, Texas, and no, we haven't decided yet where we're going to settle down. And we were thinking of getting married sometime around Christmas."

"That's great. That's just great. Congratulations." Diz turned on her heel and stormed out. The screen door clattered closed behind her.

She paced back and forth on the porch. Everything she'd feared, everything she'd despaired of—all of it was coming true. All of her plans for the future were for naught. She crossed her arms over her chest.

"Hey," Frannie said, coming out to join her. "Want to tell me what that was all about? Elsie's in there crying, and everybody is trying to console her."

"Don't you see?" Diz rounded on Frannie. "This is exactly what I was afraid of. You said everything would be all right. Elsie would come home and I could have the life I wanted. Now she's planning to marry a guy from Dallas at Christmastime and go off and make her own life, and I'm going to be stuck here caring for Mother. Everything I ever wanted, a college degree, a teaching job, a life with you in a place of our own... All that goes up in smoke now."

"You don't know that."

"Sure, side with her. You've been siding with her from the beginning."

"I'm not siding with anyone," Frannie said. "Listen, maybe those were Elsie's plans before your father died. That doesn't mean that's still what she's going to do. This is all just happening now. Why don't you give it a little time to see how it unfolds?"

"You know full well that when Elsie went off to join the WASPs, that meant I had to put going to school on hold so that I could make enough money to help out at home. You know, because I told you, that she promised me then that it would only be until the end of the war—that when the war ended, she'd come home and do her fair share and I could go to ASU and get my teaching certificate. She promised."

"Things change, Diz."

"Yeah," Diz said bitterly. "Elsie's going to marry some flyboy and move to Texas, and you want to move away to God-only-knows-where." In her heart, Diz knew she was being unfair, but the ground was shifting so fast underneath her...

"Look," Frannie said, "I know you're feeling overwhelmed with everything right now. And I didn't help by bringing up the idea of moving out last night. I shouldn't have said anything. I'm sorry. That was my mistake. How about if we forget about that for right now and just deal with one thing at a time? Let's just get through tomorrow's memorial service and then figure out the rest later, okay?"

Diz stopped pacing.

"Okay?"

"I guess."

"Good. Now let's go back inside, seeing as how the team came to see you."

"They came to pay their respects to my mother."

"You are impossible, you know that? They came because they care about *you*, Diz. Don't you get it yet?"

At the moment, Diz wondered if she really understood anything about anything. In less than the span of a week, her entire world had turned upside down.

Phoenix, 2014

"So, that's where we left off last time," Julie said. She switched off the tape recorder. "What happened after that? Did Elsie get married and move to Texas? Did Frannie move out? Did you get to go to ASU and get your teaching degree?"

It was a picture-perfect spring day, and Julie and Diz were sitting at a picnic table in Chaparral Park.

"Easy, there, Tiger," Diz said. "Don't get ahead of yourself. Ah, the impatience of youth."

"Hey! I'm not that young."

"I'm glad you said that and not me." Diz winked. "Do me a favor and hand me my bag, will you?"

Julie unhooked the bag from the back of Diz's wheelchair and put it on the table where Diz could reach it.

"Let's see now..." Diz poked around in the bag. "Ah! There it is." She pulled out a wrapped package and handed it to Julie.

"What's this?"

"Well, I guess you'll never know unless you open it."

"It's for me?"

"Is there anyone else sitting here?"

Julie turned the package over in her hands.

"It isn't going to open itself, you know."

Julie laughed. "I know." She turned it over again. "You got me something?"

"I did." Diz's eyes twinkled in the sunlight. "It's our two-month anniversary."

Julie looked up, surprised. "It is?"

"It is. Are you more surprised that I knew that and you, apparently, didn't, or that I got you something?"

"Both, I think."

"It was two months ago today that you sat down with me in that restaurant with your fancy iPad, your tape recorder, and your notebook. I didn't know you were going to become someone I looked forward to seeing all the time back then, but you're growing on me."

"Lucky me. Thank you, Diz."

"Don't thank me yet. You don't know what it is."

Julie put the package to her ear. "It's not ticking."

"No. I would be a lot more subtle than that."

Julie laughed. "Now I'm worried."

"Just open it, smart-aleck."

Carefully, Julie slid a finger underneath the tape and eased open the wrapping.

"At this rate, we could be here until next year. If my fingers weren't so darned arthritic, I'd reach over there and rip that paper for you."

"Now who's impatient?" Julie peeled back the wrapping paper to reveal a framed five-by-seven picture of Diz and Frannie in their Ramblers uniforms. They were standing with their arms around each other, gazing into each other's eyes and laughing. The date on the back said the picture was taken at an exhibition game in the spring of 1944.

"This is beautiful, Diz." Julie ran her fingers over the glass. "Thank you so much for this. It's a treasure."

"I thought you might appreciate it."

"Are you sure you want me to have it?"

"Of course I'm sure. If I wasn't, I wouldn't have given it to you."

"You both look so happy."

Diz smiled wistfully. "We were, I thought. As it turns out, that was just before all Hell broke loose."

"What do you mean?"

"You wanted to know what happened after my father died, right?"

"Yes."

"The answer is, everything."

CHAPTER FOURTEEN

Phoenix, 1944

The sun sparkled in the brilliant blue sky, the outfield smelled of freshly cut grass, and the sound of softballs thwacking against leather gloves reverberated throughout the ball park.

Diz paused for a moment to take it all in. Here, on this diamond, was the first time she'd felt anything akin to normal in weeks.

All of the girls were in fine spirits for the inaugural practice of the year. True, it was only April, and the season wouldn't get underway for another month, but there was something magical about this first outing. Maybe it was the promise of a fresh start, a clean slate, and the possibility of a second national championship. Or maybe it was simply that they all shared a deep love for the game and affection for each other.

All of the volleyball and basketball games in the off-season were great, but every girl here lived and breathed for softball.

"Okay, bring it in, everybody. That's enough for the first time out," Dot called.

"Did you all hear about those two scouts being in town?" Jessie asked while they all gathered up their gear.

"You mean the ones for Wrigley's league?" Marjorie asked.

"Yeah."

"I heard they were cherry-picking girls from all of our teams," Jean Hutsell said.

"I heard you couldn't have a job all summer long if you played in that league," Delores Low said. "Those four teams each played one hundred eight games last year!"

"I heard that you had to go to 'charm' school and learn how to walk like a lady," Peanuts said. "Whatever that means."

"I sat down with them," Dot said.

"You did?" Diz asked.

"Sure, why not. They sent me a letter and said they wanted to meet, so I thought it would be interesting to hear what they had to say."

"And?" Marjorie asked. "I got a letter too, but I declined the meeting."

"And they offered me a contract. Eighty-five dollars a week."

"And?" Diz asked. "What did you say?" Dot was the Ramblers' heart and soul. She was the acting manager while Mr. Hoffman was fulfilling his Navy obligations. Diz couldn't imagine the team without Dot.

"I told them to stick their contract where the sun don't shine! Charm school? Beauty tips? Are they kidding? When is ball not about playing the game? They're wearing skirts on the field, for crying out loud. Once a Rambler, always a Rambler."

Diz said a silent prayer of thanks. She already had suffered enough losses to last a lifetime, to lose Dot… Well, she couldn't fathom it.

"Ramblers for life!" Peanuts shouted.

"Ramblers for life," everyone answered.

Diz turned to Frannie. "That's someth… Frannie?"

"What?" Frannie made a show of stuffing her cleats and glove in her bag.

"You tell me."

"Tell you what, Diz?" Frannie zipped the bag and headed for the parking lot.

"Hey, you gals going out to South Mountain?" Zada asked.

Diz continued to stare at Frannie as they walked. "Tell me what you're not telling me." Panic crept into Diz's voice. After almost three years together, Diz knew when Frannie was hiding something, and she was most definitely hiding something now.

"Sure," Frannie answered Zada. "Last one there is a rotten egg." Frannie threw her bag in the trunk, grabbed Diz's, and tossed that in the trunk, as well. "Anyone need a ride?"

"You're avoiding me," Diz said. "You don't want to be alone with me."

"I'll ride with you," Jessie said, walking toward Diz and Frannie. "Margie has to run a few errands. No reason for me to tag along with her, when I could be at the Mountain with everyone else."

"Great, come on, then." Frannie headed for the driver's door.

Diz noted that Frannie still had neither answered her, nor looked her in the eye. The idea of the two of them spending an afternoon with all the girls, pretending as though nothing was amiss... Diz just didn't have the strength for it.

"You know what? You two go ahead. I'm going to see if I can catch a ride home from Margie. I'm sure Mother would appreciate the company."

At Mrs. Hosler's urging, Elsie had gone back to the WASPs last week, with the promise that she would return home, with Pete in tow, for a long weekend soon, so that her mother could get to know him.

With Elsie gone, it fell to Diz to take care of her mother. Although the memorial service was weeks ago, Mrs. Hosler remained prone to crying jags and fits of depression.

"Diz? You're not coming with us?"

"Go ahead," she said to Frannie, waving her off. "Have fun. There's no reason for both of us to babysit. I'll see you at home later. Hey, Margie," Diz called, "is my house on your way? I should go check on Mother."

"Sure, I can drop you off. Come on."

"Have fun, girls," Diz said to the group at large, as nonchalantly as she could muster. "Don't get too sunburned." She trotted over to Margie's car and hopped in. "Thanks for the lift."

"No problem. Everything okay?"

"Sure. Why wouldn't it be?"

Margie checked her mirror before pulling out. "I don't know. You and Frannie are like glue. It's not like you to—"

"It's no big deal. Mother hasn't really gotten out of the house since the memorial service. I'm worried about her, that's all." Margie glanced at her sideways, and Diz added, "It would be selfish and silly to expect Frannie to give up a perfectly beautiful afternoon at the Mountain just because Mother shouldn't be alone right now."

"How are you doing with all that?" Margie asked.

"I'm fine. I miss Daddy like crazy, and there are nights when I cry myself to sleep. I still fall to pieces every time I see a man who looks like him coming toward me, or someone comes into the store wearing the same aftershave."

"I bet."

"I wonder how I'll feel when the war is over and everybody else's loved ones are coming home…"

Margie reached across the seat and squeezed Diz's hand. "I know there's nothing I can really do, but I hope you know that every one of us Ramblers feels for you. We're a family, and families stick together."

"Yes, they do," Diz said, thinking, yet again, about the look on Frannie's face back at the field.

"Did you think…?" Margie was saying.

"What?"

"I'm sure I'm being ridiculous, but you know her better than anyone. Did it strike you as odd that Frannie didn't join in when we all said, 'Ramblers for life?'"

Diz's eyes opened wide. "She didn't?"

"No." Margie said. "Didn't you notice?"

"No." Diz thought about it. She'd been standing in front of Frannie and so couldn't see her and wasn't listening that carefully. Frankly, she'd been more concerned about Dot's revelation that she'd met with the scouts than anything else.

But, now that she thought about it, she hadn't heard Frannie's voice in the mix. The thing that had struck her as odd was the look on Frannie's face immediately afterwards.

"Here you go," Margie said. "Tell your mother I said hello."

"Will do, and thanks for the lift."

"Any time. Pick you up for work tomorrow?"

"You bet." Diz strode up the driveway and into the house.

"Girls? Is that you?"

"Just me, Mother." She followed her mother's voice into the sewing room.

"You're all by yourself?"

"Yes."

"Where's Frannie?"

"She went to South Mountain with the girls. Can't it just be me for once?"

"Of course, dear. It's just that... You and Frannie are inseparable. It surprises me, that's all."

Diz decided it was time to change the topic. "Did you eat anything?"

"I'm not that hungry."

Diz came and sat on the hassock. "You have to eat something, Mother. You're getting too thin."

"When did you start to become my mother?" Mrs. Hosler reached out and smoothed a lock of Diz's hair that had fallen onto her forehead. "It's supposed to be the other way around."

"We care for each other. That's what Daddy would want."

Mrs. Hosler put a hand to her chest. "Yes, I suppose that's true." Her eyes misted over. "Your father would be very proud of the woman you're becoming, Theodora. Very proud, indeed. I know you and I haven't always been very close—you really were Daddy's little girl—but I hope you know how much I love you and care about you."

"I know. What are you working on?" Diz asked, more to change the subject than out of genuine interest.

"I'm altering my wedding dress. I thought maybe Elsie might like to wear it on her special day."

"Oh." The words slammed Diz hard in the chest—yet another reminder that Elsie was not going to be coming home to this house to care for their mother. "I-I'm sure she'll love it."

"I hope so. We don't have the money to get her a new one."

Diz stood abruptly. "Is there anything I can do for you, Mother?"

"Hmm?" Mrs. Hosler bent over the dress to examine a seam.

"Is there anything you need me to do?"

"You could dust your room and Elsie's, please."

"Great." Diz found the dust rag and trudged up the stairs. Briefly, she thought about Frannie and the girls having a blast at the Mountain and wished she were there instead.

She decided to start in Elsie's room, since it was orderly and easier to clean. Frannie's clothes and personal items were neatly stacked on shelves she and Frannie had built for the purpose. Diz carefully moved each pile, dusted the shelf, and put everything back as it was.

When she got to the third of four piles, some books on top of the clothes became unbalanced and clattered to the floor. "Damn it!" She bent down to pick them up.

That's when she spotted it—a single sheet of typing paper with words printed in precise paragraphs and a line at the bottom with something scrawled on it.

Diz picked up the paper and started to put it back. Then she saw the words, "$85 per week for the duration of the 1944 season of the All American Girls Professional Baseball League. Season to commence with Spring Training on 14 May, 1944, in Peru, Illinois."

Diz's knees buckled and she sank to the floor. The writing on the line at the bottom was Frannie's signature.

⋘⋙

Diz blinked as the brightness of the light invaded the dark room. She put a hand up to shield her eyes.

"Why are you sitting on the floor in the dark? Are you all right?"

Frannie's alarmed tone rang hollowly in Diz's ears. "Why do you care?"

"Why do I...?" Frannie's eyes tracked to the piece of paper on Diz's lap. "Diz—" Frannie moved toward her.

"Don't." Diz held up a hand. "Don't take another step." Diz shook her head sadly. "When were you planning to tell me? The day you moved out? Or maybe you were going to drop me a note once you got settled in Chicago, or wherever it is you're going."

"Diz—"

"No. No, Frannie." Mindful of her mother down the hall, Diz lowered her voice. "Everybody else had something to say today about being scouted. Not you. You didn't say a word. I knew something was off. I knew it." Diz jabbed a finger in Frannie's direction. "But I tried to ask you, and you cut me off. You deliberately changed the topic."

"I—"

Diz talked over Frannie. "You had every chance to be honest. You had every opportunity to tell me, and you didn't." Diz stood up and handed Frannie the contract. "More than that, you didn't even think it was worth talking to me about it ahead of time so that we could make a decision together."

"You don't understand."

"Oh, I understand perfectly fine. Three years together, and I didn't even deserve a conversation."

"Diz—"

"It's not enough that I lost Daddy." Diz willed the tears not to fall. She would not cry again. She wouldn't. "It's not enough that Elsie is gone and she's not coming back here—not to live, anyway. It's not enough that Mother can barely function. Now I'm losing you too."

"Please—"

Diz brushed past Frannie without making eye contact. "For the record, I dusted your room for you. I wasn't looking for anything. I was just cleaning like Mother asked me to. In case you thought I was 'spying' or 'snooping.' I wasn't."

"I didn't—"

"Goodnight, Frannie." Diz walked down the hall into her room and closed and locked the door behind her. When she was safely inside, she collapsed face down on the bed, gathered her pillow and hugged it to her. Apparently, she was going to have to get used to sleeping alone again after all.

When Diz groggily awoke for work at four o'clock the next morning, she was still fully dressed from last night and very much alone. She rubbed the spot in the center of her chest with the heel of her hand, as if somehow the action would ease her pain.

Maybe it was all a bad dream. Maybe she'd read the contract wrong. Maybe... Maybe nothing. Frannie had made a choice—and that decision was tearing them apart.

Diz covered her face with the pillow.

Why was Frannie so desperate to get away? Was it something Diz said? Something she hadn't said? Was she griping too much about work? Were they not getting enough time alone together? Was Frannie sweet on someone else—someone whom she might have agreed to go to Chicago with?

Diz's heart stuttered at that last thought. Could it be? No, she would have known. She would've seen the signs. Besides, she and Frannie constantly were together when they weren't working. There wouldn't have been any time.

Maybe Frannie would change her mind and rip up the contract and tell Wrigley to stuff it like Dot had done. Could she do that now? Or was it already too late? Maybe none of this ruminating was getting her anywhere except late for work.

Wearily, Diz rose and straightened the covers, grabbed a pair of jeans and a shirt from her closet, and laid them out on the bed. Was Frannie awake? Was she regretting her decision?

Stop it. It doesn't matter. She signed the contract.

Diz unlocked and cracked open the door. She peeked down the hall—all was quiet. She made her way to the bathroom, took a quick shower, and crept back toward her room. The door to Elsie's room was closed. She laid her palm flat against the wood, as if touching it would bring her closer to Frannie. She put her ear to the door. There was no sound from within.

Reluctantly, Diz continued on to her room, dressed for work, went downstairs for a quick bowl of oatmeal, and was waiting outside at 5:00 a.m. when Margie arrived to pick her up as usual for the drive to Goodyear. Jessie and Amelina already were in the back seat of the car, so Diz took the passenger seat.

"'Morning, sunshine."

"Hi."

"What's wrong, Diz?" Amelina asked.

"Nothing."

"It doesn't look like nothing," Jessie said. "It looks like you lost your best friend. Is your mom doing all right?"

"She's okay. When I got home yesterday, she was working on a wedding dress for Elsie." Diz stared out the window. Elsie, who was never coming home to live so that Diz could go to college.

"Elsie bought a dress?" Margie asked.

Diz forced herself to turn and make eye contact with Margie. "No. Mother was altering her own wedding dress to give her." At least their interest in Elsie had shifted the attention away from her.

"Is that going to be weird?" Amelina made a face. "With your Dad and…"

Jessie put a hand on Amelina's arm and shook her head.

"Oh, sorry. I didn't mean anything by it."

"It's okay. I know what you mean." Diz tried for a sympathetic smile. "I don't know. I haven't talked to Elsie about it." In fact, Diz hadn't talked to Elsie about anything since she'd left. The one time she had called, Diz handed the phone to her mother without saying more than hello.

"Did she—"

"C'mon girls, change the topic. Poor Diz must feel like she's being grilled like a hamburger."

If Margie hadn't been driving, Diz might've kissed her for intervening. Maybe it was the fact that Margie now had kids of her own that made her more sensitive than the others. Diz didn't know, but at this moment, she was grateful for the assistance.

The remainder of the car ride was quiet.

"See you gals back here at three," Margie said. "Keep all your fingers and toes today."

For once, Diz was happy that the drill press was loud and no one would try to make conversation with her. She allowed herself to be lulled by the noise and the repetitive nature of the job.

Briefly, she wondered if Frannie would be home when she got there, and if she would plan to go to practice, and if, and when, she would tell the other girls she wasn't going to be a Rambler anymore.

Diz willed herself to stop focusing on Frannie. She would have plenty of time to think and feel later.

CHAPTER FIFTEEN

Phoenix, 1944

Warily, Diz opened the screen door and walked into the house. All of the emotions she'd been holding in throughout the workday pushed their way into her consciousness, and she struggled to take a deep breath. What if Frannie already was gone? Would she go without even saying goodbye?

Diz leaned against the wall for support. Surely Frannie wouldn't do that.

Diz tuned into the house. It was quiet, almost too quiet. She listened for the sound of her mother's sewing machine but heard nothing. A search of the downstairs proved fruitless.

Her mother had left the house only twice since the memorial service—once to go to church to thank the minister for everything he'd done, and once to pick up some things at the store. Maybe she was upstairs taking a nap.

Diz climbed the stairs and peeked into her mother's bedroom. The bed was empty, fully made, and undisturbed.

"Some of the ladies—"

Diz gasped and jumped, her heart racing.

"I'm sorry," Frannie said. She started toward Diz with her arms open, then stopped and dropped them to her sides. "I didn't mean to startle you."

"Startle me? You scared me half to death!"

"Like I said, I'm sorry."

Frannie's voice was subdued, and Diz noticed for the first time that she had circles under her eyes, as though she hadn't had enough sleep.

"It's okay. I just wasn't expecting... Well, I don't know what I was expecting." Diz shifted from foot to foot. Why did this have to be so awkward?

"What I started to tell you, was that some of the ladies came by and asked your mother to go with them to help them set up tables for a fundraiser they're doing."

"Really?"

Frannie nodded. "I think they were trying to take her mind off of...things."

"Good. She needs to get out some."

"I guess—"

"Can I—"

Frannie motioned to Diz. "You first."

"No, you go ahead. Can you...what?"

"I was going to ask if it was okay if we talked for a little bit?"

"Oh. Um, sure, I suppose."

"Can we go in your room instead of standing out here in the hallway?"

Diz led the way, sat down on the bed, and waited as Frannie sat down on the bed facing her.

"First, thanks for letting me say something today." Diz started to protest, and Frannie held up a hand. "Please, just let me say what I need to say. After that, you can have a turn."

"I'm listening." Diz crossed her arms across her chest defensively.

"I know you're hurt. I know that you're sore. And you have every right to be. I should have said something sooner. I should have told you right away. I just..." Frannie ducked her head. "I was afraid. I was afraid that you'd react exactly like you did last night. I didn't want to lose you, Diz."

"Yeah, well, you sure have a funny way of showing it."

Frannie winced. "I understand how it looks, but there are things you don't know."

"You mean, like why you're so damned determined to get away from here? Why you can't wait to leave me?" Diz felt the anger rise up in her throat. "How many times have I asked you that since Daddy died? You never answer me."

She clasped her hands together to keep them from shaking. "Everybody I love, everybody I care about, is leaving me." She started listing the names on her fingers. "Daddy. Elsie. Mother will never be the same; she's like a completely different person. And now you. Why does everybody have to leave me?"

Again, Frannie raised her arms as if to envelop Diz in an embrace. Again, she dropped them back to her sides. "I'm not—"

"You signed a contract, Frannie! That's your handwriting on the bottom. The contract doesn't lie!"

"I know. I did sign the contract. You're right. But you don't understand why I did it."

"You're damned right I don't understand! How..." Diz swallowed the lump in her throat. "How could you? How..."

This time, Frannie did take Diz in her arms. She pulled her in and hugged her hard against her chest.

Diz wanted to resist, she wanted to stay as mad as she was. But the feel of Frannie's strong arms, the scent of her, the sound of her heart beating in Diz's ear... All Diz wanted to do was to stay like that forever.

Frannie kissed the top of Diz's head and stroked her hair. "There are some things you need to know. Some things I should have told you years ago, when we first started going together. But I thought I had everything under control. I thought I was past it."

"Past what?"

Frannie continued to talk as if she hadn't heard the question. "I thought if I just didn't allow myself to feel too deeply, or get too involved, I'd be all right. Then I started living here and sleeping with you every night."

"What are you talking about? Why is that a problem? That's why you're running away? Because you don't want to sleep with me anymore?" Diz sat up so that she could see Frannie's face. Her gaze was focused somewhere over Diz's head and she had the same faraway look she had that day they'd fled her aunt and uncle's place.

"The night of the fire—"

"The night your parents died?"

177

"Yes. That night, I was sleeping over at a girlfriend's house."

"So you said."

Frannie smiled sadly. "What I didn't tell you was that I was in love with that girl. She was sweet, and pretty, and smart. That night was the first time I kissed a girl. I thought I'd died and gone to Heaven."

Diz fought against a surge of jealousy. "You never told me you'd been in love—"

"Actually, I sort of did. You asked me on our first date if I had ever kissed a girl before. I told you I'd kissed two—but that only one of them mattered. Hazel was my best friend. We did everything together. We were fourteen and planned to conquer the world.

"That night, we were lying on her bed doing our homework. We had our heads close together and we were giggling about something—I don't even remember what. And then she just leaned forward...and I leaned forward... And, well, it happened. I think we both surprised ourselves." Frannie smiled wistfully.

"What does that have to do with anything now?" Diz didn't want to know this, didn't want to hear it. Was this Hazel a ball player? "Is this girl the reason you're leaving? Is she going to Chicago too?"

"What? Why would you think...? You think I'm cheating on you? That I'm sweet on someone else?" Frannie laughed derisively. "You've got it all wrong, sweetheart."

"Well, help me understand."

"I'm trying, if you'll stop interrupting." Frannie sighed. "So Hazel and I kissed, and when bedtime came, we snuggled under the covers together after her mother turned the lights out."

"Did you...?"

"We were fourteen, Diz. We didn't have a clue what we were doing. It just felt good to hold each other. Well, we must've fallen asleep that way, because the next thing I knew, her parents were in the room, yelling at us and carrying on."

"They caught you?"

Frannie nodded. "They came in because a policeman came to the house to get me to tell me that my parents were gone."

"Oh."

"All the way down the stairs, her parents were screaming that my parents' death was my fault because I was 'like that,' and that I corrupted their daughter. I was never to see her, or step foot in their house, again."

"Oh, my God. That's horrible," Diz said. "You'd just lost your parents, for cripe's sake."

Frannie shrugged. "For a long time, I believed them, that it was my fault. Maybe a part of me still does. If I hadn't been so wrapped up in Hazel, I might've been home..."

"You don't know that that would've made any difference," Diz said. "You could've been killed too." Her heart ached with the knowledge that Frannie might've died that night. She took a deep breath to dispel the thought. "Did you ever see Hazel again?"

Frannie shook her head. "No, her parents made sure of that. And when I moved in with my aunt and uncle, I was in a different school district."

"That's sad."

"Anyway," Frannie said, "for a long time, I believed my house caught fire and my parents got killed because I did a bad thing by kissing a girl."

"That's not true!" Even as she said it, Diz wondered if she would've come to the same conclusion.

"I completely shut down. I felt nothing, willed myself to feel nothing for anyone, and I thought the world and I were better off for it. I never let anyone get close." Frannie caressed Diz's cheek with her thumb. "And then, you came along. I was so intrigued by you, so attracted to you... I just couldn't stop myself. I told myself you were younger—it wouldn't be deep, it would just be fun."

Diz's ears turned red with anger. "So I was just a cheap thrill? A dalliance?"

"That's the whole thing—you weren't. Right from that first moment I kissed you, I knew I was in trouble. And then you had to go and step in and get all noble and chivalrous on me and 'rescue' me from my uncle. Nobody had ever stood up for me before like that."

"They should've."

"Oh, Diz. Where were you when I was fourteen?" Frannie's gaze was filled with love. "At first, when you were so worried whether anyone would find out we were queer, I was super hard on you because your fear was a reminder of my own. Every time you brought it up, all I could see was Hazel, and the look on her parents' faces when they found us snuggling together. The sound of their accusations kept echoing in my mind."

"I-I didn't know."

"I know you didn't. That's not your fault. I never told you the story, so you couldn't possibly understand why I was so raw about that."

"I'm better about that now," Diz said.

"You are. And I'm so glad." Frannie trailed her fingers along Diz's jaw line.

"So, if you're serious about me, and my insecurities aren't what's driving you away, why are you leaving me? Why is it so important for you to go?"

Frannie broke contact. "It's complicated. After Hazel and my parents were ripped away from me, I felt like the only person I could rely on was myself. And that's how I lived my life. I hung around with girls who wanted to go out and have a good time without getting all clingy or demanding."

Diz remembered the girls Frannie used to arrive to practices and the games with early on. They had all seemed to fade into the background once Diz and Frannie started spending more time together.

"Am I too clingy and demanding?" Diz asked.

"It isn't that." Frannie picked up Diz's hand and interlaced their fingers. "Do you remember how reluctant I was to stay that very first day you brought me home?"

"Do I!"

"Right, well, I didn't want to feel like I was part of a real family again. It wasn't safe. When you have a family, you have the chance of losing them. Families—nice, healthy families—don't last. But you were so determined for me to stay, and sleeping with you by my side was divine, so I let myself be lulled into believing I might've been wrong."

"And then Daddy died," Diz said.

"Yes, then your father died. And you, Elsie, and your mother have been completely torn up about it."

180

"Well, how are we supposed to feel?"

"Easy, Tiger," Frannie said. "You're supposed to feel exactly as you do. But that's the thing—I just can't go through it with you. Not again. I've tried. But it takes me right back to my parents' deaths and all that time I spent being pretty much an emotional wreck. I'm falling apart all over again. I want to be there for you, but I just can't be. And because I can't be, I feel like I'm failing you. And because I'm failing you, you'll grow to resent me."

"You don't know that," Diz protested.

"I do, because I know myself. You, your mother, and Elsie have to heal. You have to find your own ways of dealing with the loss. Right now, it hurts too much for me to be here."

"And that's why you signed the contract?"

"Partly."

A sense of dread filled Diz. "What's the rest of the reason?"

"Diz, it's eighty-five dollars a week. I can actually afford to live on that. Plus, they're offering housing and a job in the off-season. I could be financially independent in a way I've never been able to be before."

"But you'd be leaving me. How can you…? Doesn't that mean anything to you?"

"That means everything to me. You"—Frannie's voice broke and she took a few seconds to compose herself—"you mean everything to me."

"Don't go."

"I have to. But I really, really hope you'll still want to be my girl, even if I'm in Chicago or some other godforsaken place."

"I don't see how that can work."

"We'll write letters back and forth all the time. And I'll call you when I can."

"You should have told me before you signed the contract."

"You're right," Frannie agreed. "I should have. But I knew you'd never leave your mother the way things are right now, and you wouldn't have agreed to me going without you."

Diz couldn't argue with the truth of that.

"You would've insisted that we could find a way to get our own place nearby, or to keep on as things are right now. And if I allowed that to happen, I would've continued to shut down more and more until we lost what we have. I didn't want that."

Diz felt her world slipping away. "When do you have to leave?"

"I guess that depends on you."

"What do you mean?"

"If you're still sore and you want to break up, I'll go right now."

Diz's breath caught and she forced the words out. "Where would you go?"

"I don't know. I'd find someplace. I hope I don't have to. I hope you'll want me to stay with you until I have to report to spring training."

"When is that?"

"May 14th."

"That's just a little over two weeks!"

"Yes."

"That's not enough time." Panic made Diz's voice sound shrill.

"It's more time than we'd have if you kick me out now."

Diz was grasping at straws. If Frannie wouldn't stay for her, surely she would stay for the team. "Are you going to tell Mr. Hoffman and the girls?"

"I will."

"When?"

Frannie looked at her watch. "Well, since practice starts in less than an hour, I guess I'll tell them then."

"Mr. Hoffman won't be there."

"I'll write him a letter."

They were both silent for a minute.

Finally, Diz accepted that she wasn't going to change the outcome. Frannie really was leaving. "I don't want you to go."

"I know. Can I stay with you until I have to report to spring training?"

Diz considered. Her heart hurt, and she was still angry that Frannie hadn't been honest and upfront with her. But the idea of having to say goodbye right now was just too much to bear.

"Will you sleep in here with me?"

"If you'll have me."

"Okay, then."

"Okay, as in, you'll still be my girl? Even when I'm over there?"

"Okay, as in, you can stay until you report, and I'll think about the rest."

"Well, it's something," Frannie said.

~§~

Phoenix, 2014

Julie squeezed Diz's hand. "I'm sorry. I didn't know Frannie ever left you."

Diz sighed and swirled a spoon in her coffee cup with her free hand. "Yeah, well, it's not a period of my life I like to talk about much."

"Did she really go? I mean, she didn't change her mind and void the contract?"

"Nope. She really went. Hardest time of my life." Diz laid down the spoon. "Even harder, I think, than when she passed away."

Julie raised an eyebrow.

"When Frannie died, she'd been so sick, it was a blessing to let her go—to know that she was free of pain and no longer suffering. When she left to play for the Racine Belles, well, she was full of life and off to chart her own course without me."

"But, she asked you to keep going steady, or whatever you called it back then, even while she was gone."

"Yes, she did."

"I'm confused," Julie said. "Did you break up with Frannie?"

"It was complicated."

Julie looked down at the framed photograph. "You looked so happy together." She let go of Diz's hand, turned the picture over again and frowned. "Diz?"

"Hmm?"

"Is this your handwriting on the back of the picture?" She showed it to Diz.

"Yep."

"But, it says this was taken in the spring of 1944, at an exhibition game."

"Right."

"If Frannie went to play in Wisconsin, how is it that she was playing an exhibition game for the Ramblers at the same time?"

"Ah," Diz said. "Well, Frannie went to practice with me that day—the day we had our heart-to-heart."

Julie jumped in. "Let me guess, she couldn't tell them she was leaving."

Diz smiled at her kindly. "Have I mentioned how much I enjoy that you're completely taken by this story?"

"C'mon! You're not going to leave me hanging here, are you?" Julie pressed her palms together in a prayerful pose. "Please? Please tell me you're not going to wait until next time to finish this part of it."

Diz's eyes twinkled. "While I do enjoy keeping you on the edge of your seat, I'll take pity on you and explain."

"Oh, thank God!"

Diz laughed. "Don't be so dramatic. The thing was, Frannie wasn't the only one who jumped at the money Wrigley was throwing around. Several other Ramblers also had committed to play in Wrigley's league, and they'd already packed their bags and left. That meant we were short of players, and we had an exhibition game scheduled against our archrivals, the Queens, that weekend."

"So Frannie played in the game against the Queens before she left?" Julie asked.

"She did. As upset as all the girls were that Frannie was leaving, nobody, including Frannie, wanted to forfeit a game to the Queens. So we kept Frannie's status hush-hush, and she started for us in left field like always. I hit a triple, and Frannie drove me home with the winning run on a sacrifice fly."

Julie clapped.

"We were quite thrilled, as you can see. This photograph was taken just after the game. I remember it quite clearly, because as soon as the flashbulb went off, I stopped smiling. It was the moment it truly struck me that this was the last time Frannie and I were going to wear the same uniform. It was her last at-bat for the

Ramblers." Diz raised the coffee cup with shaking hands and slurped. "At least she went out a winner."

"But—"

"Don't get ahead of yourself, or the story," Diz cautioned. "I promise to tell all."

CHAPTER SIXTEEN

Phoenix, 1944

The party was in full swing at the 902, as it always was any time the Ramblers beat the Queens. It mattered not that this was an exhibition game. The fact was, the Ramblers were on top going into the season.

Diz stood off to the side, watching as Mickey Sullivan, their third baseman, demonstrated for an appreciative audience the tag she had placed on the Queens Charlotte "Skipper" Armstrong.

"Attention, everyone." Dot yelled to be heard over the din.

When the noise level failed to abate, Jessie put her fingers in her mouth and whistled.

"Thanks," Dot said. "I propose a toast." She raised her beer bottle. "To Frannie." Everyone raised their glasses and bottles. "Safe travels. Play great ball. And know that we all love you and wish you the best."

"Here, here," came the chorus.

"Wait," Dot said. "There's more. And thanks for going out on a high note by helping us stick it to the Queens!"

Everyone clapped and whistled. Someone bought Frannie a fresh beer and thrust it in her hand. Several of the players lifted Frannie up and carried her around the bar on their shoulders for a victory lap.

Diz wished a hole would open up in the floor so that she could crawl into it. The last thing she wanted to do was to celebrate.

"You're going to miss her." It wasn't a question. Margie leaned on the bar next to Diz.

Diz didn't trust her voice just then, so she nodded.

"I get that. We're all going to miss how much fun she brings to the team, not to mention that killer swing. But you," Margie turned to face Diz directly, "you've lost so much this year. I'm sure this one hits especially hard."

Diz swallowed the lump in her throat. Did Margie know what she and Frannie were to each other?

She tuned back in to hear Margie say, "She's your best friend. She's like your other sister. It's natural for you to be down in the dumps. I want you to know that I'm here for you. And so are all the other girls."

"Thanks," Diz managed.

"Anyway, for what it's worth, I think she's making a big mistake."

"You do?"

"Of course. There's no better team than the Ramblers. Not in any league. Period. Who would want to play anywhere else?"

"Right," Diz said.

"I bet she comes crawling back after half a season."

As much as she wanted to believe Margie, Diz highly doubted that Frannie would quit the Belles and come home. Besides, it would be impossible now. "She can't."

Margie stopped talking.

"I mean, she'd have to sit out a whole season here if she did," Diz said. "The rules are clear—if you go off and get paid to play, you're a professional. The only way to regain your amateur status is to sit out a whole year."

"I can see you've given this some consideration."

Diz blushed. "Well… I mean… What I'm trying to say is…"

Margie laughed and put a hand on Diz's arm. "It's okay. I'm sure you tried every argument you could think of on Frannie. I'm glad. I really hate to lose her."

"Hey," Frannie said, as the girls lowered her from their shoulders and set her on her feet right in front of Diz and Margie.

"Hey, yourself," Margie said. "I was just telling Diz here how hard it's going to be to lose you."

Frannie addressed Margie, but her eyes were on Diz. "Yeah, well, I wish I could take you all with me. I'm sure going to miss you."

Diz turned away and found something interesting to look at across the bar. If Frannie continued to look at her like that, she would surely risk bursting into tears.

"How about if we get out of here?" Frannie asked.

Diz glanced around. Margie had moved away, and most of the other girls were busy dancing or playing pool. "Now?"

"Sure."

"But the party's just really getting started, and everybody wants to send you off in style."

Frannie inched closer. "There's only one person I care about right now, and I'd much rather have a private party with her."

The heat started in the pit of Diz's stomach and spread throughout her entire body. She shifted uncomfortably, and Frannie laughed.

"Come on." She grabbed Diz by the hand. "Let's say our goodbyes."

∽⤙⤚∾

The moon was high in the star-filled sky as Diz and Frannie sat on the hood of the car in their special spot. The cicadas sounded especially loud in the stillness. Somewhere in the distance, a coyote howled.

Frannie put her arm around Diz. "Do you remember the first time I brought you here?"

"How could I forget? I thought we were going out with a group of girls. Instead, we ended up here, dancing in the moonlight."

"I didn't want to share you. Not then, and not now." Frannie turned so that they were facing each other. Their mouths were inches apart. "I love you, Theodora Hosler. You haven't answered whether or not you'll still be my girl while I'm away, but I think you should know, I'm not going to give you up without a fight."

There it was—that look that Frannie got in her eye—the one that made Diz's insides turn to mush. Frannie closed the rest of the distance between them and claimed her lips.

Just as she had that very first night, Diz yielded to the insistent pressure, to the pounding in her heart that demanded her to let Frannie in, to let love in. Nothing in her life had ever felt so good. She couldn't imagine that anything—or anyone—else could rival what she and Frannie shared.

They kissed for what seemed like hours; they kissed alternately with urgency, with tenderness, with passion, with desperation, and always with the knowledge that this could be the last time.

"We should get home," Frannie finally said.

"Mother will be worried." But Diz didn't want to move. She needed this night to last forever. Until this moment, she always had looked forward to each new day and what it would bring. Now... Now, it would be just fine with her if the dawn never came.

Reluctantly, she slid off the hood and got into the car. All the way home, they clung to each other. Diz sat glued to Frannie's side and Frannie held on tightly to Diz's hand.

Once home, they silently crept up the stairs, donned their pajamas, and got ready for bed.

"I don't want to go to sleep," Diz said.

"Me, either." Frannie gathered Diz into her arms, pillowing Diz's head on her shoulder. "I love you."

"Love you too." Diz spent several moments simply listening to the steady beat of her girl's heart and feeling the rise and fall of her chest as she breathed. "Are you really sure?"

Frannie was silent for a long time, and Diz wondered if maybe she'd dozed off. "I'm not really sure of anything right now, except that I'm going to miss you like crazy."

Diz tightened her arms around Frannie. "Me too."

"We'll make it work."

"Mm-hmm." Diz wanted to believe her, wanted to have the kind of faith Frannie seemed to have about all this, but at the moment, all she could think was that tomorrow night, she'd be going to sleep alone.

As dawn broke over them, Diz closed her eyes, breathing in Frannie one last time.

"I have to go. It's a long drive."

"I know."

"Diz?"

"Yeah?"

"It's not going to be forever."

Diz opened her mouth, but no words came out. "Mm-hmm." It was the most she could manage.

When Frannie slipped out from under the covers and headed for the bathroom, Diz moved into her spot and hugged her pillow. It still smelled like her shampoo. She squeezed her eyes shut. How was she ever going to live without Frannie?

"Come outside with me? See me off?"

Diz wasn't sure she could, but she knew she had to, so she climbed out of bed, threw on a pair of jeans and a shirt, and followed Frannie outside.

The sun's rays made the clouds iridescent. Hues of pink, orange, and red reminded Diz of that first sunset with Frannie.

"What are you doing?"

"Hmm?"

"Why are you staring at the sky?"

"I was just..." Diz took a moment to compose herself. "The colors are the same as that first night. I can't see a sky like that now and not think of us."

Frannie stepped closer and glanced toward the house. Tears were poised on her eyelashes. "I know your mother will be getting up soon, so I won't kiss you the way I want to out here in the open." She caressed Diz's cheek tenderly with her fingertips. "I'm glad we created those kinds of memories together, sweetheart. I hope every time you look at a sunrise or a sunset—every time you see the stars twinkling overhead—you think of me, of us. I know I will."

"Mm-hmm."

Frannie shook her head at Diz. "Are you ever going to answer me with more than one syllable?"

"Mm-hmm." Diz smiled at the reference to their early days. She'd been so shy, so young then.

Frannie must've been thinking the same thing, because she said, "You've come a long way, you know that? Back then, it was hard to get you to say anything at all."

"Bet you liked that better, huh?"

"What? Are you kidding me?" Frannie's gaze was filled with affection. "I am so proud of the woman you're becoming, Diz. You're more self-assured, more outspoken, more mature. You're amazing, and I love you."

"Yeah, well, I wouldn't be any of those things without you." Diz toed the dirt with her shoe. "I was so intimidated by you. You were so pretty, so much more mature, and a much better ball player than I was."

"That's not true, and you know it."

"You were," Diz argued. "That very first day—the day we tried out and you made that neat catch out in center field and then came up to bat and hit the cover off the ball—I knew if it was a choice between us, the coach was going to choose you."

"But he didn't, did he? He chose both of us." Frannie put a finger under Diz's chin and made her lift her gaze. "You are a fantastic ball player. Never forget that. You're the starting center fielder for the P.B.S.W. Ramblers, one of the best teams in the country. How many people can say that?"

Frannie kissed Diz on the forehead and hefted her suitcase. "I really do have to go now."

"I know."

"Am I still your girl?"

Diz hesitated. She loved Frannie more than anything in the world, but how could this possibly work? They were going to be separated by almost two thousand miles.

"Well, at least I know where I stand," Frannie said. "Goodb—"

"What? Wait!" Diz clutched at Frannie's arm. "No. No, no, no. I can't... You can't..." Diz's throat tightened, so she simply shook her head.

"Diz..."

She held on harder and tried to breathe. "I-I need you. I don't know how to be without you."

Frannie put the suitcase down. "You'll be fine. You're stronger than you know. All the girls will be here—Dot, Margie, Jessie, Dobbie, Amy—"

"They're not you."

"No, they're not." Frannie glanced at the sky, where the sun was now almost fully risen, and then at her wristwatch. "I really have to go now, Diz." She extricated her arm from Diz's grasp and put the suitcase in the backseat.

"Yes."

Frannie turned around. "What?"

"Yes." Diz said it with more force this time. She stood up straighter. "Yes, you're still my girl."

"Yes?" Frannie asked.

"Yes." Diz lifted her chin. "So you'd better be true."

"I will." Again, Frannie stepped closer. "I promise."

"And you'd better write... Every day."

"What if I can't? What if I can't find a stamp, or we're on the road playing?"

Diz considered. "Okay. How about at least three times a week?"

"It's a deal."

"And you'd better call."

Frannie smiled. "Every chance I get."

Diz bit her lip. "Maybe we should set a schedule or something."

"A schedule?"

"For calling. You know, so we don't miss each other."

"Okay."

"What do you think about Wednesday nights?" Diz asked. "It's the one night we don't practice."

Frannie shook her head. "I'll probably be playing games then. How about Wednesday afternoons right after you get home from work? Most of our games are at night, and I won't have any job except for playing ball during the season."

"Okay, Wednesday afternoons between three o'clock and four o'clock."

"It's a deal." Frannie opened the driver's side door and started to get in.

"Wait!"

Frannie paused with her hand on the door. "Now what?"

"Aren't Chicago and Wisconsin in a different time zone than us here?"

Frannie laughed and got in the car. "We have a standing telephone date every Wednesday afternoon that we can, between three and four o'clock your time, sweetheart. Better?"

"Yes." Diz closed the door for Frannie, who rolled down the window.

"I'm going to miss you."

"I'm going to miss you too. Drive carefully."

"I will."

"Stop if you get tired."

"I will."

"Let me know that you got there all right."

"I will." Frannie reached out and covered the hand Diz had on the car door. "It's going to be fine. You'll see. Take good care of yourself, Tiger."

"You too." Diz searched Frannie's face, desperate to memorize every detail. "I love you."

"Love you too. Tell your mother I said goodbye, and thanks for everything."

"I will."

Diz backed away and Frannie put the car in gear. As she pulled away, Diz waved. She kept waving until the car was almost out of sight, then continued to stand there, watching the dust settle. Eventually, she went back inside, trudged up the stairs and into her room, kicked her shoes off, and threw herself back on the bed.

She imagined Frannie, still there with her, holding her close and whispering in her ear, and dropped off into an exhausted slumber.

∽⟡∾

"Theodora? Can you come in here, please?"

"Yes, Mother." Diz set aside the shoe polish she'd been using to shine her cleats and joined her mother in the kitchen. "What do you need?"

Mrs. Hosler was standing on tiptoes, her arm fully extended, her fingertips still several inches from the top shelf of the cupboard. "I need you to reach the cinnamon."

Diz dragged over one of the kitchen chairs and stood on it.

194

"Our Frannie could have gotten that without using a chair."

Diz's heart clenched. It had been almost a week since Frannie had driven away. In that time, Diz had gotten one letter telling her that Frannie had arrived safely in Chicago, and that all of the girls—one hundred twenty-six of them—were being put up in a pair of hotels in the area. Frannie was ensconced in the Peru Hotel in Peru, Illinois.

"Have you heard from her? How is she getting along?"

"I got a letter the other day saying that she arrived on the thirteenth and got settled in her hotel." Diz retrieved the cinnamon and handed it to her mother.

"Well, I still don't understand why she had to go off so far away. Wasn't she doing well on the Ramblers?"

Diz closed her eyes and willed herself to be patient. This was at least the third time she'd had this conversation with her mother.

"They were offering her a lot of money to play, Mother. She needed to support herself." Diz saw no reason to explain Frannie's more personal reasons for leaving.

"She could have stayed here with us. We were all making do."

"Is there anything else you need? I should finish polishing—"

The phone rang and Diz's pulse jumped. "I'll get it!" She ran to the phone and picked up the receiver. "Hello?"

"Do you know what day of the week it is?"

"It's Wednesday." Diz smiled into the phone.

"Do you know what time it is?"

"Three o'clock."

"Right, and here I am, just like I promised I would be."

"Who is it, Theodora? Is that Elsie?"

Diz put her hand over the receiver. "No, Mother. It's for me."

"Well, who's calling?"

"It's Frannie, Mother."

"Our Frannie?"

Diz growled. "Yes."

"Please tell her I said hello and I miss her height around here."

"I will, Mother. Now can I get back to the call? This must be costing her a fortune." Diz uncovered the receiver. "Sorry about that."

"Your mother?"

"Who else? She says to tell you she misses your height."

Frannie laughed. "That's what she misses?"

"Well, I just had to get on a chair to get the cinnamon out of the cupboard." Diz wrapped the phone cord around her finger and lowered her voice. "How are you? I miss you."

"I miss you too. I'm doing okay. I ran into Skipper Armstrong, Pauline Crawley, and Carolyn Morris yesterday."

"No kidding. Wow, I wonder what kind of team the Queens are going to field without them in the lineup."

"You know them, they'll find someone."

"How's everything? What's it like?"

"Didn't you get my letter?"

"The only letter I got was the one where you said you'd arrived and were staying at the Peru Hotel."

"I don't want to ruin the surprise for you, wait until you get the letter and read for yourself."

"Okay."

"How are things there? Did you guys hold tryouts yet?"

"Yeah. We had a few show up."

"Were any of them cute?" Frannie asked.

"What? No!"

"It's okay if they are, as long as they're not making any moves on my girl."

Diz blushed. "It's not like that. Besides, none of them made the team."

"Good."

"How about you?"

"What about me?"

"You're meeting new girls from all over the country…"

"Theodora Hosler. I promised I'd be true to you, and that's the end of that story. Understood?"

"Yes," Diz said.

"Good. Listen, I have to go. We have etiquette class in less than an hour."

"You have…what?"

"You heard me. Read the letter when it gets there." There was a pause on the line. "I miss you like crazy, Diz."

Diz made sure her mother wasn't in hearing range. "I miss you too. I love you."

"Love you too. I think about you all the time."

"Me too."

"Good. Keep it that way. Don't go getting all wild on me at the 902 and dancing with all the girls."

Diz chuckled. "Yeah, because you know how much I like to stay out and carouse."

"Okay. Well, like I said, I have to go. Talk to you same time next week?"

"Sure. Bye."

"Bye, Diz. See you in my dreams."

Diz continued to hold onto the receiver for a long time after the line had gone dead.

CHAPTER SEVENTEEN

Phoenix, 1944

Hey, Diz, hey Diz," the girls chanted from the dugout as Diz stepped into the batter's box in the bottom of the sixth inning against the Chicago Match Maids.

"Show 'em how we do it here in Phoenix, Diz!"

"Steee-rike one," the umpire called, as the first pitch sailed past her knees on the inside corner.

Diz took a deep breath in and let it out slowly. She was mired in the worst slump of her career, and badly needed a hit. Jean Hutsell was standing on first base. Mildred Dixon, who had taken Frannie's place in left field, was due up after Diz. Dixon already was two-for-two with two doubles and the only two RBIs in the game so far.

Diz narrowed her focus, shutting out all the chants, all the taunts, all the distractions. As the next pitch came in, dead center, she planted her right foot, transferred her weight to the lead leg, and swung. At the last second, the ball dropped like a rock, directly into the catcher's mitt.

"Damned drop ball." Diz stepped out of the batter's box and rolled her shoulders.

"You've got her number, Diz. Like you can," Mildred called from the on-deck circle.

Irrationally, the words of encouragement angered Diz. She bit back a sharp retort. It wasn't Mildred's fault she wasn't Frannie.

Not only that, but she'd been playing well and was a real asset to the team.

Diz took another practice swing. *Keep your eye on the ball. Forget about Frannie for a minute, forget about everything except hitting the damned ball.* She stepped back in. This time when she swung, she made solid contact. The ball flew off the bat, whizzed past the pitcher's head, and skidded toward the deepest part of the ball park. Diz took off for first base, rounded the bag, and headed for second.

"Down!" Dot yelled from the third base coach's box.

Diz slid, cleats high, aiming directly for the shortstop's glove. The metal of her cleat connected with the glove and the ball, dislodging both.

"Safe!" the umpire called.

"Time, Ump!" Diz yelled. She popped up, dusted off her hands, shook the dirt out of her shorts, and looked to the dugout, where all the girls were cheering. Jean, who was standing on third base, gave her a big thumbs up.

"Atta girl, Diz!"

"Way to go!"

Mildred, who was getting ready to hit, whistled her approval.

Diz looked in. Would they intentionally walk Mildred to get to Peanuts? The catcher set up in a squat on the outside corner of the plate, answering Diz's question.

"Like you can!" Diz yelled.

On the very first pitch, Mildred lashed a single to left field, scoring Jean. From third base, Diz applauded loudly. No, Mildred wasn't Frannie—no one was. But she was her teammate, and Diz would be as supportive as she was for any other of the girls.

The game, the sixth in the ten-game series, ended with a 3-0 Ramblers victory, tying the series three-games-to-three.

"You coming out, Diz?" Peanuts asked.

Diz hadn't been to the 902 since Frannie's departure. Her ready excuse had been that her mother was home alone, and that was true. But it was also true that Diz simply wasn't feeling social. She preferred to sit in her room and read and re-read Frannie's letters.

"C'mon, join us for once," Dot said, clapping Diz on the shoulder. "Dobbie says she'll buy your first beer."

"I did?"

"You did."

"I guess I did."

It couldn't hurt to go out for one beer, she supposed. "Sure."

⋘⋙

The bar was jam-packed on a Saturday night and the music was blaring from the speakers.

"What do you hear from Frannie?" Zada shouted to be heard above the din.

Diz was standing in the corner, leaning against the bar, sipping her beer. Although she heard what Zada asked, she cupped a hand to her ear indicating that she hadn't. The last thing she wanted to do was dwell on Frannie's new life.

"Hi, there. Haven't seen you here in a while."

Diz turned to find the same blonde girl with the obnoxious perfume that Frannie had accused of flirting with her that night so long ago. Diz wished she was anywhere but here.

"Where's your friend?" The girl made a show of looking around.

"My friend?"

"You know, the one who's always hovering around you like a body guard."

Diz's nostrils flared and the tips of her ears turned red with anger. How dare this girl...

The girl tipped her head back and laughed. "You're cute when you're all worked up, you know?"

"I don't know what you're talking about," Diz mumbled, no doubt too low to be heard over the beat of the Glenn Miller band. She started to walk away, but the girl blocked her path.

"Want to dance?"

"What? No."

"Why not?"

"Because." Diz knew that was lame, but the audacity of this girl had her off-balance. Last time she'd been in this position, Frannie had come to her rescue.

"Hey, Diz," Dot said. She positioned herself between Diz and the girl like she was blocking home plate. "It's too loud in here and we're all hungry. Want to come next door with us to eat?"

Diz thought she'd never been so grateful in her life. She wasn't sure if Dot knew what she was interrupting, but it didn't matter. "I'd love to." She didn't look back as she followed Dot out the side door of the bar and next door to the diner.

"You okay?" Dot asked.

"S-sure. Why do you ask?"

Dot shrugged. "Just seemed like that girl was hassling you. I don't like anyone hassling my teammates."

"Thanks. I think she was pretty harmless."

"Still," Dot put an arm around Diz, "it didn't seem right."

"Thanks for taking care of me."

They walked through the door, and Dobbie flagged them down. Almost the entire team had commandeered three long tables and put them together.

"Sit here, Diz." Jessie patted the seat next to her. "What's the latest from Chicago?"

"What?"

"What do you hear from Frannie?"

"Oh." This time Diz couldn't argue that it was too loud to have the conversation. "Actually, she's not in Chicago. She's in Racine, Wisconsin, playing for the Belles."

"Same thing," Peanuts chimed in.

"Shh. Let Diz talk," Jean said.

"Well, there's really not much to say."

"Come on. I hear they've got all kinds of rules and regulations off the field that they have to follow. Is it true?" Zada asked. "Give, Diz. Surely, Frannie would've told you if that was true?"

Diz could see that she was going to have to say something. "Yeah, it's pretty crazy."

"Spill." Jessie sat forward.

"Well—"

"Can I take your order?" A buxom, gum-snapping waitress stood just behind Diz's chair.

"I'll have a Spanish omelet and toast, please."

The waitress disappeared into the kitchen.

"Well?" Jessie asked.

"For starters, each girl was issued a *Charm School Guide* during spring training."

"What the heck does that mean?" Dobbie asked.

"And they have to have a beauty kit fully stocked at all times."

"What's in it?" Jessie asked.

"Face cream, lipstick, rouge, deodorant, astringent, hand lotion, and hair remover."

"You've got to be kidding."

"Oh, it gets better." Diz stood up and fished in her pocket for the car keys. "I'll be right back. I didn't get a chance to take the mail inside before I left for the game. I have Frannie's last letter in my bag. She actually sent me a page out of the book." Diz went to her car, rummaged through her softball bag, and found the letter.

By the time she returned, her food had arrived. Diz took a bite of toast and opened Frannie's letter. She couldn't let the girls see the letter, of course, since it was personal, but she unfolded the pages and pulled out the sheet of paper titled, League Rules of Conduct.*

"Take a look at this." Diz smoothed the sheet of paper out on the table and several of the girls got up and came to look over her shoulder.

"Read it out loud," Jean said from the other end of the table, as she shoved a bite of scrambled eggs into her mouth.

"How about if I just hit the highlights?" Diz asked. She began to read:

```
THE MANAGEMENT SETS A HIGH STANDARD FOR
THE  GIRLS  SELECTED  FOR  THE  DIFFERENT
CLUBS AND EXPECTS THEM TO LIVE UP TO THE
CODE  OF  CONDUCT  WHICH  RECOGNIZES  THAT
STANDARD.  THERE  ARE  GENERAL  REGULATIONS
NECESSARY AS A MEANS OF MAINTAINING ORDER
AND  ORGANIZING  CLUBS  INTO  A  WORKING
PROCEDURE.
    1.  ALWAYS  appear  in  feminine  attire
when  not  actively  engaged  in  practice  or
playing  ball.  This  regulation  continues
through  the  playoffs  for  all,  even  though
your  team  is  not  participating.  AT  NO
```

TIME MAY A PLAYER APPEAR IN THE STANDS IN
HER UNIFORM, OR WEAR SLACKS OR SHORTS IN
PUBLIC.
    2. Boyish bobs are not permissible and
in general your hair should be well
groomed at all times with longer hair
preferable to short hair cuts. Lipstick
should always be on.
    3. Smoking or drinking is not
permissible in public places. Liquor
drinking will not be permissible under
any circumstances. Other intoxicating
drinks in limited portions with after-
game meal only, will be allowed. Obscene
language will not be allowed at any time.
    4. All social engagements must be
approved by chaperone. Legitimate
requests for dates can be allowed by
chaperones.

Diz glossed over number five and continued reading:

    6. All living quarters and eating
places must be approved by the
chaperones. No player shall change her
residence without the permission of the
chaperone.

"Moving right along." Diz scanned the page and jumped to
number twelve.

    12. Baseball uniform skirts shall not
be shorter than six inches above the
knee-cap.
    13. In order to sustain the complete
spirit of rivalry between clubs, the
members of different clubs must not
fraternize at any time during the season.
After the opening day of the season,
fraternizing will be subject to heavy
penalties. This also means in particular,
room parties, auto trips to out-of-the-

```
way eating places, etc. However, friendly
discussions in lobbies with opposing
players are permissible. Players should
never approach the opposing manager or
chaperone about being transferred.
```

"Oh, wait until you get a load of number fifteen," Diz said.

```
    15. Players will not be allowed to
drive their cars past their city's limits
without the special permission of their
manager. Each team will travel as a unit
via method of travel provided for the
league.
    FINES OF FIVE DOLLARS FOR FIRST
OFFENSE, TEN DOLLARS FOR SECOND, AND
SUSPENSION FOR THIRD, WILL AUTOMATICALLY
BE IMPOSED FOR BREAKING ANY OF THE ABOVE
RULES.
```

"Oh, my," Zada said. "Could you just imagine us—"

"Not if you paid me in gold nuggets," Peanuts said.

"No liquor? No obscene language? No smoking? The chaperone has approval over who I date? I don't think so," Dobbie said.

"Did you get a load of number thirteen?" Dot, who'd been standing behind Diz, reached over her shoulder and put her finger on the paper. 'No fraternizing.' Guess that means we couldn't take the other team out to Blue Point or South Mountain anymore."

"Or hang out in each other's hotel rooms," Jessie said.

"Heck, we couldn't have any friends who played for any other team," Jean added.

"Don't forget the 'no jeans or shorts in public' clause," Zada said. "They have got to be joking."

"Frannie says it's no joke," Diz said. "Some girls have already been fined, and two were sent home."

"That's ridiculous," Dot said. "How is she putting up with that?"

"Four words," Peanuts said, and counted them off on her fingers, "Eighty-five dollars per week."

"Is that four words if one is hyphenated? Or is it five?" Jessie asked. Peanuts smacked her good-naturedly in the arm. "Wait, it's illegal to hit me in public. You just got yourself kicked out of the league."

Both Jessie and Peanuts dissolved into laughter.

Diz let the comments roll off her. She had no intention of sharing Frannie's opinion of the rules, nor the fact that Frannie expressly said that the policies were designed to prevent the general public from thinking that any of the girls were queer. Poor Frannie.

◈◈

Phoenix, 2014

"I saw the movie," Julie said, as she poured syrup on her pancakes. "I guess I just never made the connection that the rules were about keeping lesbians out of the baseball league.

Diz squeezed the ketchup bottle over her country potatoes with both hands. Because her hands were shaky, some of the ketchup bled onto her omelet. She scraped it off with her fork.

"It wasn't that they kept lesbians out," she said. "It was simply that they were well-camouflaged."

"From everything you've said about Frannie, I can't imagine her going along with it."

"She had her share of run-ins with the chaperones, that's for sure."

"Surely she didn't stay long, right? Maybe a season or two? Did she get kicked out?"

Diz shook her head. "You have this endearing habit of getting ahead of yourself all the time. Patience is a virtue, or so I'm told."

"I'm not feeling very virtuous," Julie said, bathing her forkful of pancakes in the syrup on her plate. "Please tell me Frannie came home to you right away."

Diz laughed. "Do you want me to jump right to the end? Or do you want to listen to the rest of the story?"

"You know the answer to that. I want to hear the whole thing. But it had better end happily ever after."

"We'll see," Diz said, winking. "I tell you what. I'll skip ahead to the 1944 National Championships. How's that?"

"Wait. Am I missing anything major if you do that? Did Elsie get married? Did she come home? Did you get to go to college? Did you move out of the house? Did you stay true to Frannie? Was she faithful to you?"

"My, that's a lot of questions," Diz said. "Remember, the war was still going on. The championships were in September. Elsie was still off flying planes, I remained home with Mother, helping her and working two jobs. As for me and Frannie..."

CHAPTER EIGHTEEN

Cleveland, Ohio, 1944

Diz laced up her cleats and tightened her uniform belt. She double-checked her bag for her favorite bat, her game glove and her back-up glove. Everything appeared to be in order.

"Everybody decent?" Mr. Hoffman called into the locker room.

"Yes, sir," Dot answered. "All clear."

The coach strode into the room wearing his Navy dress blues. "All right, everybody. Gather 'round." The girls formed a loose circle around him. "I know I don't have to tell you how important this game is. We shouldn't have lost that game to Toronto, but we did. Now we've got to play our way out of the loser's bracket.

"The Jax are two-time defending national champions. If we want to win this thing, we're going to have to go through them. That means the Savona sisters."

Some of the girls grumbled under their breath.

"Hey. Chins up, ladies. The Jax can be beat. Cleveland proved that last night. Don't get me wrong, Cleveland has a good team, but we're the Phoenix Ramblers. I expect you to go out and play like that."

Dot chimed in, "Okay, bring it in." All the girls put their hands in the middle of the circle. "Ramblers, on three. One. Two. Three."

"Ramblers!"

"Let's beat the socks off 'em."

Diz stuffed everything back in her bag and jogged out of the locker room and onto the field with the rest of the team. The lights in the stadium were bright, and the stands were filled to capacity.

"Theodora." Mr. Hoffman, who had changed out of his Navy uniform, pulled her aside. "This is a huge stage. I know you know that. It's not the first time you've been in a big game."

"No, sir."

"You've been pressing too hard. The hits will come; I don't want you to worry about that. Do you hear me?"

"Yes, sir." Diz wished she believed him. It was hard not to see the box scores and get depressed. This was her worst season ever.

"Eyes on me, please, Miss Hosler."

Diz raised her gaze from her cleats to the coach's face.

"That's better. I know this has been a difficult year for you. Losing your father, Elsie being away, having to take on a bigger role at home… It's a lot to take on at your age."

"I'm fine, sir." Diz lifted her chin.

Mr. Hoffman put a hand on her shoulder. "I believe you will be. I know I haven't been around much—"

"You're serving our country, sir. It's all right."

"Let me finish, please."

"I'm sorry, sir."

"I hear you've been wanting to go to college."

"I have to help my mother out. I can't afford—"

"I understand. That's why I want to talk to you after the season's over. I want to help you."

"I—"

"Miss Hosler. Why are you interrupting me?"

Diz clamped her mouth shut.

"Today, right now, I want you to focus only on this game, on this moment. We'll talk about everything else at a later date. Okay?"

"Yes, sir."

"I've got you leading off. I believe in you. All I want you to think about is getting on base. Can you do that?"

"Yes, sir. I'll do my very best."

"I know you will." He released Diz's shoulder. "Now get out there and give it your best shot."

"Yes, sir!" Diz trotted out to center field. She supposed Mr. Hoffman's words should make her feel better. She was sure that was his intent. But being singled out only made her feel more self-conscious than she already did.

"Coming, Diz." Mildred held up a practice ball so that Diz could see it, then tossed it to her.

Diz caught it easily. The coach wanted her to put everything aside except the game. And yet, there was Mildred, warming up with her instead of Frannie. Diz threw the ball back to Mildred. "I'm good," she said.

She'd missed a phone call from Frannie on Wednesday because the team was on the road to the championships. The previous Wednesday, Frannie had been the one traveling for a game. Between their softball schedules, Diz's jobs, and helping her mother, their letters had become sporadic.

Diz blinked. Focus on the game. She rotated her torso first to the right, then to the left, loosening up. Maybe after the season was over, she could find a way to visit Frannie. She bent over and touched her toes.

"Welcome to Elks Field," the announcer boomed, "home of the 1944 World Softball Championships, and tonight's tilt between the former-champion Phoenix Ramblers, and the reigning champion, New Orleans Jax."

Diz took a deep breath in and released it. Time to play ball.

The score was still knotted at zero when Diz stepped into the on-deck circle in the bottom of the eighth inning. All game long, Jax pitcher Lottie Jackson had stymied the Ramblers' hitters.

Diz bent over, picked up a handful of dirt, and rubbed her hands together. Then she ran her hands along the bat.

"Hey, good-looking."

The remark emanated from the stands immediately behind the circle. Diz, who was used to being heckled and hassled, paid no attention.

"Wow. You have really good powers of concentration. Okay, let's try this. Jackson likes to throw the change-up on an oh-and-two count. She's done it the last four batters in a row. Let her go oh-and-two on you and blast it up the middle."

Diz, who was mid-practice swing, whipped around. Frannie— *her* Frannie—was right there, leaning over the railing that separated the stands from the field of play, just feet away from where Diz stood.

Diz's heart pounded so hard she thought it might burst out of her chest. She opened her mouth to say something, but no words came out. At the plate, Jean Hutsell was waiting for the delivery from Jackson.

"How...? W-what are you doing here?"

Frannie's smile lit up her face. She summoned Diz with a crook of her index finger. Despite the situation, Diz didn't hesitate.

"I can't believe you're here." She faced forward, her back to Frannie so that to anyone else who was watching, she was paying attention to Jean's at-bat.

Frannie leaned farther over the railing so that her mouth was close to Diz's ear. "I miss you like crazy. I had to come."

Diz's skin turned to goose flesh. She took a step back so that her backside was touching the railing. She was close enough that if Frannie reached out, her arms would encircle Diz.

Diz put her hand in front of her mouth. "I love you like crazy."

"Yeah? Well, hurry up and win the game, will you?"

Diz laughed. Just then, Jean took ball four.

"You might want to follow the advice I gave you. And make sure you wait on the ball. You're rushing."

Diz shook her head and headed for the batter's box. Frannie was here, right here, watching her. Warmth spread through her as she settled herself and waited for the first pitch.

"Ball."

Diz took a practice swing.

"Steee-rike one!"

Although it was normally a pitch Diz would have swung at, she let it go. She stepped out and looked down the line to Mr. Hoffman, who was coaching third base. He clapped his hands together and ran through a series of signs. She was surprised that he hadn't asked her to bunt to move Jean to second. Instead, he was telling her to swing away.

"Steee-rike two!"

Again, Diz let the pitch go by. Like the first two, it was a fastball.

"C'mon, Diz. Give it a ride!"

"Hey batter, hey batter, no batter!"

Diz took a deep breath in and blew it out. She rotated her neck to the left and to the right to ease the tension. If Frannie was right, this pitch would be a change-up. If she timed it right…

Lottie Jackson reached back and started her wind-up.

"Wait for it. Wait for it," Diz muttered to herself.

Jackson released the ball, and Diz counted to three in her head, strode forward, and swung.

With a satisfying, "crack," the ball jumped off the bat. Diz took off for first base. She glanced up to catch a glimpse of the ball as it caromed off the base of the wall in right field, then she lowered her head and picked up speed rounding first, where the coach was waving her on to second.

Almost to the bag at second, Diz spied Mr. Hoffman, who was animatedly waving her to third as the throw came in to home plate, where Jean was just starting her slide.

As Diz slid hard into third base with a triple, she heard the umpire yell, "Out!"

She turned her head in time to see a cloud of dust at home plate and the umpire standing over Jean, making the call.

"Time!" Diz yelled to the umpire covering third base. She stood and shook the dirt out of her shorts.

"Way to go, Miss Hosler. Nice hit, good running." Mr. Hoffman clapped Diz on the back. "You just got the Ramblers' first hit of the game."

Diz beamed and immediately looked to the stands to find her girl. There was Frannie, whistling and clapping. She held up a fist and shook it in Diz's direction.

"Okay," Mr. Hoffman was saying, "Listen for me. We've got one out. Let's be smart. I'll talk to you on a fly ball."

Diz clapped her hands. "Here we go, Mildred. Give it a ride!"

At the plate, Mildred Dixon was getting ready to hit. Mr. Hoffman gave her the signs. The fans were on their feet and the noise level was deafening.

After two straight balls, Jackson threw a strike on the outside corner.

"C'mon, Mildred. This one's yours!" Diz screamed. She readied herself to run.

Mildred took a huge cut at the next pitch, and missed. The count was two-and-two. She swung again at the next pitch, a drop ball that fell away and outside, and missed badly.

"Okay. Two outs. You're running on contact no matter what," Mr. Hoffman told Diz, as Dot stepped up to bat.

She's a contact hitter. Be ready. Crack of the bat. You're the winning run. You're standing between the Ramblers and the championship game. Diz wiggled her fingers and dug her foot into the base for better traction.

Dot let the first two pitches go by for balls, and Diz wondered if Jackson would even risk throwing Dot a strike. Then again, Amy was on deck, and she was sure the pitcher wouldn't want to face the clean-up batter with two runners on base.

"Show 'em where you live, Dottie!"

"Steee-rike one!"

Dot glared at the home plate umpire and stepped out of the box. She rubbed some dirt on her hands, wiped them on her shorts, and re-gripped the bat.

"This one's yours, Dot!"

Dot adjusted her hands on the bat. She was a picture of concentration. Jackson went into her wind-up and released the ball; it was a rise ball up and in, right where Dot liked it.

Dot swung with all her might and smashed the ball into right-center field. Diz took off for home plate on contact. Both the center fielder and the right fielder converged. The center fielder dove...and the ball landed on the grass, just past her outstretched glove.

Diz stepped on home plate as Dot crossed first base, and the entire stadium erupted. Every player on the Ramblers bench bolted for home plate to congratulate Diz. In the middle of the swarm, Dot, who had run in from first, picked Diz up in a bear hug.

"You did it, kid. You did it."

"No, you did it, Dot. You got the game-winning hit."

"It wouldn't have happened if you hadn't smacked that triple. I'm proud of you."

Diz's heart swelled with pride. She remembered that trip to New York in 1938 where all she had wanted was to be a Rambler. And here she was, with the captain of the team congratulating her on scoring the game-winning run and knocking the two-time national champions out of the tournament. If this was a dream, Diz sure didn't want to wake up.

She came up for air and scooted underneath Dobbie's arm and around Margie. She scanned the crowd in the stands. All that was missing from this beautiful moment was Frannie.

Diz found the spot where Frannie had been sitting. She wasn't there. Where was she? Diz let her eyes roam the entire section, and the section next to that, and the one next to that. No Frannie. Her smile faded. Surely Frannie wouldn't leave? Not now. Surely she hadn't come all the way from Wisconsin just to whisper a few words to Diz before her at-bat?

"Hey, Diz. C'mon. Mr. Hoffman wants to talk to us."

Diz followed Zada to the pitcher's mound, where Mr. Hoffman was waiting with the rest of the team.

"I'm really, really proud of you gals," Mr. Hoffman said. You fought hard. You never gave up. And, despite getting only two hits all day, you came away with a big W. That's great."

The team cheered.

"Wait a minute." Mr. Hoffman held up a hand. "We're not done yet. Not by a long-shot. The way I see it, we've still got Chicago and Cleveland standing in our way before we can even get to the championship game. So go, enjoy tonight. But when we walk on that field again tomorrow, I expect you to be all business."

Dot signaled for everyone to put their hands in the circle. "Ramblers on three. One. Two. Three."

"Ramblers!"

"Don't stay up too late, get a good night's rest. Good job, everybody." Mr. Hoffman walked off the field.

"Party in Peanuts' room!" Dobbie called.

All of the girls returned to the dugout to grab their gear and head for the parking lot.

Diz lingered on the field, hoping that Frannie would come find her. Eventually, when everyone cleared out and Frannie failed to show herself, Diz headed for the dugout to gather her stuff.

Where was Frannie? And how had she gotten to Cleveland? Was she waiting in her car in the parking lot? If she'd driven, according to the rules, she would've needed her chaperone's permission.

Diz had caught a ride to the field in Dot's car, so, unless her girl was outside waiting for her, she assumed she'd be heading back to the hotel in Dot's car, as well, which meant she'd better get a move on.

Diz trotted down the dugout steps, and ran directly into the bat girl. "Geez. I'm sorry. I didn't see you there."

The girl was holding out a neatly folded piece of paper. "That's okay. The lady in the green dress said to give this to you. 'Only give this to her,' she said. 'Don't show it to anyone else.'"

Diz raised an eyebrow.

"She gave me a nickel." The girl held out her hand with the shiny nickel in it, and Diz smiled.

"I see. That was very nice of her. What are you going to buy with your nickel?"

"Ice cream!"

"Good for you," Diz said. She took the note from the girl. "Thanks. You did a good job."

"I know." The girl skipped up the steps and out of sight.

Diz checked to make sure she was alone, sat down on the bench, and greedily read the note.

Tiger, great job out there. I'm so proud of you. Nice legs, by the way. I'm not supposed to be here, so it wouldn't do for the girls to see me. I'm staying at the Statler Hotel, Euclid Avenue and 12th Street, room 337. I asked around, and I know that you are staying at the Hollenden Hotel. That's just six blocks away, and so in walking distance. Please come see me as soon as possible. I miss you. Always, F.

Diz held the paper to her chest. Frannie had come all the way from Racine just to see her.

"Diz, you coming?" Peanuts poked her head in through the fence gate. "We're leaving."

"Coming." Hastily, Diz slipped the note inside her bra, gathered up her bag, and hustled through the gate to the waiting car.

All the way back to the hotel, Diz schemed in her head. How would she slip away without anyone knowing? The party would be going on in the room shared by Peanuts, Dot, Dobbie, Zada, and Jean. She was sharing a room with Margie, Amy, Mildred, and Mickey. She just had to hope that all of them would be in a celebratory mood. That way she could pretend to have a headache and sneak out.

The car came to a stop and all of the girls piled out. Diz made sure to move slowly, as though she wasn't feeling well.

"What's the matter, champ? This is your night. You scored the winning run. Put some pep in your step," Zada said.

"You know? I'm not feeling that great. I've got a headache."

"What's going on?" Dot joined the conversation.

"Diz says she's not feeling well."

"I'm fine. Really. I think I'm just a little dehydrated. I'll go get some water and lie down. I'm sure I'll be right as rain by the morning."

"You need someone to go with you?"

"No." Diz said too quickly and too forcefully. "I mean, that was a big win. You guys go ahead and party for me. I'll grab a shower and turn in early."

"Are you sure?"

"I am. Go ahead."

Dot narrowed her eyes and crossed her arms. "If I didn't know better, I'd say you were lying."

"What? Why would you think that?"

"I don't know. You tell me."

Diz tried her hardest not to squirm. "There's nothing to tell. Like I said, I have a headache."

Dot pointed a finger at Diz. "I'd better not find out that you were sneaking around."

Diz swallowed hard. She made an X over her heart with her left index finger. "I swear."

After one more intimidating glare, Dot relented. "Okay. Feel better. If you need anything, come get one of us."

"I will, but I'm sure I'll be fine."

Diz grabbed her toiletries and some clean clothes and locked herself in the bathroom. Within minutes, she was showered, dressed, and ready to go. She checked her watch. It was almost 9:30 p.m. She and Frannie wouldn't have much time together. Lights out would be at 12:30 a.m., and Diz would need to be back and in her bed before that.

Diz went to the door and cracked it open. The hallway was clear. She took a step over the threshold, changed her mind, and turned back around. She ran to her bed, hefted her dirty laundry bag, and stuffed it under the covers. After stepping back to survey her handiwork, she fluffed it up more. There, now it could be a body in the bed, facing away from the door.

She scouted the hallway in both directions, slipped out, and took the stairs down to the street level. When she made it through the lobby and out the front doors, Diz began to run. Frannie was here, and time was a precious commodity.

CHAPTER NINETEEN

Cleveland, Ohio, 1944

The corridor on the third floor of the Statler Hotel was empty. Diz stood outside the door of room 337 for a moment, trying to catch her breath. She'd run the entire six blocks with just one thought in mind—to hold Frannie in her arms again. Three months. They'd gone three whole months without seeing each other; it felt like an eternity.

Diz fussed with her hair and smoothed a palm down her blouse. Why in the world should she be nervous? Frannie had come all this way, just to see her. She raised a hand and knocked softly.

Seconds later, the door flew open and there was Frannie. Diz got her first good look at the green dress, the upswept hairdo, and the lipstick, and her mouth went dry.

"Are you going to stand out in the hallway, or are you going to come in, Tiger?"

Diz stumbled into the room and Frannie closed and locked the door behind them.

"You look… Wow." It was all Diz could think to say.

"I'm glad you like it."

"I do. I really, really do."

Frannie laughed and stepped closer. Diz's knees nearly buckled.

"I missed you so much. Like I said, I just had to come." Frannie wrapped her arms around Diz. "Even if it was only for a few hours—"

"Wait," Diz leaned back so she could see Frannie's face. "What do you mean, 'only for a few hours?'"

"I have to be back for work tomorrow. I was only able to get away today by telling them I needed to visit a sick relative in Cleveland." Frannie kissed Diz's forehead and Diz leaned into the contact.

"B-but, that's a really long drive."

"Eight hours, but who's counting." Frannie swept a lock of hair off of Diz's forehead, and ran her fingers along Diz's cheekbones, her jaw, her lips.

Diz closed her eyes. This was home. Right here, in Frannie's arms. This was where she belonged. She sighed with pleasure when Frannie closed the distance between them.

That first tender kiss, the first taste of her sweet mouth, and Diz was completely undone. "I miss you so much."

"I know. That's why I'm here. I feel the same way. I couldn't stand the idea of being apart for one more second," Frannie said.

"You're coming home?" Diz's heart skipped a beat.

"What? Oh, no. I'm sorry. I-I just meant to visit."

"Oh." Diz's shoulders slumped.

"Hey," Frannie tipped Diz's chin up. "Let's make the most of our time together, okay? We can worry about the rest later."

Diz allowed herself to be guided to the bed. Frannie sat down on the edge, and Diz sat next to her, without relinquishing her hand.

Suddenly, every pent up emotion Diz had been holding in for the past few months coalesced into a simple sentence. "This has been the worst season ever."

The comment surprised a laugh out of Frannie. "I could see that from the newspaper clippings you sent. Why are you having so much trouble hitting? Apart from the fact that you're rushing, like I told you earlier." Frannie kicked off her shoes and tucked her legs underneath her.

"I miss my girl. Every time I look over and see Mildred in left field, or in the on-deck circle, I'm reminded that you're not here. It makes me so sad." Diz stroked the back of Frannie's hand with her thumb. "The game just isn't the same without you in it."

"I know what you mean. I've met all these new girls..."

Diz stiffened. "You don't need to remind just how many girls you've met out there."

Frannie claimed Diz's lips again. This kiss was gentle, loving, and filled with affection. "None of those girls is you. You're the only one for me. Why do you think I drove all this way? I needed this. I needed to touch you, to kiss you, to feel your heartbeat." Frannie placed the palm of her hand on Diz's chest, and Diz savored the warmth.

"I can't hit because all I can think about is you."

"I don't know. That was a pretty nice shot today. I was very, very proud of you."

"Thanks. But that's the first hit I've had in forever."

"Well, then, it'll be the first of many," Frannie said. "Not to change the topic, but how are things at home, really? I know your mother is there every time we talk and you can't say much. How are you holding up? Is she doing any better?"

"She still falls asleep in the chair a lot. I think she doesn't like being in the bed without Daddy." Diz paused, an ironic smile playing on her lips. "I know a little bit about how she feels."

"Me too. I sleep like hell without you." Frannie pulled Diz hard to her and they tumbled backward.

Diz landed on top of Frannie. Her pulse hammered in her ears. "I'm wrinkling your dress." She barely recognized the low timber of her own voice.

"I hardly noticed."

They stayed like that for several heartbeats, their mouths inches apart.

Knock, knock. "Room service!"

Diz jumped up so fast she got her fingers tangled in the belt of Frannie's dress. "Ow!"

Knock, knock. "Room service!"

"Coming," Frannie called. She covered her mouth to mute her laughter. "Stay still for a second," she whispered to Diz. "Let me get that."

Diz stopped struggling and allowed Frannie to help her. When she was clear, she ran into the bathroom, and peeked through the crack in the door as Frannie rose, straightened the covers and her dress, and answered the door.

"It's all clear, scaredy-cat."

Sheepishly, Diz emerged from the bathroom. "You ordered room service?"

"I thought you might be hungry after the game, and I knew you weren't going to get to eat with the girls, so, yeah. I ordered us room service." Frannie placed the room service tray on the desk.

"Oh." Diz lifted her nose in the air and sniffed. "Burgers? You got us burgers?"

"I did, with extra French fries and ketchup. And a chocolate milkshake."

"Yum!" Diz glanced around. There were two winged-back chairs in the far corner of the room with a little table between them. "How about if we eat over there?"

Frannie picked up the tray and moved it.

"This is a really nice room." Diz tucked a napkin into her shirt. "How did you afford this?"

"$1.50 per night, and I thought I'd splurge on us, seeing as how I haven't been taking my girl out to the movies and to the diner lately."

"True. You do owe me." Diz winked. She reached over and took Frannie's hand in hers. "Thank you."

"Don't thank me until you taste the burger."

"No." Diz frowned. "That's not what I mean. I mean thank you for today. Thank you for coming to the game. Thank you for coming all this way just to spend a little time with me. Thank you for dinner. Just... Thank you."

"Don't"—Frannie cleared her throat—"don't go getting all emotional on me now. I love you, Diz. I can't imagine not doing everything in my power to see my girl when she's this close."

"But you said you have to drive back tonight."

"I do." Frannie disentangled their hands and picked up her burger. "Eat, before it gets cold."

"All that way. And the gas..."

"Eat." Frannie pointed at Diz's untouched burger.

Dutifully, Diz picked up the burger and took a bite.

"A couple of the gals gave me their gas rations so I'd have enough."

"You *told* people?"

"Easy, Tiger. I only told them that I had to get to Cleveland, and I didn't have enough gas rations to make the roundtrip."

"Oh." Diz swiped a French fry through the ketchup on her plate and ate it. When she looked back up, Frannie was grinning at her.

"What?"

"I'm glad to see you eating, that's what."

"You told me to."

"I know." Frannie took a sip of the milkshake. "You're too thin. I'm worried about you."

"Am not."

"Are too."

Diz opened her mouth to say something, but Frannie held up a hand. "Don't say a word, and for Heaven's sake, don't argue with me. You've lost a lot of weight, sweetheart, and you didn't have a lot to lose to begin with."

Diz averted her gaze. How could she eat when her heart was hurting so much? Sitting at the dinner table alone with her mother was painful. The conversations were stilted. Diz found herself sneaking glances at the two empty chairs once occupied by her father and Elsie. She wondered if her mother was doing the same thing.

"Hey, Diz?" Frannie ran her fingers down Diz's forearm.

"Huh?"

"Where are you? You just disappeared. Where'd you go?"

"Nowhere. I'm here, and I'm not too thin."

"You are."

Again, Diz started to say something and Frannie stopped her.

"Ah, ah. I'm the one who had her arms around you. I know how my girl feels, and you're nothing but skin and bones." Frannie held the straw toward Diz so that she could taste the milkshake. "It's no wonder you can't hit. There's nothing to you."

"Is too," Diz muttered, around the straw. It was time to change the topic. "How about you?"

"What about me?"

"Well, what's it like? All you ever do is complain about all the rules, the dress code, the curfew, the uniforms... Is there anything good about playing for the Belles?"

"The money." Frannie laughed.

"Be serious."

"I am being serious. The money is the best part. The crowds are good too, and there are some good ball players. Sophie Kurys can run like nobody's business and she gets on board a lot. Because she hits behind me in the order, I get a lot of good pitches. Nobody wants to put me on base with her coming up." Frannie took another bite of burger and wiped her mouth. "So my average is up."

Diz snagged a fry off Frannie's plate.

"Even though the pitchers are throwing underhand, we get to lead off and steal like in baseball, and the pitcher is so much farther away, we've got more time to see the pitch. Makes it easier to hit, that's for sure. Of course, the bases also are farther apart, so it means more running, and you know how much I love to run." Frannie rolled her eyes.

"I always told you, you should've tried harder to keep up with me."

"You'd be an ace base-stealer in that league, that's for sure. You? With your speed and the freedom to lead before the pitch? You'd be unstoppable."

"Only if I could get on base first."

"True. Which brings me back to why you're not hitting."

"I just can't concentrate up there. I'm thinking about you, about Mother, about Daddy..." Diz's voice broke. "I'm thinking about Elsie—"

"What's happening with her? She still off flying around the country?"

"She is. And, she's busy planning for the wedding."

"I know. I got my invitation. Christmas Eve, eh?"

"Yeah." Diz sighed. "It's the only time Pete could get leave. It's also the one thing that has Mother excited. She's been busy coordinating the food, the flowers, and helping with the guest list. She and Elsie have been sending letters back and forth like crazy."

"I bet." Frannie slurped the last of the milkshake. "Have Elsie and Pete decided yet where they're going to live?"

"Not yet. They're waiting until he's done with the service and she's done with the WASPs."

"Well, if you listen to the latest reports on the radio, things are going well. Hopefully, the war will be over soon."

"I sure hope so."

"He's a pilot, right?"

"Pete?" Diz asked, polishing off the last of her burger. "Yeah."

"Maybe, when the war's over, he could work at Sky Harbor, like your father did."

"Yeah, maybe."

Frannie got up, skirted the table, and put her arms around Diz. "I'm sorry. I should be more sensitive. I know thinking about your dad still hurts."

"It's okay. It's just... Thinking about Daddy and flying together in the same sentence makes it worse, you know?"

"I do." Frannie checked her wristwatch. "What time is your curfew?"

"12:30 a.m."

"You need to get going."

"What?" Panic welled up in Diz's chest. "No. Not yet. It can't be time already."

"It's almost midnight." Frannie cocked her head. "How did you sneak out, anyway?"

"I told the girls I had a headache and I was going to take a shower and go to bed."

"You'd better hope nobody goes back to the room to check on you."

"I hope not. But, just in case, I stuffed my laundry bag under the covers."

"Yeah, like no one's ever tried that one before." Frannie kissed Diz on the forehead again. "My little non-rule-breaker."

"Is it really time?"

"Uh-huh."

"I don't want it to be."

"I know, but if you go now, you'll beat the curfew and maybe get back to the room before the rest of the girls do. Who are you sleeping with?"

"I've got the quiet room this time. Margie, Amy, Mickey, and Mildred."

"Lucky for you in terms of actually getting some sleep, but you know those girls—they're not going to stay out late."

"Mm. I know."

"So, what's your plan if they're already back in the room when you get there? What are you going to tell them?"

Diz bit her lip. What would she tell them? That she'd rested for a while, then got hungry and went out to get something to eat? Would they believe that? She hated to lie, and really, really hoped she wouldn't have to. "I don't know. What do you think I should tell them?"

"I think you should pray that you get back to the room before anyone figures out that you haven't been there all along."

"Right. But if—"

"If you get caught, try telling them that you started feeling better and decided to go out to get something to eat. Downstairs, you ran into some of the players from the Jax or some other team that we've partied with before and they invited you to their room."

Diz felt miserable. She really, really hoped she could sneak back in time. Finally, she decided to ask a question that had been nagging at her from the outset. "Why can't the girls know you're here, anyway?"

"Well, for one thing, because it's not where I said I was going to be. For another, how would I explain that I only wanted to spend time with you, alone?"

Diz had to admit that made sense.

"Besides, some of the old Queens play with us. If any of the Ramblers blabbed to them about seeing me, I'd probably get kicked out of the league."

"Oh. I didn't think about that." Diz frowned again. "You don't think any of them saw you at the game? While we were talking?"

"Did any of them say anything to you about it?"

"No."

"Don't you think they would've mentioned it?"

"Yeah. I guess."

"You know they would have." Frannie pulled Diz closer and erased the lines in Diz's forehead with her thumb. "You worry too much."

"I do?"

"Mm-hmm. How about instead of worrying right now, you kiss me?"

Diz reluctantly opened her eyes when Frannie finally pulled away. Her lips were still vibrating and her body was humming.

"You need to go now, or I'll never let you go," Frannie said.

"That's okay with me," Diz answered.

"I need to be awake to drive, so I have to get going too."

"You got a hotel room you're not going to sleep in? That's crazy."

"I took a nap here before I came to the game so I could stay awake now."

"Oh," Diz said. "That makes sense."

"Plus, I needed a place where we could be alone." Frannie dipped her head and kissed Diz one last time. "I love you. You must always remember that."

"I will," Diz said, around the lump in her throat. "When am I going to see you again?"

"The wedding is in two months. I'm going to work some overtime so that I can get a few days off around Christmas."

"That's a whole two-and-a-half months away."

"I know, but it's the best I can do."

Frannie stepped out of Diz's embrace, took her hand, and led her to the door. "Remember, I'm crazy about you. And stop rushing at the plate."

Just as Frannie unlocked the door and was about to open it, Diz flew into her arms. "I love you." She held Frannie hard against her, clinging tightly to her, breathing her in one last time.

"I love you too, sweetheart. I'll see you so soon you won't have time to miss me."

"Liar."

"Maybe a little." Frannie kissed Diz's nose. "Skedaddle, and be careful out there. Go win us a championship."

"You drive carefully. Stop if you're too tired. Apex Machines can do without you for a day if you can't make it in time."

"I'll be fine. You worry too much." Frannie shoved Diz affectionately so that she was standing in the hallway. She blew her one last kiss and closed the door.

∽ↁ∾

Phoenix, 2014

Julie dabbed at her eyes with a Kleenex.

"Why are you crying?"

"That was so sad."

"What was?"

"The way you had to say goodbye all over again in the hotel room. It's heart-wrenching."

"You're a softie."

Julie sniffed. "Oh, so you didn't cry when you were standing on the other side of that hotel room door and all the way back to where you were staying?"

"I didn't say that, now did I?" Diz fumbled in her bag.

"Do you need my help? What are you looking for?"

"Busy-body," Diz joked. She dug a little deeper into the bag. "Aha! Here it is." She pulled out an entire unopened packet of tissues. "I figure you might need these." She tossed the pack to Julie.

"Very funny. Oh, my God. Please tell me this all has a happy ending. I can't take it anymore."

"You already know it has a happy ending."

"I do?"

"Well, you know that Frannie and I were together all those years…"

"True, but I have no idea how you got there."

"That's why you're here, isn't it? Isn't that why you keep coming back? So I can tell you the story?"

"That's part of it, yes."

"What's the other part?"

"There's this really cute, sometimes cantankerous old ball player… You might know her, her name is Theodora, but everybody calls her Diz."

"Oh, go on now. Surely you don't expect me to believe you've fallen for me."

"Yep, it's true. I'm sweet on you, Diz."

"As if…"

Julie leaned over and planted a kiss on Diz's cheek. "Darned if you haven't wormed your way into my heart. My girlfriend, Tracey, is very jealous."

"Your girlfriend, Tracey, has nothing to worry about. I'm a harmless old lady."

"Somehow, the words 'harmless' and 'you' should never be in the same sentence." Julie blew her nose and checked her notes. "Okay, so I have two more questions for today."

"Shoot."

"Did you get caught back at your hotel? Were the girls already in the room when you got there?"

Diz laughed. "I had to be the luckiest gal alive that night."

"Why? What happened?"

"There I was, running back to the hotel, trying to sneak my way through the lobby, up the stairs, and into the room, and as I hustled up the first flight of stairs, the fire alarm went off."

"No way!"

"It did," Diz said. "And I didn't pull it, either. Well, next to an air raid, a fire was everybody's biggest fear in those days. So I turned around and headed back to the lobby. I waited in a corner until I saw the girls go out the front door, then I followed them out. They said they'd been worried about me. They were afraid I wouldn't wake up for the alarm."

"Didn't they try to poke you?"

"They were all still in Peanuts' room. So I acted as groggy as I could, and when we got the all-clear, I ran up ahead of everybody else so that I could get the laundry bag out from under the covers."

"Sneaky, Diz. That was really, really, sneaky."

"It was. And lucky too." Diz winked. "What was your other question?"

"Did you win the championship?"

"Not in 1944 we didn't. We won two more games after beating the Jax and got to the finals against Portland. Well, their pitcher hadn't allowed a single run all tournament. We fought 'em for eleven innings. In the end, they beat us one-to-nothing."

"Ouch."

"You're telling me. Boy, that was one quiet ride home to Phoenix."

"I bet." Julie consulted her notebook. "So, that was in September, 1944, right?"

"Yep."

"Didn't I hear you say Elsie was getting married around Christmastime that year?"

"That's more than two questions."

"What?"

"You said you only had two more questions for me today."

"You're too sharp for your own good."

"I have to keep you on the edge of your seat. Otherwise why would you keep breaking me out of that joint?"

"Aren't you the one who chose the assisted living community?"

"I did. I didn't really have much of a choice, did I? Being stuck in this chair means I can't go up and down stairs reliably by myself anymore."

"I'm sorry, Diz."

"Me too. Getting old isn't for sissies."

"So, you want me to save Elsie's wedding for next time?" Julie jotted a note in her notebook.

"That's a good place to pick up. Maybe I'll see if I can't make you cry again."

"You wouldn't..."

"We'll see, now won't we?"

CHAPTER TWENTY

Phoenix, 1944

Mrs. Hosler flitted from room to room, arranging, re-arranging, adding, and subtracting various flower vases, doilies, and placeholders. Diz watched it all with a sense of bemusement.

"You could help instead of sitting there smirking."

"I'm not smirking, Mother. I'm in awe of your eye for detail."

"Don't be smart with me."

"I'm serious."

"Your sister will only get married once, you know. Everything needs to be just right."

"And it will be."

"When will Frannie be here?"

Diz's stomach did a happy flip. "She should be here within the hour."

"Well, it will be nice to have her under our roof again. Maybe you'll stop moping."

"I haven't been moping."

Mrs. Hosler paused in her fussing. "Please, Theodora. You've done nothing but mope ever since Frannie left. It's okay. I understand. You don't make friends easily and you need someone your age for companionship. That's natural."

Diz found something interesting to look at on the floor and hoped that the blush creeping up her neck wasn't noticeable.

"You know what, Mother? I should go see how Elsie is doing. I'm supposed to be helping her with whatever it is she needs."

"You're a good maid of honor, Theodora. I know your sister appreciates all you are doing for her and Pete."

"I only have one sister, and, as you said, she's only going to get married once." Diz excused herself and bounded up the stairs.

Diz knocked on the partially opened door. Elsie was sitting on the bed in her room. "Can I come in?"

"Sure." Elsie hastily dried her eyes and hid the handkerchief behind her back, but not before Diz saw it.

Diz walked to the bed and nudged Elsie with her hip. "Move over."

Elsie obliged, and Diz sat down. "What's wrong?"

"I don't know what you're talking about."

"C'mon, Sis. I know you. Talk to me. Is it that the WASPs sent you home? Is it Pete? What is it?"

Elsie burst into tears and Diz wrapped her arms around her. For a long while, they stayed like that, with Diz rocking Elsie and rubbing her back. Finally, Elsie pulled back. She wiped her eyes with the backs of her hands.

"Want to tell me what that was all about?"

"Everything." Elsie sniffed and blew her nose. "And when did you get to be so grown up that I'm the one crying on your shoulder?" She smiled through her tears.

Diz shrugged. "Miracles happen."

That surprised a laugh out of Elsie. "I guess they do, at that. Who thought I'd be getting married?"

"I know. It's—weird."

"It is, right?" Elsie crinkled her nose. "He really is a swell guy, Sis. Wait until you get a chance to know him. I think you'll like him, and I know he'll like you."

"Then why are you crying?"

"All my married friends told me that I'd get all emotional for no reason. I didn't believe them; turns out, they were right."

"If that was nothing, I'd hate to see what something looks like."

"It's just been such a crazy time. One day we're flying P-51s and B-17s and helping with the war effort, and the next thing we know, the government is telling us they don't need us anymore, and sending us packing on our own dime. It was so sudden."

"What happened?"

"I don't know, really. Something to do with politics, I guess. But that means Pete is getting reassigned, God only knows where."

"You'll go with him, right?"

"Not if he gets sent overseas, though that seems unlikely. He's in line for an officer's position with Air Transport Command at Love Field."

"Where's that?"

"Dallas."

"I see. You'd go with him to Dallas, then, right?" Diz tried not to sound petulant. It was exactly what she feared—she would be stuck here with Mother, and all of her dreams for the future would be put on hold indefinitely.

"Yes, probably." Elsie took Diz's hand. "Never mind all that. There's something else I wanted to talk to you about."

The tone of Elsie's voice, so serious, set alarm bells off. "Okay." Diz stared at the bedspread.

"When I joined the WASPs, I made you a promise. I want you to know I haven't forgotten." Elsie paused. "Look at me, Sis."

Diz forced herself to make eye contact.

"I know this past year has been hell for you. With me leaving, and Daddy..." Elsie's voice broke on a sob. "Somehow, it was less real for me because I wasn't here, having to watch Mother struggle. And I know that you were having a hard time too. You and Daddy had such a special relationship. And you and Mother... Well, you were never particularly close."

"We're better. Mother is much more relaxed than she used to be. I think Daddy's death just took all the fight out of her." Once the words were out, Diz realized with a start just how true they were. She'd been trying to put her finger on it for a while now. All the strictness, the intractability, the rigid rules...all gone.

"And then Frannie left for Chicago, and that was another blow."

Diz closed her eyes. She'd made it through the year by not thinking too much, not feeling too much. Now here was Elsie, laying it all out in black and white, and it was all too much.

"...so I just want you to know..."

Diz tried to focus on what Elsie was saying.

"Even though Pete and I don't know yet where we're going to land after the war, and it probably won't be here in Phoenix, we've got a plan."

"Why are you telling me this?" The last thing Diz wanted to hear was all about the wonderful life Elsie and Pete had planned with each other. It wasn't that she begrudged them their happiness; it was that she wanted a happy ending too.

"Why...? Because it has everything to do with you, silly. It's about the promise." Elsie squeezed the hand she was holding. "I told you that I would come back after the war was over and help out so that you could go to ASU."

"Yeah, but that was before—"

"Let me finish." Elsie dabbed at her eyes again with her free hand. "You know I have my teaching certificate, and Pete is a pilot, so he'll probably get a job with an airline like Daddy. Financially, we're going to be doing just fine."

"I'm happy for you—"

"I swear, if you interrupt me one more time, Theodora Hosler..."

Diz closed her mouth on her next words.

"We're going to ask Mother to come live with us."

"What?" Diz was sure she hadn't heard right.

"We're going to get a place with a mother-in-law apartment and bring Mother to live with us."

"She'll never leave here."

"She will if she wants to spend time with her grandchild."

Diz's eyes grew large. "You're—"

"Not yet, silly. But Pete and I agree that we want to start a family right away. And Mother could come help me with the baby."

"You can't teach and be a mother at the same time."

"When the baby comes along, I can quit and stay home."

"You wouldn't be able to afford to feed and house Mother on just Pete's salary, would you?"

"I can work part-time and Mother can watch the baby, or Mother can take in sewing like she does here." Elsie let go of

Diz's hand. "I thought you'd be over-the-moon about this. You'd be free to go to school and have everything you want."

Diz thought about the conversation Mr. Hoffman said he wanted to have with her. It never happened after the championships because he had to get back to his base. He had said something about wanting to help her with college. What had he meant, and had he forgotten all about it in the interim?

"What about this house? Mother wouldn't just leave the house."

"She would if you were going to stay in it. You could live here while you go to ASU. That way, you wouldn't have to pay room and board at school."

"You've really thought this through."

"I have."

"And Pete is okay with all of this?"

"Like I said, you're really going to like him. He's a family man, Sis, and he's a big softie. He reminds me a lot of Daddy."

"You're going to talk to Mother about it?"

"Yes. As soon as we know where Pete's orders are going to take him."

Diz cocked her head. "You'd do all this for me?"

"Well, technically, I'd benefit too. I'd get to have more of my family around me, and a built-in babysitter to boot. But, to answer your question, a promise is a promise, Sis. I keep mine."

"You're the best big sister I could ask for."

"I'm the only big sister you've got." Elsie threw her arms around Diz and hugged her. "Now, if you don't mind, I have a wedding to get ready for, and I must look a-fright."

"How can I help?"

"Hand me my beauty kit and get the dress out of the closet and hang it up on the door. The car will be here soon to take us to the church."

Diz did as Elsie asked, then wandered back downstairs.

"Theodora, look who's here." Mrs. Hosler, never a demonstrative woman, stood with her arm circled around Frannie's waist.

Diz knew she was grinning like a fool, but she didn't care. Frannie was home. "Hi."

"Hi, yourself. Your mother here was just telling me that you were probably upstairs helping Elsie with her makeup. I was trying to picture what Elsie might look like when you were done."

"Very funny," Diz said.

"I'll just leave you two girls to get caught up. I've got so much to do. I never should have let your sister talk me into having people back to the house after the wedding." Mrs. Hosler bustled off in the direction of the kitchen, leaving Diz and Frannie completely alone in the vestibule.

"Hi." Diz said.

"You already said that." Frannie grabbed Diz by the hand and practically ran with her out the front door and toward the barn.

"Are you crazy?" Diz asked.

Frannie slid open the barn door, yanked Diz inside, and closed the door after them. "I am crazy, as a matter of fact. I'm crazy about you." She pinned Diz against the near wall and kissed her hard.

Diz could never remember her girl being this aggressive, and her body responded as if it were on fire.

"We can't... I have to help... Oh. Um, Elsie will be... Ah. I need to..." If only her brain could function. Diz pushed off the wall. "Wait."

"I don't want to—"

"Hold on," Diz tried again. "I have to button Elsie into her dress in less than two minutes, and I can't think clearly." Diz straightened her blouse. "Let me get my wits about me."

"I'm sorry," Frannie said.

"Gosh, I hope not." Diz kissed her softly. "I missed you so much. But I'm the maid of honor, and Elsie is an emotional wreck. I've got to be there for her."

"Of course you do."

Diz risked stepping back into Frannie's arms. "Merry Christmas eve, by the way. I love you."

"Merry Christmas Eve, Tiger."

"Do I look presentable?" Diz touched her fingers to her hair.

"Let me do that." Frannie settled a few strands of hair that were out of place. "Perfect."

"Thanks." She quickly kissed Frannie, one last time. "Can I get a rain check?"

"You bet."

Diz put a hand on the door. "Let me go first, then you can follow in a minute or two when the coast is clear."

Diz opened the door and peeked both ways. She was alone. All the way back into the house and up to Elsie's room, she struggled to wrestle her uncooperative hormones under control. When she was certain she had won the battle, she knocked on Elsie's door and stuck her head in the room.

"Are you ready to get dressed? It's time."

Elsie turned to Diz. "Ready as I'll ever be."

"Okay, then, let's do this. Then I've got to get into my own dress." First, Diz helped Elsie into the corset and laced it up in back. "Can you breathe in this thing? Geez."

"I keep telling myself, it's only for a few hours. I can handle anything for a few hours."

"If you say so. Better you than me." Diz retrieved the dress off the hanger and held it for Elsie to step into. "Does it bother you that this was Mother's gown?"

"It did when she first mentioned that she wanted me to wear it. I thought it would be kind of creepy, or bad luck, you know?"

"And now?" Diz fought with the satin buttons and the tiny, fragile, loops they hooked through.

Elsie shrugged. "It's a beautiful dress. I guess, in a way, wearing this makes me feel like Daddy is here. He danced with Mother while she was wearing this dress. It was probably one of the most joyful occasions in his life. Does that make sense?"

"Actually, it does." Diz finished buttoning the last button and stood back. "Turn around." Elsie did. "You look radiant."

"I do?"

"You make a beautiful bride," Diz said. "Look in the mirror and see for yourself."

Diz ushered Elsie to the standing mirror in the corner. She beamed at the expression of wonder on Elsie's face.

"I'm getting married today."

"You certainly are."

"I can't believe it."

"Whatever you do, don't start bawling again. You'll ruin your makeup."

"Elsie, Theodora? The car is here!"

"Yes, Mother." Elsie called.

"Oh, my gosh. I'm not even dressed yet." Diz hustled out the door, down the hall and into her room, slammed the door shut, stripped off her clothes, and only belatedly realized she wasn't alone.

Frannie stood next to the closet, her head cocked to the side, eyebrows raised, and a big smile on her face.

"What are you…? Why are you…?"

"I needed a place to change. Assuming I'm back to sharing a room with you while I'm in town, this seemed like the logical place."

Diz's face turned hot, thinking about what had happened between them in the barn just a short while ago.

"Here." Frannie held out Diz's dress. "You look a little frazzled, and the car is already outside."

"Thanks." It certainly hadn't been what Diz expected, but she was grateful, at the moment that Frannie was helping her into clothes instead of out of them.

Phoenix, 2014

Diz lifted one leg off the footrest and stretched it out, then did the same with the other. "My circulation's not what it used to be."

"You can't stop there!" Julie exclaimed.

They were sitting in the gardens at the assisted living facility. The sky was a brilliant blue with nary a cloud in sight. A turkey vulture flew overhead and Diz pointed up at it. "Not yet, buzzard."

Julie shook her head. "You have a twisted sense of humor sometimes, you know that?"

"Better than no sense of humor, don't you think?"

"I do." Julie picked up the tape recorder again. "And no changing the subject."

"Who was changing the subject?"

"You were. So, you and Frannie were in your room, alone, just before the wedding."

"I didn't think you were that kind of girl." Diz's eyes twinkled. "You don't think I'm going to tell you intimate details of our shenanigans, do you?"

"Well, no. I mean, of course not. It's just…" Julie scrubbed her face to hide a blush.

"Oh, my goodness. You are so easily flustered." Diz chuckled. "You don't want to hear every detail of the wedding, trust me. It was a beautiful wedding—the kind you read about in the fairy tales. I even managed not to step on Elsie's dress."

"What happened after that?"

"What do you mean?"

"Did Elsie and Pete move to Texas? Did you ever find out what Mr. Hoffman wanted to say to you? Did you get to go to college?"

"Whoa," Diz said. She held up a hand. "There you go again. What is it with you and instant gratification? You'll find out everything you need to know, all in good time."

"You're maddening."

"No. I'm savoring the memories, and the fact that you find them so interesting. It's been a long, long time since anybody cared about any of this stuff."

"That's a shame." Julie sat still for a beat. "Now will you answer my questions?"

"Like a dog with a bone, you are," Diz said. "Okay, let's see. Did Elsie and Pete move to Texas? Indeed, they did. Everything happened almost exactly the way Elsie laid it out for me that day. Pete got a command post at Love Field, and Elsie was able to move there with him. She continued to fly for pleasure—did so for many years, in fact, well into her sixties, before her eyes started failing."

"Did you find out what it was Mr. Hoffman wanted to tell you?"

"Ford Hoffman was probably the most generous man alive. He helped all the girls with almost every aspect of life. He knew I couldn't afford to go to ASU—not after my father died and Elsie left. So he got ASU to take me in, on an academic scholarship, no less. I studied at the Teacher's College and got a degree in education. But I didn't want to teach."

"What did you do instead?"

"While I was a student at ASU, I took a part-time job in the library. Turns out I had an aptitude for that. Really, it was no surprise. I'd always loved books, from a very early age."

"You became a librarian?"

"Don't act so surprised. You think I'm not smart enough for that?"

"Of course you are," Julie said. "I don't know why, I just never pictured you as a librarian."

"From the time I was twenty-three until I was seventy. I retired when Frannie got sick the first time."

"The first time?"

"Breast cancer. She had a mastectomy and did well for a little while, before it showed up in the other breast."

"I'm so sorry, Diz."

"Yeah, well, me too." Diz undid the brakes on her wheelchair. "I think that's enough for today."

"But, I didn't get my happy ending yet."

"No? The wedding, Elsie and Pete moving to Dallas, knowing I got to go to college in the long run... What more could you want?" Diz smiled slyly.

"You and Frannie. And before you say anything else smart, just remember, I have the key to your room." Julie dangled the key in front of Diz.

"Blackmail will get you nowhere with me." Diz started to use her hands to get the wheelchair moving, but Julie jumped in to push the chair instead. "On the other hand, bribery might."

Julie laughed. "What's the price? And what am I getting in return?"

"You're getting your happy ending, that's what."

"And the price?"

"I might be able to use your help to get a few things squared away. I need some muscles. Got any of those?"

Julie made a muscle. "What do you think?"

"I think mine is more impressive, but you have working legs and hands, so you'll do."

"Thanks for the compliment, I think."

"Take me home, young 'un, before I turn into a pumpkin."

"It's the middle of the day, everybody knows you don't turn into a pumpkin before midnight."

"I think I liked you better before, when you were still busy being deferential to me."

"You're the one who started giving me a hard time, remember?"

"I do. I just didn't suspect you had it in you to give it back."

"I take after my mom," Julie said.

"Speaking of which, we still haven't solved that mystery."

"No. Nothing you've said in all these months tells me anything about her time with the Queens, or why she kept that a secret."

"I wish I could help you with that."

"Me too." Julie continued to push Diz along the concrete path that wound around the grounds and back toward the residences. "Here's a question I haven't asked you yet."

"Oh, boy. Now what?"

"No, really. Your family was so impacted by the war. You lost your father, Elsie left home and found a husband, Frannie went off to play in a women's baseball league formed during the war... What happened when the war ended? What was that like for you?"

"Good question." Diz pointed toward a bench under a shade tree. "Stop over there for a bit and I'll tell you."

Julie did as requested, positioned Diz so that they would be facing each other as she sat on the bench, and set the brakes on the chair.

"Work-wise, when the men started to come home, we women lost our jobs, me included. It was just, 'thanks for everything, now you can go home and go back to being homemakers.'"

"That's horrible."

Diz shrugged. "That's just the way it was. It was the times we lived in."

"You lost your job at Goodyear?"

"Yep."

"What did you do?"

"Mr. Hoffman came home from the service after V-E Day, in May, 1945. That's when he started his own real estate business.

It's also when he got me the scholarship to ASU. So I went to school and continued to work part-time at Woolworth's, and I started working part-time at the ASU library."

"And you played softball too? My God, you must never have been home."

"I didn't mind. It was a way to fill up my time without Frannie home."

"What about your mother?"

"My mother? She continued to take in sewing, even after the war, and that kept her busy."

"And Frannie?"

"She was still in Racine, playing for the Belles during the summer months, and working at Apex."

"She didn't lose her job to the returning soldiers?"

"Well, she lost the position she had, so they just moved her to a secretarial position."

"I can't believe she didn't come home to you after the war," Julie said.

"I couldn't believe it, either. Trust me, we had plenty of discussions about it."

"I can imagine."

"But I understood. She was making better money there than she ever could have here, my mother was still in a deep depression about my father's death, and it would've been hard to explain why we needed to keep sharing a room with Elsie's room empty. So, as much as I missed her and she missed me, part of me recognized that it would just be too emotionally difficult for her to be in our house."

"That must've been so hard." Julie frowned. "I am going to get my happy ending, right?"

Diz poked Julie. "You already know the answer, why do you keep asking me?"

"Because I want you to be happy. I want you two to be together."

"You're a hopeless romantic."

"I am, and I make no apologies for that. But I suspect underneath all your bluster, you are too. I just want you to get the girl."

"I already had the girl, remember?"

"But you were living thousands of miles apart. That hardly counts."

"Well, it counted for us, as difficult as it was." Diz closed her eyes. "I really do need a rest, dear."

"I'm sorry." Julie jumped up and released the brakes on the chair. "I'll take you back right now. That was selfish of me."

Diz reached back and patted Julie's hand. "I love that you care about us."

Julie rolled Diz up a slight incline. "So, when did Frannie come home?"

"Sounds to me like a good place to start next time."

CHAPTER TWENTY-ONE

Phoenix, 1947

Diz sealed the box closed and swiped her forearm across her brow to keep the sweat from dripping into her eyes. She surveyed her mother's bedroom and the remaining stacks of clothes and groaned.

"Theodora? I need you to..." Mrs. Hosler bustled into the room, stopped, and put her hands on her hips. "Oh, dear. I guess I never realized how many clothes I had."

"No kidding." Diz dragged over another box and began loading piles of slacks into it. "What did you need, Mother?"

"Pete and Elsie will be here soon. I was going to ask you to make sure their room was ready."

"It is."

"I really don't like the idea of her driving all this way in her condition."

"We've been over this before. They decided it was better for her to make the drive than to be home alone, in case anything happened. Which it won't," Diz hastened to add. "She's still almost two months away from her due date."

"I'm going to be a grandmother." Mrs. Hosler's voice was filled with wonder. She sat on the one open space on the bed. "I just wish your father was here to see it." Her voice broke on a sob.

Diz paused in her packing and hugged her mother awkwardly. They still weren't accustomed to showing affection toward each other, but Diz was trying to make more of an effort. "I know. I wish he was too."

Mrs. Hosler cleared her throat. "He would be very proud of you, you know."

"He would?" Diz leaned back so that she could see her mother's face.

"Of course he would. He always wanted you to get a degree and make something of yourself. You were so fiercely independent. We both knew you would need to be able to support yourself. It will take a very special man to be able to keep up with you. I can't imagine it."

Diz made a conscious effort not to stiffen, nor to react in any way.

"That's why I wish Frannie would come home. I don't like the idea of you being all alone in this house. It's not right."

"I'll be fine, Mother." Diz wasn't sure she should trust her hearing. Her mother wanted Frannie and her to live together? Her stomach fluttered happily at the thought.

"And she shouldn't be so far away. I know you two miss each other. We're her family now. Family sticks together."

"I'll talk to her about it."

"You will? Good." Mrs. Hosler smoothed her dress. "Do you think I should talk to her? Would she listen to me?"

Diz's eyes widened at the suggestion. "I don't know, Mother. Why don't you let me talk to her first."

"Very well." She touched her palm to Diz's face. "Are you sure you'll be all right?"

"I will."

"I'm going to call you to check up on you."

"I know."

"Oh." Mrs. Hosler abruptly stood up. "This is impossible. I feel like I'm abandoning you to run off and play with my grandchild."

"Don't feel that way, Mother. I don't look at it like that at all. I think it's great that you're going to live with Elsie and Pete. You can have all the time you want with the baby, and that will really help Elsie out. She needs you."

"Are you sure?"

"We've already had this conversation. I'm positive. I'll be fine. I want you to go. And I promise you that I'll take excellent care of this place."

"I know you will. You've been such a help these past few years. I can hardly believe how grown up you are."

"I'm twenty-two. I'll be fine."

"I hear Dallas is so dreary in March."

"It's almost April, Mother. The blooms will be coming out any time now."

"I suppose you're right. And who will have time to notice with the baby coming? There's so much to prepare. I don't think your sister has any idea what she's in for."

"Probably not, so I'm sure she'll be grateful to have you there to help out."

"I won't have any idea about what?" Elsie stood in the doorway, her belly impossibly large and round.

"You're here!" Mrs. Hosler enveloped her in a heartfelt hug. "Let me look at you." She stepped back and held Elsie at arm's length. "You're radiant."

"She's right about that." Diz took her turn hugging Elsie. "You look fantastic."

"You look too thin. Still. Why aren't you eating, Sis?"

"I am eating. Why does everybody think I'm not eating?"

"Well, I hope you've figured out how to cook if you're going to be on your own."

"I'll be just fine. You both need to stop worrying about me."

"It's a sign of love," Elsie said.

Pete came up alongside his wife and put a proprietary arm around her waist. "Who was talking about love?"

"I was." Elsie gazed with naked adoration at her husband, and Diz was struck by how perfect they were together.

Her heart ached with longing for Frannie. Were they as obviously in love as Elsie and Pete? On the one hand, she hoped it wasn't that plainly written on their faces. On the other hand, she hoped they still felt for each other everything these two did.

It had been months since they'd seen each other last—Christmas, to be exact, when Frannie came home to spend the holidays with them. Diz wasn't sure how much more she could take of being apart like this. Especially now that she was going to be on her own in this big house.

"Sis?"

"Huh?" Diz mentally shook herself.

"I asked, how's school going?"

"Oh, it's going good. Lots of studying and reading."

"I know you don't mind the reading part. You always had your head stuck in a book."

"But that was reading for pleasure. This is different."

"Yes, it is. But I bet you're the smartest student in the class." Elsie looked up at Pete. "My little sister was always the smartest kid in any room."

Her voice was full of pride. It reminded Diz of those early days on the Ramblers when Diz was sure she was going to be cut in favor of Frannie and Elsie gave her pep talks. They'd come a long way since then.

"Pete, why don't you go help Mother finish packing up the sewing room? I'll help Sis in here."

When they were alone, Elsie said, "How are you doing, really? I know we don't get to talk much, but Mother says you're always alone."

"That's not true. You know I hang out with the girls up at South Mountain and out at Blue Point, and the season's going to start in a couple of months."

"Speaking of softball, what happened to you guys? Since when do you go two years in a row without making the national tournament?"

"Don't remind me. Sore subject."

"Is everything okay on the team?"

"Yeah, sure. We'll be fine. We've got the usual suspects coming back this year. It's those damned Jax. The Savona sisters and Nina Korgan...they're hard to beat."

"I know."

"We'll get 'em this time."

"You'd have a better chance if Frannie would just come home."

Diz sighed. Not Elsie too. "I've tried to convince her to come back. It wouldn't matter for this year, anyway. She'd have to sit out a year to get her eligibility back as an amateur."

"Well, she should do it."

"I'll be sure to tell her you said so." Diz picked up another pile of slacks and placed them in the box. "How about you? Everything all right?"

"You mean, except for the fact that I'm fat as a house and can't see my own feet? Everything's great."

"Thank you, again, for making a place for Mother. She really needs this. It's all she's been talking about."

"I should be the one thanking you. Thank you for taking care of her for so long. Thank you for putting your dreams on hold to do it, thank you for holding down the fort when I know you would rather have been off doing something else. I owe you."

"No, you don't."

"I won't argue with you about it, but I will say this. I'm so glad you're my little Sis." Elsie put her arm around Diz's shoulder.

"Don't go getting all mushy on me."

"Heaven forbid. Oh." Elsie put her hand to her stomach.

"What? What is it? Is something—"

"Put your hand here." Elsie guided Diz's hand to her belly. "Do you feel that?"

"Wow!" Diz's face lit up with wonder. "That's a powerful kick."

"Uh-huh. Pete thinks we're going to have a ball player on our hands. He's convinced it's a boy and that he's going to be the next Ted Williams."

"I'd rather he was Dizzy Dean." Diz placed her ear against Elsie's belly. "Are you in there, Dizzy? What are your mama and daddy going to do if you're a girl?"

Elsie laughed. "She could be the next Dot Wilkinson."

"She could be," Diz agreed. She resumed packing. "Get to work, Mama. We've got a lot to do before you guys leave in the morning."

They worked side-by-side in companionable silence until every article of clothing was safely tucked in a box.

Elsie picked up one of the boxes.

"Stop!" Diz yelled. "What are you doing?"

"Taking a box out to the porch so the moving van can pick it up."

"Put that down." Diz took the box from her. "Are you crazy? You're seven months pregnant. You shouldn't be lifting like that."

"You're worse than a mother hen. I'm fine."

"You may be fine, but you're not carrying heavy boxes. I'll do it. I'm sure Pete will help." Diz carried the box out to the front porch and returned for the next one. "How in the world did you convince a Texas moving company to come all this way to move Mother?"

"Armstrong just started up this year. They move people all around the country. It was just luck that they're based in Texas."

"It must be costing you a fortune."

"It's not too bad. And don't you worry about it. It's not your concern." Elsie lowered herself to the bed. "I feel like such a lump. My ankles are so swollen."

"Stop complaining."

"You're right. We've been trying ever since our wedding night to get pregnant. I can't believe how long it took us. I thought it would just…happen."

"Well, it's happening now."

"It sure is."

⋖⋗

Phoenix, 2014

"Was it a boy or a girl?" Julie asked. She passed Diz the ketchup for her burger.

"It was a healthy baby boy, born May the 4th, 1947. They named him Theodore, for my father, but they called him Teddy."

"Aww. That's so sweet."

"I like to say they named him for me too."

"Did they?"

Diz laughed. "No. But I like to pretend." She took a bite of a French fry and glanced around the diner. "This place reminds me a little of the diner Frannie and I used to go to. I like it."

"Speaking of Frannie…"

"How did I know you were going to work the conversation around to that?"

"Come on. Your mother moved to Texas to be with your sister and the baby. Please tell me Frannie stopped being so pig-headed and came home. I mean, you had the whole place to yourselves. You didn't have to hide anymore."

"Ah-ah." Diz pointed a finger at Julie. "We always had to pretend back then. People who didn't know us thought we were sisters."

"But you didn't look anything alike."

"No, we sure didn't. But that didn't matter. We were always together. That's the way it worked. If you spent that much time together, why, you must be family." Diz ate another fry.

"So, back to my question…"

"You had a question?"

"Aargh! You're maddening."

"So you keep saying. It's just so much fun to tease you. I can't seem to help myself."

"Frannie. You. An empty house. 1947." Julie motioned with her hand, encouraging Diz to pick up the story.

"Okay, I'll take pity on you."

"Thank you. Finally."

Diz laughed. "I had been alone in the house for a couple of weeks. It was April 1st—April Fool's Day. I'll never forget it, because I thought it was a joke."

Phoenix, 1947

"Hello?"

"Hi there. I'm looking for my girl. Maybe you've seen her? Not too tall, really adorable, but too thin?"

"Hm. I might've seen her around here somewhere."

On the other end of the line, Frannie laughed and Diz smiled into the phone.

"Why are you calling me? What's wrong?"

"Does something have to be wrong?"

"No, but we're not due to speak until tomorrow. It's only Tuesday."

"Don't be so rigid. Can't I just call my girl to say hello because I miss her?"

"You could, but generally you don't."

"True, but I'm making an exception."

"Why?"

"So suspicious."

"Well, it's April Fool's Day."

"I forgot about that," Frannie said.

"I don't believe you."

"Okay. Let's see if you believe this. I quit the Belles, I quit Apex, and I'm coming home to you, if you'll have me."

Diz blinked. Surely Frannie didn't just say...

"Diz? Say something." Frannie's voice was edging toward panic. "Tell me I didn't just—"

"You're serious?"

"Cross my heart."

"You're not just trying to—"

"I'm more serious than I've ever been in my life. I was just sitting there, at my desk, typing something for my boss, and it hit me like a ton of bricks."

"What hit you?" Diz croaked.

"I hate my job at Apex. I love softball, but I don't want to play this half-softball, half-baseball game they're playing—that's not real softball. They're leaving next month for spring training in Havana, Cuba, and I don't want to go. All I want to do is come home and be with you."

Diz slid down the wall and onto the floor. For so long she'd been praying to hear these words. Now that Frannie was saying them, she wasn't sure she should trust it.

"Tiger? Please, say something here."

"Yes." It was the only word Diz could formulate.

"Yes?"

Diz swallowed hard as tears of joy threatened to spill from her eyes. "Yes. Please come home. Now. Today. Yes. A thousand times, yes."

"Okay, then."

"Okay." There was silence on the line.

"Diz? Are you still there?"

"Uh-huh."

"Why aren't you saying anything?"

"Why aren't you already in a car on your way here?"

Frannie laughed. "Soon, sweetheart. Very, very soon."

Phoenix, 2014

Julie sighed happily. Smiling broadly, she sat with her chin on her hands. "That's the most romantic thing I think I've ever heard."

"You don't get out much, do you?" Diz joked.

"Don't ruin this moment. It's beautiful. Frannie came home to you."

"My girl came home," Diz agreed.

Julie frowned.

"Now what?"

"Didn't you say she couldn't play for the Ramblers for a whole year after she quit the Belles?"

"That's right."

"She must've been miserable, having to sit on the sidelines and watch you gals play without her."

"She wasn't happy, that's for sure. Especially at the national championship game."

"What happened there?"

"We were playing the Jax, of course. I remember that it was freezing that night—forty-nine degrees. Even the fans were shivering. And there we were, out there in our short-shorts and uniform tops. I don't ever recall being as cold as I was during that game. I kept blowing on my throwing hand in the outfield to warm it up." Diz shook her head.

"Three times we had the lead. Three times." She held up three fingers. "And three times we lost it. In the end, we lost the game and the championship, six to four."

"Ouch."

"It was heartbreaking and demoralizing. We had such a good team that year."

"That must've been hard to come back from."

"It was the damnedest year though."

"What do you mean?" Julie asked.

"We got home from the tournament, and the bigwigs from the ASA—the Amateur Softball Association—had a meeting. Before the tournament, the Jax announced that they were going to turn professional after the tournament was over. So the ASA executive committee got together and voted to strip them of the championship."

"But they weren't professionals when they beat you, were they?"

"Nope. That's the thing. It didn't make any sense." Diz shrugged. "So, two days after we got home from the tournament, the ASA awarded us the championship."

"That's great. So you won."

Diz shook her head. "Not really. And none of us felt as though we'd won. After all, we blew the lead three separate times." Diz took a sip of water. "We had our picture taken with the trophy and everything, and then they changed their minds."

"What do you mean?"

"I mean the ASA changed their minds and reinstated the Jax as champions for 1947."

"That's insane."

"Yeah, but it's true."

"So you still hadn't won a championship since you joined the Ramblers."

"Nope. And I badly wanted one."

"I bet."

"The good news was, we were getting Frannie back for 1948, and the Jax were ineligible to play, since they'd turned professional."

"Oh, the plot thickens!"

CHAPTER TWENTY-TWO

Phoenix, 1948

L isten up," Dot said. She was pacing in the cramped locker room. "We've worked too hard in this tournament to go home empty-handed. We let these gals beat us once and push us into the losers' bracket. I know this is Portland's home field and almost every voice in those stands is going to be cheering for them. But, if we can get to them tonight, we earn the right to play 'em again tomorrow night for the championship. Who's with me?"

"We are!"

"All right. Hands in. On three. One. Two. Three."

"Ramblers!"

Diz, Frannie, and the rest of the girls piled out of the locker room, up the dugout steps, and onto the field. They were greeted by the boos of more than seven thousand Portland fans.

By the fourth inning, with the game still scoreless, Diz was getting a little nervous.

"Hey." Frannie came up alongside her in the dugout. "Stop worrying."

"How do you know I'm worrying?"

"Because I know you. We've got this. Watch. I promise."

Diz had to admit that Amy was pitching a great game—her fourth in a row. But the hits just weren't coming.

"This is our inning," Zada shouted. "C'mon, Ramblers. Here we go!"

Amy stepped up to the plate to lead it off. She smacked a single right up the middle past Portland pitcher Betty Evans.

"That's what I'm talking about," Peanuts shouted. "Let's go, Dobbie!"

Dobbie dutifully sliced another single to the left side. That brought up Frannie.

"You can do it, Frannie!" Margie called.

"C'mon, Frannie. C'mon, Frannie." Diz stood in the on-deck circle chanting it to herself.

Frannie took two balls and a strike. On the fourth pitch, she cracked a line drive single over the head of the leaping shortstop. Amy took off on contact. She rounded third and headed for home. The throw from the cutoff was on line. Diz, who was still standing in the on-deck circle, hollered, "Down!"

Amy slid hard, dislodging the ball from the catcher's mitt.

"Safe!" the umpire yelled.

"Yeah!" Diz slapped Amy on the butt. She headed for the batter's box and surveyed the field. Dobbie and Frannie had both advanced on the throw home, so first base was open with runners on second and third.

"Like you can, Diz!" Dot shouted.

"Show 'em where you live, Diz!" Jean yelled.

Diz rolled her shoulders and dug her cleats into the dirt. She intentionally let the first pitch go by for strike one. She preferred never to swing at a first pitch if she could help it. The second pitch was way outside, moving the count to one-and-one.

"This one's got your name on it," Diz mumbled to herself. She locked in on Betty Evans' motion, waited, kept her hands back, stepped in with her lead leg, and nailed the ball with the sweet spot of the bat. She tossed the bat aside and hustled down the first base line, peeking up to see the ball headed deep to center field.

The center fielder turned and ran back, back, peeked over her shoulder, stepped all the way to the warning track, turned, and made the catch.

Frannie, who had tagged at third, barreled toward home plate. She slid, cleats high, knocking the catcher out of the way. Two to nothing, Ramblers.

Amy shut Portland down the rest of the way, and the Ramblers earned the right to play for the national championship.

"Good job out there tonight, ladies," Mr. Hoffman said. "I'm proud of you. But we're not done yet. Tomorrow night is going to be harder than tonight. The crowd will be bigger and louder, the stakes will be higher. You know all this. You don't need me to tell you. Dot? You take it from here."

"Okay. No partying tonight. No late night. No celebrating." She looked at every girl in turn. "We'll save that for tomorrow night when we whip 'em again. Let's go get some dinner, turn in early, and be at our best tomorrow night. Ready? On three. One. Two. Three."

"Ramblers!"

Delores Low, a young second-year player, walked out with Diz and Frannie. "That was some game, huh?"

"Sure was," Diz agreed.

"What was it like when you played them in '44?"

"Pretty much the same. They're a good, solid team. They're not the Jax, but we sure can't take them for granted." Diz glanced at Frannie. She wondered if Frannie, like her, was thinking about their hotel-room rendezvous during that tournament. She smiled. Thank God they didn't have to worry about a long-distance romance anymore.

Living together made so many things easier. No longer did they have to sneak off and steal kisses, or drive to the middle of nowhere, or worry about sleeping arrangements while they were on the road. Because they lived together, everyone assumed they should room together for away games. The hardest part for Diz was remembering not to throw an arm across Frannie's waist in the middle of the night.

When they took the field the next night, the Ramblers were all business. For the first four innings, Betty Evans stymied every hitter in the lineup except for Dobbie. Twice she got stranded on base.

Diz came into the dugout from the outfield for the top of the fifth. She looked up and down the bench at all the glum faces, and knew she had to say something.

"Hey! I don't know about the rest of you, but I'm tired of watching another team celebrate at the end of this tournament every year. This is our time. This is our year." She jabbed a finger in the air for emphasis. "Now let's get up there and wail on that ball. C'mon. Who's with me?"

A dozen set of shocked eyes stared at her nonplussed. The only one who apparently wasn't surprised by the outburst, was Frannie. She winked.

"Well? Who's with me?" Diz repeated. "Ramblers, on three. One. Two. Three."

"Ramblers!"

"That's better." Diz threw her glove on the bench and sat down.

Frannie came and sat next to her. "That was some speech."

"Well, it needed to be said."

"It did."

"So why shouldn't I be the one to say it?"

"Why, indeed," Frannie agreed.

"So, you think it was all right?"

Frannie threw back her head and laughed. "I think it was aces."

Dobbie once again led off with a single.

"Just like that," Zada shouted to Dot, after Betty Harris, the second baseman, sacrificed Dobbie to second.

"Here we go, Dot!"

Dot stared down the pitcher. But Betty Evans was a veteran. She'd shut down the Ramblers in '44 for Portland's first championship, and she wasn't about to be rattled by a runner in scoring position. She went into her windup, and let loose a vicious rise ball that backed Dot off the plate.

Undeterred, Dot stepped back in. This time, Evans threw a drop ball. Dot stayed with the pitch and stroked it to right field for a base hit. That moved Dobbie to third—the Ramblers' most serious scoring threat of the game.

After another out, Margie stepped to the plate with two down. "This one's on you, Margie. Show 'em how it's done."

As she'd been doing for many years, Margie came through with another single. Dobbie crossed home plate with the game's first run, Dot slid safely into third, and Margie stood on first.

"That's what I'm talking about!" Diz jumped up and down at the dugout railing.

Amy followed Margie and pounded yet another hit, chasing Dot home and advancing Margie to second.

That brought Frannie to the plate. "Keep it going!" Peanuts called.

"Lots of room out there," Delores yelled.

Evans ran the count to one-and-two on Frannie.

"C'mon, c'mon, c'mon," Diz chanted quietly in the on-deck circle.

The pitch came in, belt-high, and Frannie smashed it hard up the middle, right back at the pitcher. Evans, always an excellent fielder, made the stop, turned, saw Margie heading for third, and let loose the throw. It sailed over the third baseman's head, allowing Margie to score.

Those three runs in the fifth were exactly what the Ramblers needed.

In the bottom of the seventh inning, with two outs, Portland slugger Roberta Mulkey came to the plate and blasted a long fly ball to center. Diz had trouble picking it up off the bat.

She heard Frannie yelling at her, "Back, back, left, back."

Diz turned and ran, angled slightly left, and turned around, praying that she would pick up the ball in the air. And there it was. She was slightly out of position, so she dove, her right arm fully extended, glove open. As she slammed against the hard ground, she felt all the air rush out of her lungs. When she came to rest several feet away, the ball was firmly cradled in the pocket of her glove.

Game over.

Diz felt arms encircle her and lift her up. Her teammates mobbed her in the outfield. People pounded her on the back, ruffled her hair, and slapped her on the butt.

All the while, she tried to catch her breath.

"You did it, champ." Frannie's mouth was close to Diz's ear.

"We did it." She grabbed Frannie and hugged her hard, twirling her around, and surprising a delighted laugh out of her.

The Phoenix Ramblers were the 1948 world champions. Diz and Frannie were champions.

꧁꧂

Phoenix, 2014

"You did it. You won the championship." Julie clapped.

"We did, two years running, in fact. We beat Portland in 1949 too."

"Now that's what I call a happy ending."

"Are you satisfied now?" Diz asked. "Turn here," she motioned to the left as Julie turned on her blinker.

"You got the girl, you won the trophy, and you got a happily ever after. Yes, I'm satisfied."

"Good."

"But where are you taking me?"

"I thought you might enjoy a little trip down memory lane with me. Plus, you promised to use those massive muscles of yours to help me with a few things, remember?"

"I do."

"Turn right and slow down."

Julie did as instructed.

"There." Diz pointed to the right. "Pull into that driveway."

"Whose house is this?" Julie asked. The house was two-story and looked to have been built a long time ago. The only modification appeared to be a handicapped ramp leading up to the front door.

"Welcome home." Diz beamed at Julie from the passenger's seat.

"What?"

"I thought you might like to see the place where so much of my story took place. This is my home. This is the home my parents raised me and Elsie in. It's the home Frannie and I shared for sixty years."

"It's…" Julie's eyes grew wide.

"Yep, it is." Diz unbuckled her seatbelt. "Come on, I'll show you around."

Julie opened her trunk, removed the wheelchair, unfolded it, and brought it around to the passenger door. With a little assistance, Diz lifted herself and transferred from the car to the wheelchair.

"Let's go inside first."

Julie pushed her up the ramp and to the front door. Diz's hand shook as she tried to put the key in the lock.

"Can I do that?"

"Damned old age." Reluctantly, Diz handed the key to Julie.

"How long has it been since you've been in here?" When Julie pushed open the door and wheeled Diz through, she was surprised that it didn't smell nearly as musty as she thought it might.

"Since I fell in the tub about a year ago. But I pay someone to come by and clean the place and keep it up."

"Why don't you sell it?"

"Sell it? Sell the place where all my memories are? No." Diz shook her head. "I can't do that."

"What will happen to it when…"

"When I die? It'll go to Teddy. He can do with it whatever he wants, but as long as I'm alive, it will remain exactly as is."

"Teddy? Elsie and Pete's son?" Julie asked.

"Yep."

"How old—"

"He's sixty-seven now. Got kids and grandkids of his own. He's a good man. He was a pilot for Southwest Airlines until he had to retire a few years ago. He kept up the proud family tradition. I guess it was in his blood."

"Does he live locally?"

"No. He's in Dallas, where he grew up."

"Are Elsie and Pete…?"

"Except for Teddy and his family, everybody else is gone—my mother, Elsie, Pete, Frannie. They're all gone. I'm the last one standing. Or in this case, sitting."

Diz pointed to her left. "That's the parlor where my mother and father used to sit every night. It looks pretty much the same as it did, except Frannie and I updated the furniture."

Diz maneuvered the wheelchair to the right. "If you want to run up those stairs, the first bedroom you'll come to is Mother's room, then Elsie's room, then mine."

Julie climbed the stairs to the second floor. "Wow. It's just like you described it," she called down.

"I certainly hope so. I lived here long enough. I should be able to remember what everything looks like."

"I love the woodwork."

"Best part of the house."

Julie bounded halfway down the stairs and stopped.

"What is it?"

"Nothing. I'm just envisioning a young Diz doing the same thing, or Frannie. This is so cool."

"I'm glad you think so." Diz wheeled herself back toward the front door. Now we've got a little work to do."

"What do you need?" Julie asked. She came the rest of the way down the stairs.

"We need to go out to the barn."

"The barn where you and Frannie—"

"That's enough of that, young lady. Yes, that barn. The barn where my father kept his car."

CHAPTER TWENTY-THREE

Phoenix, 2014

Julie slid open the door. "Is there a light in here?"

"On the wall to your right."

Julie flipped the light switch. "What is all this stuff?" In the corner was a desk and an office chair. Several filing cabinets lined the walls, along with bookshelves filled with hardcover books.

"This 'stuff,' as you call it, was my life." Diz lifted her feet off the footrest and put them on the ground.

"I thought we talked about that," Julie said. She rushed over and steadied the chair.

"I need to get closer to that cabinet over there." Diz pointed.

"Okay, I'll wheel you there."

"This chair is too damned bulky for this space. I can walk."

"No. Please, Diz. I don't want to worry about you and I don't want you to fall. I can get whatever you need."

Diz relented and resettled herself in the chair. "Okay. Open that cabinet and bring over the stack of papers and scrapbooks that are inside. And be careful. That stuff is a lot older than you are."

Julie opened the cabinet and pulled out a pile of old papers and scrapbooks. She laid them at Diz's feet. "There's something else in there." She stuck her head in the cabinet. "It looks like an old lock box or jewelry box. Do you want me to bring that too?"

"Let me see it," Diz said.

Julie liberated the box from its cubbyhole and brought it to Diz. "What is it?"

Diz turned the wooden box in her hands, examining it from every angle. "I have no idea. It isn't mine."

"It's not?"

"Nope."

"Could it be your mother's?"

"I don't think so." Diz blew the dust off the top. The corner of the box was singed, as though it had been in a fire. "Oh." Diz put a hand to her heart.

"Are you all right?" Julie put a hand on Diz's shoulder. "Diz? What is it?"

In a hushed whisper, she said, "This must've been Frannie's. She told me once that her keepsake box was the only thing the firemen were able to salvage from the fire at her parents' house. I had no idea she kept it."

"You didn't know it was here?"

"No. She must've grabbed it that day we made a run for it from her aunt and uncle's house." Diz stroked the top of the box.

"Do you want me to put it back?" Julie reached out for the box. "I mean, if it's too painful—"

"No." Diz held the box to her chest and closed her eyes. "Frannie and I had no secrets from each other. I'm sure there's nothing in here that will cause me pain. It's just a shock, that's all."

"Do you want me to give you some time alone with it?" Julie turned to go.

"No." Diz put a gnarled hand on Julie's arm. "No. I think we should look at it together. It's an adventure."

"You're sure?"

"Sure I'm sure. Let's take it inside and we can lay it out on the dining room table."

Julie replaced the papers and scrapbooks in the filing cabinet, then wheeled Diz back inside, the box still firmly in Diz's grasp.

"Help me up. I don't want to be in the chair for this."

Julie supported Diz under the arm while Diz leaned heavily against her.

Clumsily, Diz placed the box on the table and sat down in one of the dining room chairs. "Damned ball-player fingers." She fumbled with the latch.

"Do you want me to get that?"

"No. I think I should be the one to open it." After several more fruitless tries, Diz finally was able to undo the catch. "Are you ready for this?" She looked solemnly at Julie who stood off to the side.

"I'm ready if you're ready."

"Right. Okay, Frannie. What was so valuable that you kept it all those years?"

Diz lifted the lid and peered inside. "Huh."

"What's in it?"

"Come over here and we'll take it out, item by item."

Julie came next to Diz. "A dog collar?"

"Looks like it. Frannie said she had a puppy she loved very much. I wonder if he was killed in the fire." Diz dug her hand into the box again and came out with a little charm bracelet. She held it up to the light so that she could see the charms. One of them was a softball glove. She smiled.

Diz peered back into the box. She lifted out a partially charred photograph. In it, a happily smiling couple stood with their arms around each other, a young girl in front of them. They each had their free hand on the girl's shoulders.

"What are you looking at now?"

"I'm guessing these are Frannie's parents. She rarely brought them up, and she never showed me a picture."

"They're a handsome couple."

"Yes, they are. No wonder they created such a beautiful daughter."

The next thing Diz pulled out was some thin writing paper. "This is the kind of paper we used when we were kids." Carefully, she unfolded the pages as Julie looked over her shoulder.

"It's a letter," Julie said. "Maybe we shouldn't read it."

"Nonsense. Like I said, Frannie and I had no secrets from each other." Diz motioned to her bag. "Get me my glasses, will you? This print is too small."

Julie handed Diz her reading glasses.

"My dearest Francine," Diz read. "Oh, my. This is starting off well." She pushed the glasses farther up on the bridge of her nose. "I count the minutes until we're done with classes so that we can be alone to study together. I watch you twirl your hair around your finger and I wish I was the one doing that." Diz put the letter down.

"A-are you all right?"

"I am now. Back then I might not have been."

"It sounds a lot like a love letter."

"In an adolescent-we-have-no-idea-what-we're-doing kind of way, it was." Diz shook her head.

"You know who this is from?"

"I have a good idea, yes."

When nothing more was forthcoming, Julie said, "You're going to share, right?"

"Do you remember when I told you about the night of the fire at Frannie's house? The night she wasn't home?"

"Of course."

"Do you remember where she was?"

"She was at her best frien—"" Julie's eyes widened. "This is from that friend she was kissing? The girl whose parents blamed her for the fire and for perverting their daughter?"

"Looks like it."

"What was her name?" Julie asked.

"Hazel." Diz picked up the letter again. When she did, an old black and white photograph fell out and fluttered to the floor. She started to bend over.

"I'll get it," Julie said, and scooped it up. Her fingers started to tremble and she put a hand to her mouth.

"What's the matter? You look like you saw a ghost."

Julie stood stock still. Finally, she put the picture on the table and slid it toward Diz. "That picture. It's my mother."

"What?"

"That's my mother in the picture with her arm around that girl."

Diz peered at the photograph. "That girl is my Frannie." Diz turned over the picture to see the handwriting on the back. "Hazel and Francine, forever." The picture was dated 1936. "Was your mother's name Hazel?"

Julie shook her head. "The only thing she ever told me was that she didn't like her given name. So she went by Elizabeth. She even had it legally changed. So Elizabeth is all I ever knew. In the Queens lineup in 1940, which is apparently the only year she played, she's listed as Elizabeth. That's what's on her gravestone too."

"What did your father call her?"

"Liz."

"But you're certain that's your mother in the picture with Frannie."

"Positive." Julie sat down. "I've got other pictures of her at that age."

"Are you okay?"

Julie shrugged. "I don't know what I am. This is crazy. My mother was kissing a girl when she was fourteen, and not just any girl, but your girl. And why would my mother have changed her name? What was wrong with Hazel?"

"I wish I knew." Diz started to return the items to the box. She paused when she picked up the letter from Hazel to Frannie and started to read again.

"Please, read it aloud," Julie said.

Diz lowered the letter. "Are you sure you want to know?"

"I've come this far, I think I have to know."

"Okay, then. 'I know I shouldn't feel the way I do about you, but I can't help it. I hope you feel it too. Sonny wants me to go steady with him, but when he says my name, it sounds almost dirty. You're the only one I ever want whispering my name in my ear. If I can't have that for the rest of my life, I think I might die. Okay, maybe that was too dramatic, but it's the truth. Always yours, Hazel.'"

"Well, that explains why she changed her name," Julie muttered. "I never knew. Heck, I'm sure my father never knew."

Diz folded the letter again, started to put it back in the box, and held it out to Julie instead. "I believe this belongs to you, if you want it."

"No," Julie said quietly. "It was meant for Frannie. You should keep it."

Diz lovingly placed the letter and all of the other items back into the box and managed to close the latch on the first try.

"I'm glad, at least, that we solved your mystery."

"Do you really think my mother was gay? Or was she experimenting?" Julie asked.

"I can't answer that. Does it matter?"

Julie shook her head. "I guess not."

Diz looked at her watch. "We need to get going. We're going to be late."

"We have someplace we need to be at a certain time?" Julie asked.

"I promised Dot we'd meet her at the cemetery at two o'clock. It's almost that now."

"Oh."

"If you don't want to now—"

"No. It'll be fine. I'd love to see Dot again. It's just…today has been a lot to take in."

"I know." Diz pushed up out of the chair and Julie moved behind her to support her as she transferred back into the wheelchair.

Both women were silent for most of the drive.

"Do you think my mother hid her Queens uniform because she was afraid people would think she was gay? Was the stigma about softball players that powerful?" Julie asked as she drove through the cemetery gates.

"I can't answer that either. I can tell you that many, many players who would've or should've been gay, got married because it was what was expected of them."

"If that's true of my mother, that would be so sad."

"It was just a reality in our time."

They came to a stop near Frannie's grave, and Julie got Diz situated in the wheelchair. Dot pulled up a moment later.

"Hey there, you." Dot leaned over and gave Diz a warm hug. "It's good to see you."

"You too, Dot. Gosh. You look great—like you could still get out there and play."

"I don't know about that, although sometimes I think about it." Dot ambled over and gave Julie a hug and a kiss. "It's good to see you again."

"You too, Dot. I can't thank you enough for introducing me to Diz."

"She's a pip, isn't she?"

"She sure is."

"She wasn't always this way, you know. She was a shy one for a long time."

"Stop talking about me like I'm not here."

"Who do you want to visit first? Ricki or Frannie?" Dot asked.

"Ricki's buried here too?" Julie asked.

"Yep. Not far from Frannie, either. All of us ball players got plots close to each other. We were a family when we were alive, we figured we'd stay a family after we were gone."

"Let's go see Ricki first," Diz said.

From her car, Dot retrieved the bouquet of flowers she'd brought for her girl. Julie pushed Diz's chair and Dot walked alongside.

They arrived at Ricki's grave, and Dot walked to the headstone and put her hand on it. "Ricki, I brought you some friends today. You know our Diz, of course, and this here is Julie." Dot bent and arranged the fresh flowers on top of the grave. "These are for you. I hope you like them. I love you and I still miss you every day. I know you know that, but I just like to come here and tell you so."

After a few minutes of silent reflection, the trio moved on to Frannie's grave. Julie helped Diz stand as she had done the last time they'd made this trip.

"Hey there, sweetheart. I finished telling Julie our story today. She loved the happy ending." Diz sighed. "I miss you, Frannie. I know it's been a long time, but you're as much my girl today as you were all the way back at the beginning."

Diz leaned over and kissed the headstone. Then she shuffled back the few steps to the wheelchair and sat down. "It's a helluva thing, isn't it?"

"What is?" Dot asked, as they headed back toward their cars.

"You and I, we're just about the only ones left, except for Dobbie."

"We are."

"Don't you ever get the feeling that we're missing a helluva good game up there?"

"Ramblers on three," Dot said. "One, two, three."

Together, Dot, Diz, and Julie said, "Ramblers!"

"We'll get 'em when we get there, my friend," Dot said. "You know we will."

THE END

All-American Girls Baseball League Rules of Conduct

THE MANAGEMENT SETS A HIGH STANDARD FOR THE GIRLS SELECTED FOR THE DIFFERENT CLUBS AND EXPECTS THEM TO LIVE UP TO THE CODE OF CONDUCT WHICH RECOGNIZES THAT STANDARD. THERE ARE GENERAL REGULATIONS NECESSARY AS A MEANS OF MAINTAINING ORDER AND ORGANIZING CLUBS INTO A WORKING PROCEDURE.

1. ALWAYS appear in feminine attire when not actively engaged in practice or playing ball. This regulation continues through the playoffs for all, even though your team is not participating. AT NO TIME MAY A PLAYER APPEAR IN THE STANDS IN HER UNIFORM, OR WEAR SLACKS OR SHORTS IN PUBLIC.

2. Boyish bobs are not permissible and in general your hair should be well groomed at all times with longer hair preferable to short hair cuts. Lipstick should always be on.

3. Smoking or drinking is not permissible in public places. Liquor drinking will not be permissible under any circumstances. Other intoxicating drinks in limited portions with after-game meal only, will be allowed. Obscene language will not be allowed at any time.

4. All social engagements must be approved by chaperone. Legitimate requests for dates can be allowed by chaperones.

5. Jewelry must not be worn during game or practice, regardless of type.

6. All living quarters and eating places must be approved by the chaperones. No player shall change her residence without the permission of the chaperone.

7. For emergency purposes, it is necessary that you leave notice of your whereabouts and your home phone.

8. Each club will establish a satisfactory place to eat, and a time when all members must be in their individual rooms. In general, the lapse of time will be two hours after the finish of the last game, but in no case later than 12:30 a.m. Players must respect hotel regulations as to other guests after this hour, maintaining conduct in accordance with high standards set by the league.

9. Always carry your employee's pass as a means of identification for entering the various parks. This pass is NOT transferable.

10. Relatives, friends, and visitors are not allowed on the bench at any time.

11. Due to shortage of equipment, baseballs must not be given as souvenirs without permission from the Management.

12. Baseball uniform skirts shall not be shorter than six inches above the knee-cap.

13. In order to sustain the complete spirit of rivalry between clubs, the members of different clubs must not fraternize at any time during the season. After the opening day of the season, fraternizing will be subject to heavy penalties. This also means in particular, room parties, auto trips to out-of-the-way eating places, etc. However, friendly discussions in lobbies with opposing players are permissible. Players should never approach the opposing manager or chaperone about being transferred.

14. When traveling, the members of the clubs must be at the station thirty minutes before departure time. Anyone missing her arranged transportation will have to pay her own fare.

15. Players will not be allowed to drive their cars past their city's limits without the special permission of their manager. Each team will travel as a unit via method of travel provided for the league.

FINES OF FIVE DOLLARS FOR FIRST OFFENSE, TEN DOLLARS FOR SECOND, AND SUSPENSION FOR THIRD, WILL AUTOMATICALLY BE IMPOSED FOR BREAKING ANY OF THE ABOVE RULES.

*The League Rules of Conduct for the All-American Girls Baseball League (see Chapter Seventeen), are courtesy of the Northern Indiana Historical Society, South Bend, Indiana.

About the Author

An award-winning former broadcast journalist, former press secretary to the New York state senate minority leader, former public information officer for the nation's third largest prison system, and former editor of a national art magazine, Lynn Ames is a nationally recognized speaker and CEO of a public relations firm with a particular expertise in image, crisis communications planning, and crisis management.

Ms. Ames's other works include *The Price of Fame* (Book One in the Kate & Jay series), *The Cost of Commitment* (Book Two in the Kate & Jay series), *The Value of Valor* (winner of the 2007 Arizona Book Award and Book Three in the Kate & Jay series), *One ~ Love* (formerly published as *The Flip Side of Desire*), *Heartsong, Eyes on the Stars* (winner of a 2011 Golden Crown Literary award), *Beyond Instinct* (winner of a 2012 Golden Crown Literary Award and Book One in the Mission: Classified series), *Above Reproach*, Book Two in the Mission: Classified series, *All That Lies Within* (Lammy Award finalist and winner of the 2014 Ann Bannon Popular Choice Award), and *Outsiders* (winner of a 2010 Golden Crown Literary award).

More about the author, including contact information, news about sequels and other original upcoming works, pictures of locations mentioned in this novel, links to resources related to issues raised in this book, author interviews, and purchasing assistance can be found at www.lynnames.com. You can also friend Lynn on Facebook and follow her on Twitter.

Other Books in Print by Lynn Ames

The Mission: Classified Series
Beyond Instinct – Book One in the Mission: Classified Series
ISBN: 978-1-936429-02-8
Vaughn Elliott is a member of the State Department's Diplomatic Security Force. Someone high up in the United States government has pulled rank, hand-selecting her to oversee security for a visit by congressional VIPs to the West African nation of Mali. The question is, who picked her for the job and why?

Sage McNally, a career diplomat, is the political officer at the US Embassy in Mali. As control officer for the congressional visit, she is tasked to brief Vaughn regarding the political climate in the region.

The two women are instantly attracted to each other and share a wild night of passion. The next morning, Sage disappears while running, leaving behind signs of a scuffle. Why was Sage taken and by whom? Where is she being held?

Vaughn's attempts to get answers are thwarted at every turn. Even Sage does not know why she's been targeted.

Independently, Sage and Vaughn struggle to make sense of the seemingly senseless. By the time each of them figures it out, it could be too late for Sage.

As the clock ticks inexorably toward the congressional visit, the stakes get even higher, and Vaughn is faced with unspeakable choices. Her decisions will make the difference between life and death. Will she choose duty or her own code of honor?

Above Reproach – Book Two in the Mission: Classified Series
ISBN: 978-1-936429-04-2

Sedona Ramos is a dedicated public servant. Fluent in three languages, with looks that allow her to pass for Hispanic, Native American, or Middle Eastern, she is a valuable asset to the super-secret National Security Agency. When she accidentally stumbles upon a mysterious series of satellite images revealing activity at a shuttered nuclear facility in war-torn Iraq, somebody wants her dead.

With danger lurking at every turn and not knowing who among her colleagues might be involved, Sedona risks her life to get the information to the one person she can trust—the president.

The implications of Sedona's discovery are clear and quite possibly catastrophic. Potential suspects include foreign terrorists, high-ranking Cabinet members, and assorted others. Whomever the president picks for this mission must be above reproach.

Vaughn Elliott is enjoying her self-imposed isolation on a remote island, content to live in quiet anonymity. But when old friend Katherine Kyle brings an urgent SOS from the president of the United States, duty trumps comfort.

Time is of the essence. Vaughn, Sedona, and a hand-picked team of ex-operatives and specialists must figure out what's really going on outside Baghdad, stop it, and unmask the forces behind the plot. If they fail at any point along the way, it could mean the loss of millions of lives.

Will Vaughn and company unravel the mysteries in time? The trail of clues stretches from the Middle East to Washington. The list of people who want to kill them is long. And the stakes have never been higher...

Stand-Alone Romances

All That Lies Within

ISBN: 978-1-936429-06-6

How far would you go to hide who you really are inside? And what do you do when you find the one person from whom hiding your true self isn't an option?

Glamorous movie star Dara Thomas has it all—an Oscar nomination, dozens of magazine covers proclaiming her the sexiest woman alive, and people of both sexes clamoring for her attention. She also has a carefully guarded secret life. As Constance Darrow, Dara writes Pulitzer Prize-winning fiction, an outlet that allows her to be so much more than just a pretty face.

Rebecca Minton is a professor of American Literature in love with the work of the mysterious, reclusive author Constance Darrow, with whom she strikes up a correspondence. A chance phrase in a letter leads her to a startling conclusion about the author.

What happens next will change the course of both of their lives forever.

Eyes on the Stars

ISBN: 978-1-936429-00-4

Jessie Keaton and Claudia Sherwood were as different as night and day. But when their nation needed experienced female pilots, their reactions were identical: heed the call. In early 1943, the two women joined the Women Airforce Service Pilots—WASP—and reported to Avenger Field in Sweetwater, Texas, where they promptly fell head-over-heels in love.

The life of a WASP was often perilous by definition. Being two women in love added another layer of complication entirely, leading to ostracism and worse. Like many others, Jessie and Claudia hid their relationship, going on dates with men to avert suspicion. The ruse worked well until one seemingly innocent afternoon ruined everything.

Two lives tragically altered. Two hearts ripped apart. And a second chance more than fifty years in the making.

From the airfields of World War II, to the East Room of the Obama White House, follow the lives of two extraordinary women whose love transcends time and place.

Heartsong
ISBN: 978-0-9840521-3-4

After three years spent mourning the death of her partner in a tragic climbing accident, Danica Warren has re-emerged in the public eye. With a best-selling memoir, a blockbuster movie about her heroic efforts to save three other climbers, and a successful career on the motivational speaking circuit, Danica has convinced herself that her life can be full without love.

When Chase Crosley walks into Danica's field of vision everything changes. Danica is suddenly faced with questions she's never pondered.

Is there really one love that transcends all concepts of space and time? One great love that joins two hearts so that they beat as one? One moment of recognition when twin flames join and burn together?

Will Danica and Chase be able to overcome the barriers standing between them and find forever? And can that love be sustained, even in the face of cruel circumstances and fate?

One ~ Love, (formerly The Flip Side of Desire)
ISBN: 978-0-9840521-2-7

Trystan Lightfoot allowed herself to love once in her life; the experience broke her heart and strengthened her resolve never to fall in love again. At forty, however, she still longs for the comfort of a woman's arms. She finds temporary solace in meaningless, albeit adventuresome encounters, burying her pain and her emotions deep inside where no one can reach. No one, that is, until she meets C.J. Winslow.

C.J. Winslow is the model-pretty-but-aging professional tennis star the Women's Tennis Federation is counting on to dispel the image that all great female tennis players are lesbians. And her lesbianism isn't the only secret she's hiding. A traumatic event from her childhood is taking its toll both on and off the court.

Together Trystan and C.J. must find a way beyond their pasts to discover lasting love.

The Kate and Jay Series

The Price of Fame
ISBN: 978-0-9840521-4-1

When local television news anchor Katherine Kyle is thrust into the national spotlight, it sets in motion a chain of events that will change her life forever. Jamison "Jay" Parker is an intensely career-driven Time magazine reporter. The first time she saw Kate, she fell in love. The last time she saw her, Kate was rescuing her. That was five years ago, and she never expected to see her again. Then circumstances and an assignment bring them back together.

Kate and Jay's lives intertwine, leading them on a journey to love and happiness, until fate and fame threaten to tear them apart. What is the price of fame? For Kate, the cost just might be everything. For Jay, it could be the other half of her soul.

The Cost of Commitment
ISBN: 978-0-9840521-5-8

Kate and Jay want nothing more than to focus on their love. But as Kate settles into a new profession, she and Jay are caught in the middle of a deadly scheme and find themselves pawns in a larger game in which the stakes are nothing less than control of the country.

In her novel of corruption, greed, romance, and danger, Lynn Ames takes us on an unforgettable journey of harrowing conspiracy—and establishes herself as a mistress of suspense.

The Cost of Commitment—it could be everything...

The Value of Valor
ISBN: 978-0-9840521-6-5

Katherine Kyle is the press secretary to the president of the United States. Her lover, Jamison Parker, is a respected writer for Time magazine. Separated by unthinkable tragedy, the two must struggle to survive against impossible odds...

A powerful, shadowy organization wants to advance its own global agenda. To succeed, the president must be eliminated. Only one person knows the truth and can put a stop to the scheme.

It will take every ounce of courage and strength Kate possesses to stay alive long enough to expose the plot. Meanwhile, Jay must cheat death and race across continents to be by her lover's side…

This hair-raising thriller will grip you from the start and won't let you go until the ride is over.

The Value of Valor—it's priceless.

Anthology Collections
Outsiders
ISBN: 978-0-979-92545-0

What happens when you take five beloved, powerhouse authors, each with a unique voice and style, give them one word to work with, and put them between the sheets together, no holds barred?

Magic!!

Brisk Press presents Lynn Ames, Georgia Beers, JD Glass, Susan X. Meagher and Susan Smith, all together under the same cover with the aim to satisfy your every literary taste. This incredible combination offers something for everyone—a smorgasbord of fiction unlike anything you'll find anywhere else.

A Native American raised on the Reservation ventures outside the comfort and familiarity of her own world to help a lost soul embrace the gifts that set her apart. * A reluctantly wealthy woman uses all of her resources anonymously to help those who cannot help themselves. * Three individuals, three aspects of the self, combine to create balance and harmony at last for a popular trio of characters. * Two nomadic women from very different walks of life discover common ground—and a lot more—during a blackout in New York City. * A traditional, old school butch must confront her community and her own belief system when she falls for a much younger transman.

Five authors—five novellas. Outsiders—one remarkable book.

All Lynn Ames books are available through www.lynnames.com, from your favorite local bookstore, or through other online venues.

Books By Parker & Dixie Ames
(Listed under Lynn Ames)

Digging for Home
ISBN: 978-1-936429-08-0
We've all done it—sat there and wondered what our canine companions were thinking while staring at the television with us during a ball game. Ponder no more! Irrepressible golden retrievers Parker and Dixie Ames have made it their mission to take you inside the dugout for a dog's-eye view of the innings and outings of the great game of softball. Assisted by their Siberian husky pal Lucy McMan-West, an obliging cast of canine cohorts, a chicken, a turtle, and a llama named LaRue, the dynamic duo reminds us that softball is not about winning or losing—it's about finding the shortest route to the concession stand.

Filled with quirky explanations and colorful photo illustrations, *Digging for Home* is a tasty ballpark treat that's packed with heart, hilarity, and plenty of doggone good fun.

You can purchase other Phoenix Rising Press books online at www.phoenixrisingpress.com or at your local bookstore.

Published by
Phoenix Rising Press
Phoenix, AZ

Visit us on the Web: Phoenix Rising Press

Here at Phoenix Rising Press, our goal is to provide you, the reader, with top quality, entertaining, well-written, well-edited works that leave you wanting more. We give our authors free rein to let their imaginations soar. We believe that nurturing that kind of unbridled creativity and encouraging our authors to write what's in their hearts results in the kinds of books you can't put down.

Whether you crave romances, mysteries, fantasy/science fiction, short stories, thrillers, or something else, when you pick up a Phoenix Rising Press book, you know you've found a good read. So sit back, relax, get comfortable, and enjoy!

Phoenix Rising Press
Phoenix, AZ